About the Author

Martin Slevin began his writing career with the *Little Girl in the Radiator*, a biography of his time spent as the main carer for his mother who had been diagnosed with Alzheimer's Disease. The book won the British Medical Association's Book of the Year (Chairman's Choice in 2013).

To Bron, my frustrated hippopotamus, in
appreciation of all his hard work,
and
to Gom, who showed me the importance of the path
behind me.

Martin Slevin

MURIEL'S MONSTER

AUSTIN MACAULEY
PUBLISHERS LTD.

A CIP catalogue record for this title is available from the British Library.

ISBN 9781786295774 (Paperback)
ISBN 9781786295781 (E-Book)
www.austinmacauley.com

First Published (2016)
Austin Macauley Publishers Ltd.
25 Canada Square
Canary Wharf
London
E14 5LQ

"If you wish to experience the wonders of the Universe, then learn to travel through yourself. A journey through the subconscious is a journey through the whole of creation; all the Universe is, and all it has to offer, is already hidden inside each of us, for we are the stuff the stars are made of."

Patrick, in The Garden of Idols.

Introduction

Make no mistake, this is a story about you. Or to be a little more accurate, it is a story about what may be called the human condition. The human being is nature's masterpiece, and it is more than the sum of its parts. There is more to man than molecules, and the events described in this book, the places and characters depicted, are all inside each and every one of us. What happens to the main character, Muriel Mason, may not happen to you, each of us has a separate destiny after all; but the mechanics of the Crucible of Creation, the main setting for the story, and the characters she interacts with there are all yours to explore and meet, as well. The journey Muriel undertakes, and the natural expansion of her consciousness due to her time in the Crucible, is a path for you to follow if you have the will. So put yourself into Muriel's shoes, and walk with her on a unique voyage of self-discovery. It is a process of development which will leave you wiser than it found you. To get the best from this adventure, read it twice.

Okay, let's go…

PART ONE

LEARNING TO WIN

Chapter One

The Crucible of Creation

Unlike her best friend, Michelle, who was just plain beautiful, with a cascading mop of flaxen tresses tumbling in waves to her shoulders, framing a flawless face with Forget Me Not eyes, Muriel Mason alas, was just plain, plain. Muriel thought Michelle was sure to either become a super model, or marry a billionaire, but Muriel had never once held that against her pal. Muriel received a lot of back-handed attention from the boys at school, mainly asking her to put a good word in for them with Michelle, but Muriel didn't mind that, as there had existed for some years now, a genuine friendship between the two girls. Muriel was not highly intelligent, but neither was she stupid.

She had a way about her though, and if people were asked to say something nice about Muriel, they would probably say she had an engaging sense of humour, she was loyal, and she was good company. Muriel was a fairly typical fifteen-year-old girl who had no idea what she wanted to do in life when she left school, and she didn't seem to care much about it either; happy to move through each day taking what life presented to her with a carefree attitude, and a laid back disposition.

"We're going to do it tonight," remarked Michelle suddenly, as the pair wandered along the footpath from the school gates.

"Oh, you're not!" exclaimed Muriel, in genuine surprise. "You only met him the other day."

"It's been two weeks, actually," argued Michelle. "And besides, there's no point in waiting, not in this day and age. It's not chocolate to wait these days."

"Apart from the fact that you're too young, and he could be arrested for rape, you mean?" Muriel thought she would just mention that.

Michelle shrugged her shoulders. "Who is going to know?"

The pair walked on in silence for a bit.

"Are you still getting those headaches?" asked Michelle.

Muriel nodded.

"You really need to see someone," continued Michelle. "It's not normal to have so many headaches."

"How many is normal?" asked Muriel smiling.

"Mo, I'm being serious now," replied Michelle. "You need to see a doctor."

"I'm alright," replied Muriel, rubbing her forehead.

"You've got one right now, haven't you?" asked her best friend.

Muriel nodded.

As she walked along Michelle began to search through her school bag, "I have some headache tablets in here somewhere," she said. "Promise me, you'll see someone, or at least tell your parents when you get home?"

Michelle handed the packet of pills across to Muriel, but Muriel was no longer beside her. Michelle stopped and looked around.

A few paces behind her, Muriel was lying on the ground. A small crowd of pupils were beginning to gather around her.

"Mo!" shouted Michelle, running back to her prostrate friend.

"She's been shot!" announced a seven year old lad, who watched far too much television.

"She hasn't been shot!" replied Michelle. "She's just fainted, that's all. I'll call her dad."

It was late in the evening when Muriel gathered her senses. The sky was a dark and dusty pink, as the light appeared subdued and gloomy, it seemed as though a storm might be coming. Muriel felt her shoes sink into the soft sand as she walked. A featureless landscape sprawled before her, with no trees, or houses, no roads, cars or any vestige of civilisation, but Muriel wasn't surprised, she hadn't really expected any.

In the distance she could see a row of tents which meant that someone was about, and instinctively, she headed towards the encampment.

"Hello!" she called when she reached the outskirts of the settlement. "Is there anybody here?"

There were no sounds from the row of tents, no noise in the landscape at all, and the air itself seemed as though *something* was about to happen, but Muriel could not say what.

"Is there anybody here?" repeated Muriel, poking her face gingerly through the opening of the largest tent, and squinting through the darkness.

A giant, brown head lunged back at her from inside, and Muriel shot backwards, falling onto the sand.

"Oh my God!" she exclaimed.

"Hardly!" replied the hippopotamus, sticking his enormous head out of the tent, and wiggling his little round ears. "Well, well, well, fancy seeing *you* here."

Muriel woke with a start.

"Here she is!" said Muriel's mother. "How are you feeling?"

Muriel blinked, and looked around her, she was in bed at home. The familiar features of her bedroom, with its bright flowered wallpaper and pastel curtains making a sharp contrast to the hippo's gloomy tent.

"I fainted at school," she said simply.

Her mother and father were in the room, her dad was sitting on the bed. "You gave us quite a scare," he said. "Michelle called me."

Muriel nodded.

"We should call the doctor," suggested Muriel's mum, "I'm not happy about this."

"There's no need," replied Muriel. "I've been studying too hard, that's all. I'm not getting enough sleep."

Muriel yawned, to illustrate the point.

"Well you're not to go to school tomorrow," said her dad. "Stay home and rest. I'll call the headmaster and let him know."

Muriel's parents began to talk to her about the importance of a proper night's sleep, and how in their day, young girls of her age were always in bed by nine o'clock, and how...but the sound of their concerned voices faded away into a meaningless hum, as Muriel began to ponder the much more intriguing question of why a talking hippopotamus might choose to live in a tent. Muriel nodded in all the right places, and when they had made their opinions quite clear to their daughter, they waited for her reply.

"Well?" said her mother at last.

Muriel tuned back in.

"Oh, I agree, absolutely!" replied Muriel, nodding her head with conviction, which is always the safest response when you haven't been listening.

Muriel's dad switched the light off when they left her room, and Muriel felt her eyes begin to close. She always seemed to be so sleepy these days.

"So," remarked the hippo casually, "you've come back then."

Muriel nodded.

"And you've brought your friend with you this time," observed the hippo.

Muriel spun around. A mop was standing behind her, one of those old fashioned ones, with a long wooden handle and thick strands of pale yarn at the end, great for soaking up puddles.

"Hello Mop," said Muriel, turning back to the hippo. "Where is this place?"

The hippo seemed to regard the question for a moment, then he rose up onto his stout hind legs and looked across the desert. "Do you mean *this* particular place, as in just these tents, or do you mean *this* place?" replied the hippo, spreading his forelegs out in a sweeping gesture, as if to include the entire desert.

"Well, just here for now," said Muriel. "And who are you?"

The hippo looked around his camp as though he were seeing it for the first time. "This is the Camp of the Hippos," he replied. "And I am Bron, chief amongst my kind."

"I'm Muriel," said the traveller, and pointing behind her, "and this is Mop."

Mop wiggled.

"Nice to meet you both," replied Bron.

"Why is it so dark here?" asked Muriel, squinting into the distance.

Bron considered the question. "Because the light of understanding has not penetrated this far in, yet," he replied thoughtfully. "But we live in hope."

"I don't understand any of this," confessed Muriel.

"On the contrary," argued Bron, "you understand all of it. You just don't know you understand it. But I suspect you will in time."

"How can I not know if I understand something, or not?" asked Muriel, becoming even more confused than she was before.

"We often know things, but don't know we know them," replied the hippo.

"Then someone points them out to us, and then suddenly we know we know them!"

Muriel shook her head. "This is a weird dream," she observed.

"A dream?" said Bron. "You think you are dreaming?"

"Yes, of course I'm dreaming," replied Muriel, "hippopotamuses don't talk in real life, or live in tents do they?"

"The plural is hippopotami," replied Bron, shaking his head. "This is all basic stuff, I thought we might be past this by now."

"Well, *I'm* not past it," replied Muriel. "Explain it to me please?"

Bron took a deep breath, he really didn't have time for all this.

"This is the Crucible of Creation" began the hippo. "It is the centre of the entire universe. The beginning of all things. It is here where the records are kept, in the great library."

"What great library?" asked Muriel looking around the camp.

"In there," replied Bron, jerking his head towards his tent.

"There is a library in your tent?" replied Muriel.

"Not just a library. *The* library, the written records of everything that has happened, everything that has been said, thought of, and done since the dawn of time."

"All that in your tent?" asked Muriel, smiling.

Bron nodded.

"Well if everything is written down in there, you should know who killed President Kennedy, who Jack the Ripper was, and stuff like that," replied Muriel.

Bron rolled his eyes and sighed in exasperation. "It's not the records of *everybody*…just of The Client. The records are all about one particular individual."

"Ah…" said Muriel, "and who might that be?"

Muriel woke with a start, blinking rapidly in the comforting familiarity of her own bedroom. The illuminated numbers of her bedside clock shone a scarlet 3.30 into the darkness. Maybe it was because she had been back in the desert with Bron, or maybe it was because she had been in bed for hours, but Muriel suddenly felt a savage thirst come upon her.

"I need a drink," she said to herself, and with a sweep of her arm, thrust the duvet away from her.

In the kitchen she sat at the small breakfast table with a second glass of milk before her. "I need to write all this down, so I don't forget any of it," she said to herself.

Muriel began to root through her schoolbag, until she found a notepad and a pencil. Once settled at the table again she began to think. "Now, what *was* his name…?"

Slowly the images began to replay in her mind, the soft sand beneath her feet, the ominous silence and the expectant gloom. The hippo suddenly standing up…

"Bron!" she said. "That was it, Bron. I must write all this down. I must begin a journal, a diary about Bron."

As soon as Muriel began to write about Bron and the Crucible of Creation the carbon point of her pencil snapped, sending the little tip across the kitchen like a tiny bullet.

"Oh, damn!" exclaimed Muriel, and she started to root in her pencil case for the pencil sharpener she knew was in there. "Now, where have you gone?" she muttered, but search as she might, the little metal sharpener was nowhere to be seen.

In frustration, Muriel threw the broken pencil into her schoolbag, put the notebook in there too and took the remainder of her glass of milk back upstairs to bed.

"You're becoming quite a regular visitor here," observed Bron.

"I can't seem to help it," replied Muriel. "As soon as I fall asleep I end up here, it's very weird."

"There is nothing weird about this place," replied Bron, "it's all extremely straight forward."

"Explain it to me, then," replied Muriel.

"What do you want to know?" asked the hippo.

"Well, first of all what is this place?" asked Muriel, who had noticed Mop following her again.

"This is the Crucible of Creation," announced Bron proudly.

"Yes, I know, you said that before. Who are you, then?" asked Muriel.

"I am the Chief Librarian," replied the hippo.

"Ah yes," said Muriel smiling, "of the great library inside your tent."

"Quite so," replied Bron. Sarcasm was lost upon the hippopotamus.

Muriel started to look at the distant horizon, past the little encampment. "What is over there?" she asked.

"Those are the Twisted Mountains," replied Bron.

Muriel just knew he was going to say something like that. As Muriel squinted at the distant hills she could see tiny lights winking on and off all over the mountains, they gave the entire range a magical effect.

"I can see lights or sparks on the slopes," she said.

"They are fireflies," said Bron. "They live on the mountains."

"How wonderful!" replied the schoolgirl.

Muriel waved her right arm towards another horizon. "And what's down there?"

"Wernicke's Magic Castle," replied Bron.

"Show her the map!" called a voice from inside one of the other tents.

"Who asked your opinion?" growled Bron. "Get back to work!"

"Who was that?" asked Muriel.

"One of my assistants," replied Bron. "I can't be expected to do *everything* on my own, can I?"

"What map?" asked Muriel.

"When the world was new," began Bron. "And all the settlers came to this place, no-one knew the terrain, and so I sent out runners far and wide across the desert, with instructions to write down every place they came to. Slowly a very special map was created. The single most important map in the entire universe. In fact...a map *of* the entire universe."

"Wow!" exclaimed Muriel. "Can I see it, please?"

"Give it to her, it's hers anyway!" called the hidden voice again.

"Nobody asked you!" shouted Bron. "Another word out of you and you'll be indexing until the end of days."

"Runner coming!" shouted another voice from inside one of the tents.

Bron looked towards the horizon behind his encampment, and Muriel followed his gaze, squinting hard in the twilight. Away in the distance a figure could be seen jogging towards them, a tall, skinny, bald man. He wore a white t-shirt and red jogging bottoms, and seemed to be carrying a bag of some kind, strapped to his chest.

"Who is this?" Muriel asked.

"A Fornix Runner," replied Bron. "He will need information from the records."

Muriel and Bron watched the figure approach. After a short while the runner entered the camp and came to a halt before Bron. The bald runner had a long serial number printed on the front of his shirt.

"Fornix Runner 512647398. Requesting information about a missing item, please," announced the runner.

"You don't have to say your number every time," sighed Bron, "it's printed on your shirt, I can read, I *am* a librarian."

"Everything has to be done a certain way, and no other way at all," replied the runner with a tone of finality.

"The invoice?" asked Bron, holding out his foreleg.

The runner unzipped his chest bag, and handed a parchment to Bron. "It is a recent loss," said the runner. "But is causing some concern."

Bron read the invoice carefully. "A lost pencil sharpener."

Muriel looked up at Bron. "I lost my pencil sharpener too!" she announced. "How odd!"

"One moment," said Bron, retreating into his tent. Bron returned a moment later with a second parchment. "It appears to be under the sofa in the living room," replied Bron. "It was dropped by The Client, and accidentally kicked under the chair. There is no reported damage to the item."

Bron held the second parchment out for the runner to take, which he placed back into his chest bag, and zipped it shut.

"Very good," said the runner, and began to jog off in a different direction from the one had come.

"Where is he going now?" asked Muriel.

"None of my business," replied Bron. "I only tell them what they want to know. Where they take the information, or what they do with it afterwards is not my concern."

They watched the runner slowly jog away into the distance.

"The map?" whispered Muriel.

"Ah, yes, the map," replied Bron. "Yes, I suppose you should have it."

Bron went into his tent again and returned with a parchment, rinsed yellow in the river of time.

"It is very old, and there are no copies," said Bron. "So, if I give this to you, you must promise to look after it. All the important places in the universe are marked on it, you can go anywhere with it. It shows the secrets of everything, it is sacred knowledge."

"I promise," said Muriel, and Bron handed over the map.

"It's not like any map I have ever seen before," said Muriel, letting her eyes slowly wander across the faded parchment.

"Nor are you ever likely to see such magnificent work again," replied the hippo, who was obviously very pleased with his drawing.

"You're a very modest hippo," observed Muriel, smiling.

Bron thought about this for a moment. "I don't think I am," he mused, as he didn't really understand sarcasm at all.

"I didn't realise there was so much to see here," said Muriel, "I will have to go exploring."

"All of creation is here," replied Bron. "All there ever was, all there is now, and all there ever can be, therefore it is the greatest map in the universe."

Muriel wasn't sure about that, but she liked her new friend, Bron, and thought this place was interesting. "Yes, I'll definitely have to go exploring," she said.

High in the peaks of the Twisted Mountains, deep within the folds of their structure could be found a small opening, a cave. Inside this cave a living thing had been born upon the floor. As yet the thing was little more than a shapeless mass, that was weak and vulnerable, and yet it pulsed and throbbed with the tempo of life. It breathed the air of the Crucible as others breathed, yet it was not like them; it was a thing apart, different, distinct, and dangerous. It lay upon the floor of the cave allowing the passage of time to caress its form, to give it strength, to recede its vulnerability hour by hour, as the tide of time washed over it, making it whole. The thing had no consciousness as yet, it merely lived, it existed as the mountain around it existed, as the desert plains below its lofty peak existed, without a sense of self, or any understanding of who or what it was. It pulsated with the drum beat of being, swelling very slowly as the tide of time allowed it to develop. It was a thing in potential, a thing that might grow into something else if it lived; if it survived the early stages of its existence it might one day become a thing to be avoided, to be feared, a predator, a demon. It might become the very creature they already said it was, a monster.

Chapter Two

The Garden of Idols

Muriel got out of bed and went downstairs. Without thinking about it at all, her footsteps seemed to carry her instinctively to the living room, where she stopped.

"What am I doing in here?" she asked herself. "I wanted my breakfast." Muriel turned to go to the kitchen but hesitated, then suddenly swung around and faced the sofa. A feeling swept over her that she could not explain, a sense of unease mixed with the promise of wonder. She felt the fluttering of butterflies in her stomach.

"No, it couldn't be," she whispered to herself, all the while hoping beyond reason that it could. Suddenly, the moment was endowed with magic.

Muriel stepped quickly toward the sofa, fell to her knees and thrust her arm under the chair. She closed her eyes and swept her arm from side to side. Her stomach lurched with excitement when her fingertips touched something small and cold. She closed her fingers tightly around the object, and drew out her arm. The lost pencil sharpener lay in the palm of her hand and she caught her breath.

"Oh, my God!" she whispered. "I have to know more about all this."

With the obsessive determination of youth, she marched to find her schoolbag, and write everything she had discovered down on paper. "That hippopotamus is going to have to give me some straight answers," she announced.

Sitting at the kitchen table she tried to redraw Bron's Map from memory, and found she could recall a surprising amount of detail.

"I usually can't remember much about my dreams," she observed, wondering why she was able to recall so many facts about her time with Bron with such a high degree of accuracy.

"I think that's it," she said, when the map was finished. "I think I've got everything."

Muriel studied her version of Bron's Map and shook her head. "Such a strange and interesting place," she said. "I have to talk to Bron again."

Try as she might, Muriel could not force sleep to come. She lay on the sofa and closed her eyes, but she just wasn't sleepy. She went upstairs and got into bed, but sleep would still not come; it kept away from her as though it had fallen out with her, and didn't want anything to do with her now. She tried to coax sleep towards her by thinking of something tedious, but sleep was a wary cat that merely stared at her and refused to approach. In frustration Muriel got up again, and went back downstairs. An idea came to her when she was wondering what to do. Muriel went into her father's study, sat in his office chair, and opened his computer.

"I wonder if Bron is in here?" she whispered, as she typed his name into the search engine.

It turned out that Bron was a suburb in the city of Lyon in France. "That can't be it," she said. It was also part of the title of a Led Zeppelin song. Muriel shook her head. There was a firm in Holland called Bron that made jewellery. Muriel sighed and carried on, then it caught her, held her, tickled her, and deepened what was already the beginning of a tantalising mystery.

Bron. Afrikaans word meaning Source. Example, the source of a river. The starting point.

"African!" exclaimed Muriel. "Hippos are from Africa as well. Now I'm getting somewhere." She also remembered a lesson in school some time ago, where her teacher had said that human life first started in Africa, that the earliest traces of human civilisation were all found in central Africa. Muriel pressed on with her searching, but couldn't get any further.

"I really need to talk to that damn hippo again," she said.

Try as she might though, she could not force herself to fall asleep. Most people try to fight sleep off, as though it were a pickpocket, trying to steal their wallet; very few try and consciously bring it closer, and when they do, it fights to get away. In frustration, Muriel sat on the sofa watching television until the headache began to inch slowly through her head, one tiny step at a time, like a rising tide. Muriel rubbed her forehead and felt her eyes start to close.

"So!" exclaimed Muriel, pointing at the hippo. "You're African!"

Bron looked mildly surprised. "Am I?" he replied, smiling.

"But then, you could say that *everybody* is African, really," replied Muriel. "That's where it all started, isn't it?"

Bron frowned. "Where all what started?"

"This, you, me, everything. Humanity started in Africa."

"Did it?" asked Bron.

"Runner coming!" shouted a voice from inside one of the tents, and both Muriel and Bron again turned to watch the tall, skinny, bald runner approach from the right.

"I wonder what it is this time?" asked Muriel.

"We'll know soon enough," replied the hippo.

"Fornix Runner 264953871, reporting a successful search," announced the runner.

"That's a different number," said Muriel, "but he looks the same."

"They all look like that," replied Bron.

The Fornix Runner unzipped his chest bag and took out a sheaf of papers.

"There is emotional contents attached to this one," said the runner. "Surprise, delight, wonder, and intrigue. All to be cross referenced, together with a lingering sense of mystery associated with the sofa. And there might be a slight impact in the Garden of Idols."

Muriel frowned.

"Interesting," replied Bron, as the runner jogged away. "Cross referencing required immediately!" shouted Bron, and several hippos who all looked like Bron came out of various tents, taking a paper each and then disappearing into their own bivouacs again.

"What is going on?" asked Muriel.

"We can't file the records in just one place," replied Bron. "That would be very inefficient. Everything is cross referenced for ease of access later on."

Muriel shook her head. She took the map Bron had given her from her schoolbag, which had mysteriously appeared on her shoulder, and began to examine the drawing.

"I would like you to explain this map to me, please," she said.

"Certainly," replied Bron. "What would you like to know?"

"Well, for instance, that runner mentioned the *Garden of Idols*. Let's start there."

"A sacred place," replied Bron. "That's where the saints and sinners are. A great deal can be learned about yourself, and your history in that place."

Muriel nodded. "Seems like a good place to start."

"As good as any," replied the hippo.

"I think I will go there, first," announced Muriel, with the conviction of youth.

"You'll meet Patrick in there, don't lend him any money, you'll never get it back," whispered the hippo, in a conspiratorial way.

"I'm a schoolgirl," replied Muriel, "I don't have any money."

"You will when he asks you for it, otherwise there's no point," replied the hippo.

"Thanks for the advice," said Muriel, wondering what Bron was talking about.

"And stay in the desert," warned the hippo. "Do not go up into the Twisted Mountains."

"Why not?"

Bron turned to face the mountain range that could be seen outlined in the gloom, far in the distance. "Something has been born up there. We have just been notified of its arrival," he whispered.

"What is it?" asked Muriel.

Bron shook his head.

"Tell me," demanded the schoolgirl.

"A monster has been born in the Twisted Mountains," said the hippo.

"A monster?" replied Muriel.

Bron nodded. "A very dangerous creature indeed. One day it will come down from its cave and destroy everything here, if it's not stopped."

"Why would it do that?" asked Muriel.

"That's what monsters do," replied Bron simply.

"Who could stop it?"

Bron shook his big, brown head. "Who knows? Maybe the Silver Knight. I don't know."

Muriel searched her map, "I can't see any Silver Knight on here," she said.

"That's because he's never in one spot for long," replied Bron. "He travels all over the place, he comes and goes."

"Where is he now?" asked Muriel.

"No idea." Bron shook his shoulders. "He could be anywhere."

"Anyway, I'm going to the Garden of Idols," said Muriel. "I've made up my mind."

"Runner coming!" shouted the voice again.

Muriel left the Camp of the Hippos and began to travel up as indicated on Bron's Map, carefully avoiding the foothills of the Twisted Mountains, and bearing Out towards her destination. There was no scale marked on the map, and so she had no idea how long it might take her to get there, and yet after only what seemed like a few paces she found herself before a large set of garden gates. *Garden of Idols*, announced the sign on the gate. The iron gates had a crest worked into the ironwork, the word *TRUTH* beside a spear tip. Muriel wondered what it meant as she turned around and could barely see the Camp of the Hippos way off in the distance. Muriel pushed the gate open and stepped inside.

A man was digging a hole and a donkey was standing beside him, eating the grass when Muriel entered. Both the man and the donkey looked up when Muriel shut the gate behind her with a metallic clang.

"Hello," said the man. "This is a pleasant surprise."

The donkey did not seem surprised at all.

"Hello," called Muriel to the man. "You must be Patrick."

The man seemed slightly offended at this. He stopped what he was doing, and placed his hands on his hips, letting the shovel fall to the ground. "Why must *I* be Patrick?" he asked.

"Well, I just thought..." stumbled Muriel.

"I am The Gardener!" announced the man proudly, "this…" indicating the donkey with a sideways jerk of his head, "is Patrick."

"Lend me a fiver?" asked Patrick.

Muriel shook her head. "Sorry, I don't have any money," she replied, remembering Bron's advice.

"She's been warned about you," said the man to Patrick.

"Would you mind if I asked you about this place?" said Muriel. "I mean, what is it for?"

The man looked around. The garden was very neat and tidy, with no litter on the paths, which had been freshly swept. There were little flower beds with a cascade of fresh and colourful blossoms displayed in each. Dotted here and there were a number of statues, or rather shapeless blocks, which would eventually become statues, Muriel thought, if the sculptor ever got around to working on them.

"This," said the gardener proudly, "is the place where we keep our beliefs and our prejudices, safe and sound. It is here where we work on what we believe to be true, and what we believe to be false. This is where The Client keeps all their motivations and fears, all their important impressions. This is the Garden of Idols."

Muriel frowned.

"I don't understand," she said.

"It's not difficult to grasp," replied the gardener. "What matters in life is what we believe. The truth is largely irrelevant."

"I don't see how that's true," replied Muriel. "The truth always matters."

"Actually the truth hardly *ever* matters," argued the gardener.

"Perhaps a couple of examples would help?" suggested the donkey.

Muriel nodded.

"Imagine a policeman believes a man to be a thief," began Patrick.

Muriel nodded again.

"If the man tells the policeman he *is* a thief, will the policeman believe him?"

"Yes, he will," agreed Muriel.

"What if the man tells the policeman he is *not* a thief, will the policeman believe him, then?"

Muriel shook her head. "No, he won't."

"So it doesn't matter what the man says," observed Patrick, "it is only what the policeman *believes* that matters."

"But what if the man really is innocent?" argued Muriel. "What if he really isn't a thief, after all, and the policeman is mistaken?"

Patrick smiled. "Will the policeman treat the man any differently if the man is innocent, as long as the policeman still believes he is guilty?"

"No. I suppose not," admitted Muriel.

"So, it doesn't matter whether he is innocent or guilty. The truth is irrelevant, only what the policeman *believes,* really counts," said the donkey.

"But that's so wrong," argued Muriel.

"No, it's so Right!" replied the gardener.

"Let me give you another example," suggested Patrick.

"Alright," replied Muriel, she was beginning to enjoy this peculiar exchange with the donkey.

"Imagine there is a great art gallery," went on Patrick. "And in this gallery hangs a very famous, wonderful painting."

"Okay," agreed Muriel.

"Then one day a rumour starts to go around that the painting is a forgery. Will the value of the painting, go up, stay the same, or go down, if people begin to think it is a fake?"

"The value of the painting will go down, if people think it might be a fake," said Muriel, fairly sure she was right.

"Correct. But what if the rumour is false, and the painting is really genuine after all? Will its value still go down if people believe it is a forgery, even though it's not?" asked the donkey.

"Yes," said Muriel. "The value of the picture will still go down."

"So, again the actual truth doesn't matter," said the donkey. "Only what people *believe* has any substance and force. The truth is actually irrelevant."

Muriel sat down on a bench that suddenly appeared behind her, just in case she might like to sit on it.

"I have to think about this," she said.

"Imagine a woman thinks her husband has been unfaithful to her," continued the donkey.

Muriel nodded.

"Will she start to treat him differently, now she thinks he has betrayed her?"

"Of course she will," agreed Muriel with some conviction.

34

"Will she still treat him differently if he has not been unfaithful, even though she believes he has?" asked the donkey.

"Yes, I suppose so," agreed Muriel.

"So, it makes no difference whether he has been unfaithful to her or not!" announced Patrick. "The actual truth is completely irrelevant. It is only what the woman *believes* that counts. It is always our beliefs that drive our actions, the truth never comes into it."

Muriel had to think about this.

"Truth is beside the point," remarked the gardener.

"Like on the gate," added the donkey.

"And so it is with this place," continued the gardener. "These statues represent what The Client believes. Whether or not those beliefs are true is completely irrelevant."

"So, what are your jobs here?" asked Muriel.

"I keep the place nice and tidy," said the gardener. "We like to keep our beliefs and prejudices in pleasant surroundings. We need to take care of their settings."

"And I eat all the weeds," replied Patrick.

"No-one wants weeds growing up through their prejudices," remarked the gardener, "that would be very unpleasant."

Muriel looked at the nearest statue, it was little more than a rectangular block of what looked like jelly.

"The statues have no shape," said Muriel. "And they're all soft."

"They are works in progress," replied the gardener.

"The Client is young," observed the donkey. "Their beliefs and prejudices have not formed into solid structure yet. In the years to come these statues will start to take shape and to harden."

"When they become solid, they will be very difficult to change," observed the gardener.

"Once our beliefs are set, and turned to stone, they cannot be altered very easily," remarked the donkey, shaking his head.

Suddenly an idea occurred to Muriel and the light in the Crucible of Creation began to slowly brighten. Both man and donkey noticed this and smiled at Muriel.

"I am The Client, aren't I?" asked Muriel.

Suddenly everywhere across the Crucible of Creation it was broad daylight. In the camp, Bron and the hippos came out and began to cheer.

"The Light of Understanding!" shouted Patrick.

"At last," remarked the gardener, smiling broadly at Muriel. "You are beginning to understand!"

"So, is all this real, or not?" asked Muriel.

"Is all what real?" asked Patrick.

"All this!" exclaimed Muriel, sweeping her arms wide to indicate the expanse of garden where they were. "Or is it all inside my head?"

"A very intelligent question," observed the gardener. "How would you define reality?"

"Reality is things that really exist," replied Muriel.

"Do I exist?" asked the donkey.

Muriel smiled. "How can I know?"

"Well, you are talking to me!" replied Patrick.

"Then you must exist at some level, I suppose," replied Muriel.

"Everything exists at *some* level," said the gardener.

"Name something in your life that you know is real," said the donkey.

Muriel thought about this. "My house is real," she said at last.

"And what is your house made of?" asked the gardener.

"It is made of bricks," replied Muriel confidently.

"And what are the bricks made of?" asked Patrick, smiling.

"They're made of clay, I think," replied Muriel.

"And what is clay made of?" replied the gardener.

"Clay is just clay, it comes from the earth."

"And what is the earth made of?" continued the gardener.

Muriel shook her head. "Atoms I suppose."

"Exactly!" exclaimed the donkey. "Everything is made of atoms, is it not?"

"Yes," replied Muriel.

"And what is an atom made of?" asked the gardener.

Muriel shook her head again.

"Almost nothing," said Patrick. "When they look inside the atom all they find is empty space, there's practically nothing there."

"Well, that's just crazy," said Muriel. "That means that everything is made of nothing!"

"Now we're getting somewhere!" observed the gardener.

"So!" exclaimed Patrick the donkey. "If everything is made of nothing, what is real?"

Muriel began to consider this, but it all seemed so confusing and complicated.

"Come with me," said Patrick, who turned away and began to wander off.

Muriel got up and followed Patrick and the gardener down the path, until they came to a small table standing beside the walkway. On the table were three brass hand bells, all of different sizes.

"Ring the bells," said Patrick.

Muriel picked up the smallest bell and shook it. There was no sound, but Muriel suddenly felt a tingling sensation run through her body.

"It doesn't make any sound," observed Muriel. "How strange!"

Muriel looked inside the bell to see if it had a clapper, which it did.

"It does make a sound," replied Patrick. "You just can't hear it."

"Why can't I hear it?" asked Muriel, shaking the silent bell again.

"Try the next one," suggested the gardener.

Muriel replaced the smallest bell, and then picked up the middle sized one.

When she shook it the bell tinkled.

"That's better," said Muriel. "I can hear that one."

"And the last one?" asked Patrick.

When Muriel shook the third, and largest bell, again there was no sound, but Muriel did feel a gentle pushing sensation in the pit of her stomach.

"Okay I give up," said Muriel. "What's happening?"

"Every consciousness in existence has a range to its sensory capacities." explained the gardener.

Muriel frowned.

"Every living creature has a limited range, within which it can detect atomic movement, light and sound," said Patrick.

Muriel was still frowning.

"The first bell sends out a sound wave below 20 Hertz, which is below the lower limit of human hearing, so you can't hear it," continued the gardener.

"And the largest bell creates a wave above 20,000 Hertz, which is over the upper limit of human hearing," said Patrick.

"So, you can't hear that one either," finished the gardener.

"But I felt *something*," insisted Muriel.

"What you felt was the sound wave hitting your body," explained Patrick. "The sound wave is still there whether you can hear it or not."

Muriel had to think about this.

"So, here's the question," went on the donkey. "If the sound isn't in the bell, then where is it?"

"In the air?" ventured Muriel.

Patrick smiled. "What colour is the grass?" he asked.

"Green of course!" replied Muriel.

"Is it though?" asked the gardener. "What is colour?"

"Ah, we've done this one at school," said Muriel more confidently. "Colour is made up of light waves."

"Exactly!" exclaimed Patrick. "So why is the grass green and not purple?"

Muriel shrugged her shoulders.

"Plants produce chlorophyll which is a chemical that helps with photosynthesis, the reaction that turns sunlight into energy," explained the gardener.

Muriel nodded, she had done this at school as well.

"Chlorophyll absorbs short light waves which are blue, and long light waves which are red, but it rejects the green light wave, it bounces it back into the atmosphere. So you only see the green light wave when you look at the grass, and so the grass looks green to you," said Patrick.

Muriel nodded. "So what colour is the grass really?"

"It isn't any colour, it's just a collection of moving atoms," replied the gardener. "All of which are empty."

"So, here's the great question again," went on the donkey. "If the sound isn't in the bell, and the green isn't in the grass, where are they?"

Muriel laughed and shook her head.

"Well, they must be *somewhere*," suggested the gardener. "So, where are they?"

Muriel looked blankly at the donkey, wondering how she had got herself into this in the first place.

"The sound is not in the bell, the colour is not in the grass, and everything is made of nothing," said Patrick. "Yet we see and feel, shape, structure, form, sound and colour, do we not?"

Muriel nodded in agreement.

"So if all that structure and shape and form, colour and sound is not out *there*, then where is it all?" asked Patrick.

Muriel felt the answer was approaching, but it wasn't near enough yet, to be seen clearly.

"They are all in your mind," whispered Patrick. "When you ask what is real, the only truly real thing in the entire universe is your own consciousness. Everything else is just vibrating atoms, light waves and sound waves. It is your brain that collects the stimulus from out there, and converts it into a picture you will understand. You create the universe you see, yourself."

"Then what *am* I?" asked Muriel. "What are *we*?"

"We are what we think we are, if we think we are what we are," replied the donkey, and the gardener nodded.

"The universe is simply a collection of atoms in motion," said the gardener, "but it needed a consciousness, so it could begin to know itself, and so it created one."

"The Client," observed Patrick.

"You are the way the universe can know itself," said the gardener.

"So am I the only consciousness in the entire universe then?" asked Muriel.

"No, of course not," replied Patrick. "But the atoms in your body are made from the same material as the

40

universe itself, therefore your consciousness is the same as universal consciousness, only on a smaller scale."

"Like a glass of water is the same as the ocean, only smaller," said the gardener.

"Your mind is the same as cosmic mind," continued Patrick, "because there is only one consciousness in the universe that is able to think."

"Universal consciousness flows through every living creature like a river," said the gardener. "And while that creature remains connected to universal mind, it can use that consciousness to think."

"We all share the same consciousness," concluded the donkey. "That's why people are telepathic. Every single thought that has ever been thought is still in universal mind, you can plug into it if you know how. It is the trigger of genius."

"One mind is all mind," said the gardener. "There is no escaping that conclusion."

"I want to know all this stuff, I really want to understand it, but it's so difficult," confessed Muriel.

"If you wish to experience the wonders of the Universe, then learn to travel through yourself. A journey through the subconscious is a journey through the whole of creation; all the Universe is, and all it has to offer, is already hidden inside each and every one of us, for we are the stuff the stars are made of," said Patrick.

Patrick could see that Muriel was completely lost. "At home think of all the things you have that run on electricity, name a few of them," he said.

"Well, there's the television, and the computer, and the lights, and the toaster."

"Do all those things have separate electricity?" asked the gardener. "Or do they all plug into the same current?"

"They all plug into the same current," replied Muriel.

"And as long as they stay connected to that current, they will be able to function," said the gardener.

"You are now plugged in to universal mind, and so as long as you stay plugged in, you will be able to think," said Patrick. "And so will everyone else who is also plugged in to the same current."

"There is only one electricity, and there is only one consciousness. One mind is all mind," finished the gardener.

"So everybody in the world shares the one mind?" asked Muriel.

"Exactly!" exclaimed the donkey.

"Living creatures are just meat!" said the gardener. "How could meat think? It has no capacity for thought. But, when it connects to an external power source, like the toaster plugging into the electricity supply, then the meat can think. The external power supply is universal mind, it is the only consciousness in the universe, we all just plug into it."

"Now, do I get that fiver or not?" asked Patrick.

Muriel shook her head. "I don't have any money with me," she explained.

"A poor excuse!" replied Patrick. "If you had a five pound note in your pocket, would you give it to me?"

Suddenly, Muriel instinctively knew the money was in there. She reached into her pocket, and was not at all surprised to feel the note, which she drew out.

"Well?" asked Patrick.

Muriel still shook her head.

"Look!" said the man, indicating a small statue of a woman's purse, which had a female manicured and bejewelled hand holding the clasp shut. "You're going to be tight with your money when you get older," predicted the gardener. "Already you don't like parting with your cash."

Muriel held the note firmly in her hand. She felt tense, she was not going to give her money away. She felt a pressure to protect the note, to hang on to it. The hand of the statue began to tighten on its purse.

Patrick wandered over towards Muriel, and looked at her. She thought the donkey had kindly eyes.

"Let me tell you a secret," whispered Patrick. "We can change our beliefs, we can modify them for the better, as long as we do it *before* they are turned to stone."

Muriel felt a lightness of being, the pressure she had felt to keep hold of the five pound note began to slip away from her, as she handed the note to Patrick. The statue of the purse had now changed; the grip of the hand had relaxed, and the purse was now open.

"Or maybe you won't be tight with your money after all," observed the gardener.

Patrick accepted the note and winked at Muriel. "I'm not going to pay you back," he said. "Can I still have it?"

Muriel looked at the statue, she preferred the version with the purse open. It made her feel less tense, more at ease in herself, less stressed. When she no longer cared so much about the money, she was liberated to enjoy the moment again.

"Yes," she replied smiling.

Patrick nodded slowly at Muriel. "You're going to become a very nice lady," observed the wise old donkey.

"We have work to do," said the gardener, and he and Patrick began to wander away.

On the floor of its cave, the thing Bron had called a monster had begun to swell and to take shape. Its soft flesh had continued to throb with the pulse of existence, it was becoming stronger as the hours passed. Slowly, over the time since its birth the sides of its mass had begun to separate from the main structure, so that it appeared to have a small arm either side of the main torso. In the twilight it resembled the letter M, as it lay on its back in the cave. A fanciful imagination might have thought the letter stood for Mutant, or maybe even for Muriel, but Bron would have disagreed. "M is for Monster!" the hippo would have said.

Chapter Three

Brocas' Language School

Muriel and Michelle were having their lunch together a few days later.

"So, how did it go?" asked Muriel.

Michelle smiled. "How did what go?" she asked, knowing full well what Muriel had meant.

Muriel laughed. "Come on, give me all the details."

"It was okay," replied Michelle. "Not at all like in the books. A lot more sordid really."

"No great seduction then?" asked Muriel.

"No great anything," replied Michelle. "All very straight down to business, then over and out, so to speak."

The two girls laughed, as the bell to announce the end of the lunch period could be heard echoing around the crowded school playground.

"I have to see the Head, now," announced Muriel.

"What for?"

"Probably to do with that time I fainted," replied Muriel.

"I'll catch you later, then," replied Michelle, as the two friends parted.

Muriel stood before the wooden door and raised her fist to knock, but her hand stayed where it was, suspended in mid-air, as the blow refused to fall. Across the glass panel which took up the top half of the door, the word HEADMASTER had been etched in plain black capital letters. The word itself made her heart flutter in a soft dread of anticipation, no-one ever came to see the

Headmaster unless they were in trouble. The word itself, etched across the glass in front of her eyes in solid chunky black letters, showed not a trace of ornamentation or playful frivolity. There was no hint of humanity in the etching at all, not a single flourish to any letter to hint to the visitor that the character behind the glass might be fun to know, or indeed someone you could talk to, just the square blocking of the word, leaving no room for doubt, self-expression or even whimsy, the way a robot would write it, or a Fornix Runner perhaps, thought Muriel.

Her fist fell forwards with a single thump upon the teak frame.

"Enter!" responded a voice from within.

Not, "Do come in, my dear," or even "please come in," just, "Enter!" Like an instruction for a website, *when you have finished, press, Enter*.

Muriel opened the door and stepped quietly into the oak panelled Headmaster's office, with her juvenile heart beating more quickly, and much more stressed than it needed to be.

"You wanted to see me, Headmaster?" she asked, closing the door behind her with a soft click.

"Ah, Mason!" said the Headmaster, who was seated behind a large, and ornately carved wooden desk, and wearing his black gown. Muriel suddenly thought he looked like a giant bat sitting there, and therefore he should have been hanging upside down from the ceiling; the thought made her smile.

"You know Nurse Patterson, of course," remarked the Headmaster, indicating a woman in a starched, all white uniform, sitting beside him.

Muriel nodded at the nurse, who made no response at all, but merely stared at the young pupil with an intensity that was both disturbing and intimidating; she displayed the caring profession's bedside manner of a starving vulture.

Muriel sat in the chair which had been strategically placed before the desk. A straight-backed, no cushion, wooden chair, designed by someone with a mortal terror of physical comfort.

"I wanted to talk to you about an incident that happened the other day outside the school gates," began the Headmaster.

Muriel looked slightly confused.

"You fainted," said the nurse, helpfully. "Right underneath the school sign!"

As though it made a substantial difference where she fainted.

Muriel nodded.

"I was rather expecting some explanation from your parents before now," continued the Headmaster, "but I have received no communication from them at all!"

Muriel wondered what business it was of the school's anyway, she hadn't been careless enough to faint on the school premises after all.

"We are concerned for your wellbeing," stated the nurse flatly. "We owe a duty of care to our pupils, under the law."

"Quite so," added the giant bat, nodding and smiling.

"I just fainted, that's all," replied Muriel, "sorry it was under the school sign."

The Headmaster shook his head. "The *location* of the faint was unfortunate," said the bat, "but that is not the real issue here."

"The real issue is *why* you fainted in the first place?" added the white vulture.

"There must be a reason."

"I am not sleeping very well at the moment," suggested Muriel, who always slept like a log, but thought the excuse sounded a reasonable one. "I've been working very hard for my exams as well." A nice final point, thought Muriel.

"That's no excuse!" replied the white vulture, shifting uneasily in her armchair, "you're supposed to work hard, that's why you're here!"

"Please, Nurse Patterson," whispered the great bat, shooing the vulture away as life had not entirely expired from the carcass of the visitor yet. "Let me deal with this."

The nurse had a pained expression on her face, it really was too much for pupils to go around fainting all over the place, especially right under the school sign, it could give the parents a very disturbing impression of the teaching methods employed here.

"We are merely concerned about you," said the Headmaster, smiling. "May I ask you what the doctor said?"

"What doctor?" asked Muriel innocently.

"The doctor who examined you afterwards!" said the nurse testily, as though they were dealing with an idiot.

"I didn't see a doctor," replied Muriel. "I was fine afterwards, it wasn't necessary."

The bat and the vulture exchanged a worried glance between themselves, as Muriel sat patiently on the uncomfortable chair, wondering when she could go.

"I have written to your parents," said the Headmaster. "Outlining our concerns."

"I'm fine, really," replied Muriel. "Both my parents agreed I didn't need to see a doctor."

The nurse shook her head at such foolishness, but knew there was nothing she could do. The white vulture wanted nothing more than to exercise her professional expertise in front of the Headmaster by examining the carcass there and then, but everyone in the room knew that would not be possible without the victim's parental consent.

The Headmaster knew too that his powers in the matter were limited by law, and the foolish pupil before him was being uncooperative. He longed for the good old days when he could beat common sense into his youthful charges with a lengthy stick.

"I don't want to have a repeat of this occurrence, Mason," said the Head at last, as though he needed to restate his authority in any way he could.

"I will do my best not to faint again," replied Muriel softly, with the tiniest trace of a smile on her young lips.

The impudence of the little smile secretly enraged the bat and the vulture, but both of them knew there was nothing they could do or even say about it.

"Then you may go," said the Headmaster at last. Muriel stood up, and without another word, went to the door.

Muriel closed the iron gates of the Garden of Idols behind her, with a solid clunk. She felt as though she had learned something about herself in there, something that was deep and important, a lesson that would serve her well in the future. As Muriel faced the iron gates she noticed once again the figurative ironwork, the word *TRUTH* next to a spear tip.

"Truth is beside the point," she said, turning away. "Now I get it!"

Muriel looked again at Bron's Map and thought it seemed a short distance from where she was now to Brocas' Language School.

"Maybe I should go there next," she said to herself, as she started to walk away from the garden. "A language school does sound a bit of a bore, though."

She was studying the map as she walked across the soft sand, when suddenly she bumped into the head of a magnificent, white horse.

"Why don't you look where you are going?" asked the rider.

"She was reading a map," said the horse, blinking rapidly after the impact on its face. "She's obviously lost."

Muriel looked up to see who could only be the Silver Knight blocking her path.

"I'm sorry," replied Muriel. "I didn't see you there."

"Because you were reading the map instead of watching the road," insisted the horse. "If I did that, *he* would never get anywhere he was going."

"Do all the animals talk here?" asked Muriel.

The white horse frowned and examined the schoolgirl carefully. "All creatures talk," replied the animal. "You don't know anything!"

"You never seem to notice me these days," replied the Silver Knight, with a touch of sadness in his voice.

Muriel noticed the crest on his shield to be a big red heart, like the heart on Valentine's Day cards. A funny crest for a knight to carry, she thought.

"Do I know you?" asked Muriel, gazing up into the square helmet of the knight. "Your voice is familiar I think," she said, "but I can't see your face."

"You have always taken me for granted," replied the Silver Knight.

"Well, I am sorry if you feel like that," replied Muriel. "I never meant to, and besides, I don't think I know who you are, anyway."

"There is both a sadness and a truth in what you say," replied the Silver Knight.

"She is clever, but she has a lot to learn," observed the horse.

"I am guessing that you are The Silver Knight," suggested Muriel.

"None other," replied the rider, "and this is Spero."

"Nice to meet you at last," replied Spero the horse.

"There is Hope for you," said the Silver Knight.

Muriel did not understand about the horse, however, she could appreciate the animal's purity, so she simply stroked his nose gently instead. As she did so, a sense of lightness stole over her, and she suddenly felt more optimistic for the future.

"Bron says you are here to help The Client," suggested Muriel.

"If I can," replied the knight. "It is my duty to do so."

"Bron also says there is a monster in the Twisted Mountains."

"Is there indeed?" replied the Knight, turning in his saddle and gazing away towards the distant hills.

"There have been rumours to that effect," replied Spero. "The future doesn't look good for this place if that is true, yet there is always Hope."

"Bron says the monster will one day come down and destroy everything," went on Muriel.

"Bron says a lot of things," observed the Silver Knight, still gazing away towards the Twisted Mountain. "But Hope will carry me forwards."

"That rather depends on the type of monster it is," replied the horse. "Some monsters don't travel at all, but their wickedness radiates out from them across the world, that is how they do so much damage by staying in one place."

Muriel didn't really understand what the horse was saying, but didn't want either of them to know she didn't understand, so she nodded as though she did.

"Maybe Bron says too much," observed the knight.

"I keep thinking I know you," said Muriel.

"I don't believe I have ever had the pleasure of your acquaintance," replied the horse.

"Not you, *him*," said Muriel, indicating the knight.

"You know me, and then you don't know me," replied the Silver Knight.

"How can I know you, and not know you at the same time?" asked Muriel, who was secretly wishing people here just gave a straight answer to a straight question.

"I didn't say you knew me, and didn't know me at the same time," replied the knight. "Your consciousness of me comes and goes, at different times. But I am *always* conscious of you."

"Because I am The Client?" asked Muriel, trying to understand.

"Something like that," replied the Silver Knight.

Muriel shook her head. "Maybe you will accept a quest?" she ventured in an effort to change the subject. "Seek out and destroy the monster!"

"I am your servant, I will do as my lady bids me," replied the knight.

Muriel smiled at the Silver Knight. There was something vaguely familiar about him. Muriel thought she ought to have known who he was, but she wasn't sure. She was about to ask him to raise his helmet so she could see his face when the Silver Knight turned on his magnificent steed Spero, and trotted away without another word towards the Twisted Mountains.

"Watch where you're going!" shouted back Spero, as it cantered away into the distance.

"How can you take someone for granted when you don't even know them?" asked Muriel to herself, as she put the map away, and started down the slope to Brocas' Language School.

The Crucible of Creation was nearly all desert, but it wasn't all flat, Muriel observed. She was definitely walking downhill when the crest of a tiled roof rose before her from below the large sand dune she was on. Muriel could hear the sound of children playing as she skirted the side of the building, and entered the school gate from the front, where she stopped dead.

In the playground before the school building were numbers of other Muriels, all different versions of herself, some of a similar age, but many were younger, and some looked to be only about five years old.

"I didn't expect this," said Muriel to herself, as she passed through the gate, and began to mingle with her other selves.

Suddenly a bell began to ring, and Muriel could see a man in a black college gown and mortar board, madly waving the brass hand bell up and down.

"That must be the middle bell," said Muriel to herself.

"Come on, come on, let's get in," shouted the professor. "No time to waste."

Muriel walked towards the front door of the little school building, and as she approached, the professor saw her, and recognised her immediately.

"Well, hello Muriel," he said. "You've come back to see us. How nice, go in."

Muriel resisted the temptation to mention the fact that she had never been here before, as far as she could remember, but decided not to. It's way too easy to make a mistake here, she thought, deciding to keep quiet for now.

"Settle down, settle down quickly," said the teacher. "Let's get the register done, then we can begin."

The professor picked up a large, black book from the top of his desk, opened it, then called out in a loud voice. "Muriel Mason?"

Everyone in the class shouted, "Here!" at once.

"All present and correct," replied the teacher, closing the register with a clap.

Muriel was standing at the back of the class, and the teacher waved at her impatiently. "Sit, sit, sit…"

Muriel found an empty desk beside Muriel aged about ten. Muriel smiled, Muriel smiled back.

"You will have noticed that an old girl has come back to see us, her name is Muriel Mason, I trust you will all make her most welcome," said the professor, and many Muriels turned and smiled at Muriel.

"I expect you have forgotten all of this already, Muriel?" asked Professor Brocas.

"I don't remember…" faltered Muriel.

"Of course you don't!" shouted Professor Brocas. "Here you learn about language subconsciously…you don't know you know it. But later when you need it, then you know you know it, you know?"

Muriel slowly nodded.

Several of the younger Muriels were not paying any attention to Professor Brocas, instead they were looking under their desks, and peering cautiously under their chairs. The Professor sighed. "There are no spiders in here today Muriel!" he announced. "Please return to your seats!"

The young Muriels, suddenly reassured that the schoolroom was an arachnid free zone, sat back on their seats and looked at the man in the black gown.

"Today we are going to begin to examine the modern trend for exaggeration, which is appalling!" shouted Professor Brocas. "People exaggerate to show emphasis, which is unnecessary, as the words themselves should convey the exact meaning to the listener, and therefore the exaggeration is pointless!"

A young Muriel at the back at the class began to yawn. Professor Brocas pointed at her and shouted, "Muriel Mason, I have told you ten thousand times not to yawn in my class!"

Everyone turned to look at Muriel who slapped a hand over her mouth and stifled the yawn mid glory, so that her eyes began to water.

"Have I told you that ten thousand times Muriel Mason?" shouted the Professor.

The Muriel with the strangled yawn nodded her head in agreement.

"Have I?" shouted the Professor. "Ten thousand times?"

The yawning Muriel shook her head to disagree.

"No, I haven't!" exclaimed Professor Brocas. "I was exaggerating!"

Professor Brocas picked up a tin tray from the top of his desk, and sweeping off his mortar board with one hand, he proceeded to bash himself over the head several times, with the tray in his other hand. As the tray crashed onto his head each time he shouted. "Naughty! Naughty! Naughty Professor!"

Professor Brocas placed the bent tray back on his desk, and his mortar board back on his head.

"If you speak with the correct choice of words my little angels, you will never need to exaggerate."

The Professor picked up a plate of spaghetti, and ignoring his pupils began to slowly wind the pasta strings around his fork. When he had wrapped the tines in a Flemish coil of pasta rope he slowly raised the fork to his mouth, and placed the food in there with such loving care he seemed to be savouring the experience as though he had never tasted the like before. Professor Brocas closed his eyes with rapture and began to hum with delight.

All the facets of Muriel could not take their eyes from their teacher, never was there a class in the history of teaching so engaged.

One single strand hung from the lips of the mentor like a yellow shoelace, which the Professor began to slowly suck up inch by inch. Several Muriels began to smile. When the last of the string finally disappeared, Professor Brocas opened his eyes, looked at his youthful charges to make sure he had their attention, and then lowered them to his plate.

"Oh my darling!" he exclaimed. "You are so beautiful, you make me so happy, and my life is complete with you in it."

Several Muriels began to stare wide-eyed at their teacher.

"I cannot live without you," said Professor Brocas to his plate of spaghetti. "I love you so much."

Several Muriels began to giggle.

Professor Brocas seemed to snap out of his reverie and smiled at the class.

Several of them laughed out loud.

"I *love* spaghetti!" said Professor Brocas laughing.

Muriel laughed and clapped as one.

"You cannot LOVE spaghetti!" shouted the Professor, finally tossing the plate away. "That's just insane!"

The Muriels got the point, and began to warm to the Professor.

"Use the correct words when you speak and do not exaggerate!" he said.

The class was his now, and the wise old Prof went on to the next subject.

"Now we are going to discuss the use of stress in language," announced Professor Brocas, taking out a bottle of pills, emptying the bottle into the palm of his hand and then cramming all the pills into his mouth; some of the little white tablets bounced on the wooden schoolroom floor. "God knows, I know all there is to know about stress these days," he shouted.

The professor took a bottle of whisky from the bookshelf behind him, opened the bottle, threw the top away and took a gargantuan swig to wash the tablets down.

No-one in class seemed to think this was odd behaviour for a teacher, except perhaps Muriel.

Professor Brocas thrust his arms straight up and out, towards the ceiling, and threw back his head, sending his mortar board flying backwards into the air, and bellowed at the very top of his voice: "I NEVER SAID SHE WAS MY FRIEND MURIEL!"

Then he lowered his head between his still upstretched arms to gaze upon the features of his startled pupils.

"Now, let's examine this sentence by laying the stress on each word in turn, and we will see how the meaning of the sentence changes as we go," said the Professor, in a much calmer voice, and lowering his arms.

"*I* never said she was my friend Muriel, means I never said it, someone else did. I *never* said she was my friend Muriel, means that someone said it, but it wasn't me, or I may have said something else. I never *said* she was my friend Muriel, means, I did mean it all the time but never said it, I may have written it down instead. I never said *she* was my friend Muriel, means I did say it but didn't mean her. I never said she *was* my friend Muriel, means I never meant to imply that she isn't my friend now. I never said she was *my* friend Muriel, means I never said she was my friend, but she could be someone else's friend. I never said she was my *friend* Muriel, means she might just be an acquaintance of mine, not a friend at all. And finally, I never said she was my friend *Muriel,* means I am telling Muriel I never said it!"

Professor Brocas took another large swig from the whisky bottle, and with one eye, owlishly scanned his mesmerised class.

"See!" shouted Professor Brocas. "Handling stress is easy!"

Muriel sat open-mouthed. Professor Brocas took another titanic swig from the whisky bottle. His eyes rolled upwards just before he lost consciousness, and fell down onto the floor with a meaty crash. The bottle rolled away and hit the wall with a solid clunk. No-one seemed shocked or even surprised, except perhaps Muriel.

Muriel in the front row leaned over her desk and gazed at her stricken teacher.

"He's out cold again!" she announced to the class. "First break!"

The entire class took this as the end of the lesson. Rising as one they filed outside to the front square, immediately organising themselves into small groups, where the older ones talked together in huddles and the younger ones began to play skipping and hopscotch.

"Is he going to be alright?" asked Muriel to her younger self who had been sitting beside her in the classroom.

"Don't worry," replied Muriel. "He often passes out when he gets stressed like this. He's trying to cram as much knowledge into us as he can in the time he has left."

"What do you mean?" asked Muriel to her classmate. "In the time he has left?" as she moved out through the school gates.

"Before the monster comes," replied Muriel, closing the gates with a soft click, and then waving goodbye to Muriel before running back to join her friends.

"I need to find out more about this monster," mused Muriel, wandering away from Brocas' Language School and consulting Bron's map once again.

The living thing, whose very appearance in the Crucible had sent alarm signals racing to every compass point, lay still upon its back, completely heedless of the consternation its very existence had caused. It had begun to develop its overall shape again, making changes to its structure as the hours of its hibernation ticked slowly past.

It had formed a bulbous mass above the main trunk, which pulsed and twitched below its skin more than the trunk itself, as though some separate creature lay within.

In the upper centre of this bulbous mass two swellings could be seen, separate and distinct from the rest of their surroundings. These swellings throbbed with a pulse of their own, flicking from left to right in unison, synchronised together. Suddenly these two swellings stopped moving and centred themselves, pausing as the seconds ticked away. Below the twin mounds two small rips appeared in the fabric of the creature, the skin above the small rips rolled back to reveal two black orbs. The monster opened its eyes and looked at the ceiling of its cave.

Chapter Four

The Great Egg and the Upside Down People

As it was a Saturday, Muriel decided a trip into town was in order. She had tried on her father's home computer several times to research exactly who or what Bron was, with only limited success, and thought she might have more luck in the reference section at the city library.

"Can I help you?" asked the librarian when Muriel stood idly at the reception desk.

"Do you have anything on interpreting dreams?" asked Muriel.

"We have a very good section on that subject," replied the librarian. "I'll show you."

Together Muriel and the librarian weaved their way through the lines of long bookshelves, until they arrived at the Right section.

"Everything along the middle shelf is on the subject you are looking for," explained the librarian. "Call me again if you need further assistance."

A man in a blue pinstriped suit was looking through the same section, Muriel thought he looked like a banker. Muriel wondered what a banker might dream about.

Money probably.

Every book Muriel looked in told her that to dream of a hippopotamus meant something completely different. One suggested she might be pregnant, Muriel knew that could not be true. Another said that to dream of a hippopotamus was a sign that she was uncomfortable with her weight, and she might consider going on a diet. Muriel shook her head. "Who writes this stuff?" she whispered to herself, and found another book. Nothing answered her questions, she was no better off than she had been before she came to the library. "Anyway," she said to herself as she left, "I'm not really sure they are dreams at all."

Muriel sat on the bus going home and noticed an elderly lady in a blue hat, sitting opposite her. Behind the old lady, scenes of life in the town whizzed by. Groups of men with brightly coloured scarves going to some sporting event. A local church, the pub. The old lady did not seem aware of any of the hustle and bustle of modern life that surrounded her on all sides. Muriel wondered what old age must be like.

Muriel got off the bus at her stop and began to walk home; she recognised the form of her friend a few hundred yards in front of her, and Muriel shouted "Michelle! Michelle!" but her friend did not hear, and turned the corner at the top of the street, disappearing from view. Muriel walked through the park as a short cut home, and had to jump out of the way of a small boy on a bicycle who was pedalling along the path as fast he could.

"I don't think I'm going to get the answers I need in any library," said Muriel to herself, "or on the internet. It sounds mad, but I think the answer to who or what Bron is, lies with Bron himself."

Muriel was thinking about this at home, when she suddenly began to feel quite tired. "I think I will have a few minutes sleep on the sofa," said Muriel.

"Oh darling!" exclaimed Muriel's mother in exasperation. "You're only out of bed a few hours, you can't be sleepy already! Muriel this isn't normal!"

"Stop fussing mother," replied Muriel, yawning. "I'll only have five minutes."

Muriel kicked off her shoes and stretched out on the sofa. She decided to follow Bron's map logically, and to visit all the places on it that she could, and since she was now just outside the gates to Brocas' Language School, it seemed a short step down to the Great Egg.

As she continue to walk downhill, she could see the giant arc of the egg become clearer to her as she drew ever closer.

"It's huge," she said to herself, as she began to realise the dimensions of the Great Egg. "I wonder what sort of creature was able to lay an egg that size? And how many Upside Down People actually live beside it? And why would people be upside down in the first place?"

As Muriel approached the egg itself, she could no longer make out its curved shape at all, as it was simply so large, it covered the entire horizon before her, and merely became like a great edifice that stretched in all directions as far as she could see. Muriel found what appeared to be a doorway in the base of the egg, and went inside.

As Muriel entered the central pathway which led from the door of the structure, she saw great lines of people coming into the egg, they just appeared through the front wall, floated through the air until they reached a glass panel, and then were flipped upside down when they emerged from the other side. None of the people seemed to be the least perturbed or surprised at now being upside down.

Muriel began to wander closer to the Upside Down People; she wanted to talk to them at least, this was all so new and fascinating for her.

"You can't go that way!" shouted a very stern voice behind her, and Muriel spun around to see a uniformed man waving frantically to her. "Come over here at once!" he called.

Muriel felt she had no option but to obey the summons, and began to walk towards the man.

"Where do you think you're going?" asked the man, as Muriel approached.

"I don't really know," replied Muriel truthfully, "I'm new here."

"Well, what do you want?" asked the man. "Move along there, don't bunch up, there's room enough for everyone!" he called to the Upside Down People. "Keep moving, that's it!"

"I don't really want anything, I was just curious," replied Muriel. "I was interested in the egg, that's all. I'm just visiting."

"Then you must be lost, we don't get visitors here," said the man, and then calling over Muriel's shoulder to the Upside Down People, "Keep moving, that's it!"

"I'm not lost, I have a map," replied Muriel.

"And what does the map tell you about the egg?" asked the man.

"Nothing. It just shows me where it is."

"Not much good then, is it?" replied the official.

Muriel didn't like the man very much. His manner seemed a little brusque for a tour guide, and he wasn't very polite at all.

"May I ask what your job is?" asked Muriel.

"Isn't it obvious?" replied the man testily. "I am here to keep them all moving in straight lines, of course."

Muriel nodded. "Of course."

"Can't have them bunching up, and getting on top of each other, that would cause confusion, which would be catastrophic for the whole world. It would throw the universe into chaos!"

Muriel was still nodding, but secretly she thought the man was exaggerating wildly. He was probably trying to make his job sound much more important than it really was. Professor Brocas would not have cared for the man's exaggerations at all.

"And why are they all upside down?" asked Muriel.

"Who knows such things?" replied the man. "They have always been upside down as far as I know, once they pass through the panel that is, and I have been here since the egg was built. I am its first and only Traffic Warden."

"Ah," replied Muriel, "so you're a Traffic Warden. Who built the egg?"

"I am *The* Traffic Warden if you please. And the egg has always been here."

Muriel knew that couldn't true, the egg must have been created at some point in time, but obviously the man didn't know everything about it.

"I don't understand the point of it," observed Muriel, "I mean what does it do exactly?"

The Traffic Warden sighed, this girl was beginning to get on his nerves, she asked way too many searching questions: questions he himself had never asked in all the time he had worked there.

Muriel continued to watch the endless procession of the Upside Down People moving steadily from the inside of the egg, down a designated path, far into the distance where they just seemed to fade away into the back wall. The strangest thing about the procession was not the fact that they were all upside down, although that in itself was indeed strange enough, but that each of them seemed to carry their own little background scene with them, which was individual to them. A child on a bicycle pedalled past

Muriel, and there were trees and upside down flowers moving past his upside down wheels; he seemed to be in a garden or a park, perhaps. Then a man in a blue pinstriped suit walked past who was reading a book, but around him were high bookshelves, he seemed to be in a library. An elderly woman passed Muriel who was wearing a blue hat, and who was sitting on a seat; behind her head, buildings were whizzing past her, as though the woman was seated on a bus. Muriel wondered what old age must be like. Some of the Upside Down People seemed familiar to Muriel, but at that moment she could not remember when or where she had seen them before.

"It's not a procession of people at all," exclaimed Muriel. "They are all separate scenes, like the individual frames of different movies. They're not connected together."

"You're a bright girl," replied the Traffic Warden. "It took me a long time to realise that."

"There's my friend!" shouted Muriel, pointing to one of the Upside Down People whom she instantly recognised. "Michelle!"

Muriel ran up a short flight of stairs leading to an elevated walkway, where the Traffic Warden could get a much closer view of the Upside Down People as they floated past. As Michelle glided down towards the far wall, Muriel stepped out onto the walkway to speak to her.

"Wait! Stop!" shouted the Traffic Warden from behind her, but it was too late.

Muriel began to hinder the progress of the other Upside Down People as she weaved her way through the collection of scenes towards her friend.

"Get off there!" shouted the Warden.

As soon as Muriel stepped onto the walkway the passing scenes began to vibrate, and then became blurred and indistinct. Several of them stopped moving, and the others coming behind began to crash into the now frozen images in front. When they touched each other the images began to fade away and disappear.

"Get off there immediately!" screamed the Warden, as though Muriel was about to bring the universe to an end.

Muriel looked through the crowd of images for her friend, Michelle, only to see that particular image crackle and then disappear.

"All right, I'm going," said Muriel, "no need to panic."

"You have no idea what you have done!" shouted the Warden. "This area is very sensitive, this is why there are no visitors, you shouldn't even be here!"

"Calm down," replied Muriel. "I only wanted to talk to my friend."

The Great Egg began to rotate slowly, and a terrible humming sound filled the air.

"Oh my God, what's happening?" asked the Warden, as he looked up with terrified eyes to the summit of the giant sphere. "What have you done?"

Over the exterior of the great edifice began to run a dribble of water, which ran like rivulets of rain down the arched sides of the egg; this tide of water could be seen from the inside as a dark shadow moving from top to bottom from where they stood.

"It's starting to water," whispered the Warden, in genuine alarm. "Maybe I should tell someone about this. It's not my fault."

"Don't worry," said Muriel in a soothing voice. "I will tell them it was all my doing."

Within seconds poured a cascade of water, like the opening of a giant sluice, as the exterior walls of the egg turned from a pale to a dark grey as the light inside the egg faded into twilight. The procession of Upside Down People suddenly disappeared, and no more scenes came through the front wall. Muriel felt the arms of the Traffic Warden encircle her waist and drag her physically off the walkway.

"Look what you've done!" shouted the Warden. "You stupid girl, look what you've done!"

"I'm sorry!" shouted Muriel. "I didn't think, I wanted to speak to my friend."

"You must never go onto the walkway, never!" yelled the Warden, "and you must never, never try to touch them!"

"They're not real!" stammered Muriel, kicking her legs frantically to get free of the Warden's embrace, as he had physically lifted her off her feet. "They're not real people, they're like photographs, that's all."

"Not photographs," replied the Warden, more calmly this time. "More like reflections in a mirror."

The Warden gently deposited Muriel back onto her feet.

The cascade of water which had flooded the outside of the Great Egg and washed all the Upside Down People away, was now dissipating. In a moment the walls seemed to dry once more and into the egg another procession of images began to emerge and as before, began to make their way down towards the glass panel, where they were all flipped upside down.

"It's started again," whispered Muriel. "No harm done."

"No harm done?" replied the Warden. "All those people are now lost forever, washed away by the egg's defence system. Those people can never be replaced!"

"You said yourself they're only reflections!" replied Muriel. "How important can they be?"

The Warden looked at Muriel as though she was some kind of master criminal.

"Anyway there's loads more coming now," said Muriel.

"That's beside the point!" shouted the Warden.

"Like the gate at the garden," replied Muriel.

"What?" asked the Warden.

"Truth is beside the point. It's only what we believe that matters. Never mind," said Muriel. "I was thinking of another place."

"I think you had better go," said the Warden, "before you do any more damage."

"I'm sorry about all this," replied Muriel truthfully, "but I do want to understand a lot more about the egg, and about the Upside Down People."

"I don't have the answers to your questions," replied the Warden.

"Who would know?" asked Muriel.

The Traffic Warden scratched his head. "The most intelligent person I know is Wernicke the Magician. Ask him."

Muriel got out Bron's Map and nodded. "That would Wernicke at Wernicke's Magic Castle, I presume."

The Warden nodded.

"Thank you, I will," said Muriel, "I'll be going now."

The Traffic Warden seemed relieved.

"I'm sorry for the trouble I caused you, I didn't mean to be a nuisance," apologised Muriel.

The Traffic Warden nodded again.

"Muriel!"

The sound of her name echoed around the Great Egg, and the startled Traffic Warden looked towards the skies. "What's that?" he asked.

"Someone is calling me," replied Muriel.

"Muriel! Wake up," said Muriel's mother. "You've been crying in your sleep.

What's wrong?"

"Nothing's wrong," replied Muriel. "I'm not crying, my eye is watering, that's all."

"What's wrong with your eye?" asked Muriel's mother, as she bent over, and gazed steadily into her daughter's face.

"I don't know," replied Muriel truthfully. "It's just happened, maybe there's something in it."

"I'll get a tissue, and have a look," said Mrs Mason.

Muriel rubbed her left eye as the tears ran over her fingers.

"There's a lot of water," observed Muriel's mother, "put your head back and let me see."

Muriel arched her neck and looked straight up at the ceiling, as her mother gazed into her daughter's eye, for a sign of something that should not be there. "I can't see anything," said her mother.

"Never mind," replied Muriel, "whatever it was, it has gone now."

In the Garden of Idols, Patrick was feeling a sense of unease. For the past week or so he had been coming to a particular spot in the garden where a new statue was emerging from its block of jelly.

"I don't like the look of this one," said Patrick shaking his head.

The new sculpture could not be identified as anything Patrick had seen before.

It did have the appearance of a living thing, as it seemed to have a head of sorts, which had eyes and ears, but no mouth. It had no neck, the sides of what appeared to be its head rose directly from its torso, but it supported itself upon two strong arms which ended in claws. The whole effect was of a thing emerging from the plinth itself, pushing itself upwards, rising out of the floor. A thing appearing from another dimension.

"What can it represent?" asked Patrick of himself.

Muriel jumped up from the sofa. "I'm going to be sick!" she announced, heading quickly to the bathroom.

Muriel's mother ran after her daughter.

In the bathroom, Muriel vomited the contents of her stomach into the toilet bowl.

"Muriel, you have to see a doctor," insisted her mother. "Something is terribly wrong with you."

"I just feel a bit light headed today, that's all," explained Muriel. "It will pass."

"Are you pregnant?" asked her mother quietly.

Muriel laughed. "No chance of that," she replied.

Again Muriel ejected her lunch into the toilet bowl.

"I'm going to make an appointment with the doctor," said Muriel's mother.

Muriel shook her head as if to reply once again that seeing the doctor was unnecessary, when the bathroom walls began to fade away, and Muriel felt herself falling.

"Muriel! Muriel!" called a familiar voice, but Muriel could not hear it properly as it seemed to be coming from a distant place; a shout from far away. Muriel felt a sense of weightlessness steal over her being as she floated away from the voice, further and further, until she could hear it no longer.

The unknown thing which lay on the floor of the cave had been looking straight up at the ceiling of rock for some time. It had fallen into bouts of sleep, and in each short period of hibernation it had felt stronger, more vital upon waking. As it slept again there appeared on either side of its bulbous mass a small opening, as though the side itself had collapsed, and after crashing inwards there was left nothing but a small hole either side. As it woke the first thing it noticed was that it could hear the sounds of the Crucible. The monster was developing slowly, day by day, hour by hour, minute by minute. It had sight and sound now, and it listened carefully to the hum of nature around its being. It heard the rocks move, scraping against each other, the breeze shifting the sands far below it on the desert plain, and the distant chatter of the inhabitants as they went about their daily chores, unaware of what this strange thing, born alone in the mountains was slowly becoming.

Chapter Five

The Arch of Pons

Muriel awoke to the sound of a squeaky wheel, rotating painfully beneath an overladen hospital trolley. The protesting wheel came to a silent stop as the middle-aged woman who had been pushing the vehicle also came to a stop at the foot of Muriel's bed.

"Oh, you're awake!" declared the woman smiling. "Would you like a nice cup of tea?"

"Where am I?" asked Muriel, trying to take in her suddenly strange surroundings.

"Oh, she's awake!" declared Muriel's mother, rushing towards the bedside and throwing her arms around her daughter.

"Why am I in hospital?" asked Muriel, endeavouring to sit up, and realising she was wearing one of those hospital gowns which ties at the back of the neck, and seemed to serve no function other than to make the wearer look ridiculous.

"You fainted in the bathroom, and we couldn't wake you," observed Muriel's dad, who had joined them at the bedside. "We were very worried about you."

"I don't remember," replied Muriel simply.

"It's alright now," assured Muriel's mother, "they're going to do some tests, they want to find out why you keep fainting, that's all. They're going to keep you in for a few days."

"I don't *keep* fainting," argued Muriel, remembering Professor Brocas' warning about exaggerations. "It has only happened twice."

"That's two times too many," replied her dad.

"And you're being sick, and you're falling asleep all over the place, it's not natural," added her mother.

Muriel tried to focus on the present moment, but it kicked and slid out of her grasp like an oily fish. Only her time in the Crucible seemed clear to her now, and images of the Upside Down People crowded into her consciousness whether she wanted them there or not.

"*Everyone* is very worried about you," said Muriel's mother matter-of-factly, and Muriel thought again of Professor Brocas, who insisted on the correct usage of language, at all times and didn't like casual exaggerations.

Muriel pointed to an elderly lady in the opposite bed who was wheezing for every breath, and sounded like she might die any second. "*She's* not worried about me," replied Muriel.

Muriel's mother's face took on a sympathetic expression which was generally reserved for advertisements on the television where tortured tigers in Africa needed £3 a month for their salvation. "You know what I mean," she replied.

Presently an elderly sage in a white coat appeared at the foot of Muriel's bed, and looked at her appraisingly. He seemed to be sizing her up in some way, assessing her value, as an estate agent might look at a house for sale.

"How are you feeling now?" he asked, stroking his white goatee beard with his index finger and thumb, and wondering at the same time what state of disrepair her guttering might be in.

"I'm fine," replied Muriel, "I don't need to be here."

The doctor smiled benignly, and nodded his head. "We just want to make sure of that," he said. "Rest now, and we'll begin the tests in the morning."

Muriel could not help wondering about the Upside Down People as she traversed the sand towards the Arch of Pons. Why they were all upside down in the first place remained a mystery, that according to the Traffic Warden, only Wernicke the Magician could unravel. Muriel wondered what Wernicke might be like; she envisioned him as an aged sage in a purple robe sporting moons and stars, flowing away beneath a broad-brimmed, tall, pointed hat. The classic, storybook wizard. Of course he would have to have a long white beard, all traditional wizards had long white beards. Yet a thought came to Muriel which made her wonder about how clever Wernicke really was. If he was in fact such a powerful Magician, why had he not simply put a spell on the monster? That was a question which troubled Muriel as she tramped across the desert sands, trying to fit the pieces of the puzzle into some interlocking whole, that might begin to form a picture of this strange and enchanting world she had lately discovered.

"Get your guide to the famous Arch of Pons, only three hundred pounds," said a voice which brought Muriel back to the present moment.

A young man was standing in front of Muriel with a single pamphlet held out towards her. "Only three hundred pounds, Miss," he said again. The young man had a handcart beside him which was full of such pamphlets.

Muriel instinctively reached forwards and took the pamphlet. It was just a single sheet of paper with a badly drawn picture of an arch on it. Through the arch was depicted a road going down to the bottom of the paper, and another road going off to the Right. *Arch of Pons* was all that was written on the sheet. Muriel looked at it, and then handed it back.

"Three hundred pounds for that?" she exclaimed. "That's way too much!" she said. "It's not worth it."

"Value is relative, Miss," replied the boy. "What is worthless to some, is a treasure to others."

"Maybe so," agreed Muriel, "but not to me. I have a better drawing than that myself, and it was given to me for nothing."

"By a hippopotamus living in a tent, I suppose!" replied the lad.

Muriel smiled and showed her map to the boy.

"As we have only just met, and we always want to create a good impression with strangers, you are reluctant to reject my offer with no explanation," replied the boy. "You feel as though you might have hurt my feelings, and so you justify your actions as being logical, and therefore understandable, by producing evidence which supports your estimation of my products' relative overcosting? It was unnecessary Miss. I am not at all insulted."

"I beg your pardon?" replied Muriel, trying to remember what the young man had just said.

"Three hundred and fifty pounds, and it's yours?" the lad replied, thrusting the same pamphlet back at Muriel.

Muriel laughed. "I have just told you that your original price was too much, now you offer it to me again at a higher price? That makes no sense."

"A thought has just passed through your mind that you might have missed a bargain," observed the boy. "Now the price has gone up. If you had bought from me only a moment ago, you could have saved yourself fifty pounds. A sense of regret is manifesting in your subconscious. You are already wondering if you have made a mistake."

"Nonsense!" replied Muriel, but she sensed the boy was right.

"Value is entirely dependent on circumstances," said the boy. "The perceived value of an item on Monday may go up or down on Wednesday, depending upon what has transpired with the perceiver on Tuesday."

Muriel thought the boy talked funny, but he was a handsome lad with an engaging smile; she caught herself smiling back at him.

A middle-aged couple appeared beside Muriel, and the boy turned his attention from Muriel to them.

"A fantastic Map of the Arch of Pons for the Lady and Gentleman, only five hundred pounds," said the boy.

The couple whispered to each other, and nodded together. They seemed to come to an agreement between themselves.

"Will you take a cheque?" asked the man, without even questioning the outrageous price.

"I will take payment in any currency, in any form, sir," replied the boy.

The man wrote out the cheque, exchanged it for the pamphlet with the boy, and the couple walked away delighted with their purchase.

"I don't believe this," said Muriel. "Who were they?"

"Tourists, here to illustrate my point," replied the boy. "Everything and everyone here serves a function engineered purely for either The Client's welfare, amusement or education."

"And who are you?" asked Muriel, as she began to realise all was not what it seemed, but then nothing was in this place.

"I am the Vendor," replied the boy. "It is my job to demonstrate to The Client the twin concepts of *quality* and *value*! Providing The Client has a mind to listen, of course."

"By selling something way overpriced?" asked Muriel coyly.

"By showing anyone who cares to understand, that everything in the world has a value, which is entirely relative to the person involved. Not only does the value have to match the individual, it also has to match the circumstances of the individual at the time."

"I'm not sure I follow," replied Muriel.

"Bottle tops!" exclaimed the Vendor.

"Excuse me?" said Muriel, wondering if she heard the lad correctly.

"Imagine you collected bottle tops," continued the boy. "Imagine you come across a rare bottle top that you have been seeking for a long time. To anyone else it is merely another bottle top just like all the others, but how much is that particular bottle top worth to you?"

"I don't collect bottle tops," remarked Muriel.

A silence fell between Muriel and her new acquaintance in which he was obviously waiting for her to participate in the game.

"Oh very well," sighed Muriel. "I suppose it would be worth a lot to me."

"Then the value of that bottle top is entirely different between you and the non-collector, is it not, Miss?"

"Yes, I suppose so," agreed Muriel.

"Therefore the value of the item is dependent on both the individual and the circumstance," explained the Vendor.

Muriel nodded in agreement, she didn't want to argue.

The boy put down the pamphlet and picked up a glass of water, which he handed to Muriel. "Here you are Miss, a lovely glass of clean, fresh water, only fifty pounds!"

Muriel laughed. "Don't be silly," she said. "I'm not paying fifty pounds for a glass of water!"

"Water! Water!" gasped a man crawling towards Muriel and the Vendor.

The man had a shock of long, dark matted hair and a beard. He was ragged like a beggar, with a walnut brown, sun-baked face, and lips swollen from the desert heat.

"Water! Water!" gasped the man as he crawled along the floor.

The Vendor looked pityingly at the man. "Here we are sir, a glass of lovely, fresh clean water to drink, only ten thousand pounds!"

"Yes! Yes!" shouted the man, who started to empty his pockets by throwing great sheaves of money at the boy. The notes floated in the air like autumn leaves.

When the man's pockets were depleted, he looked imploringly at the glass of water.

"Is there enough money there?" he gasped, through painfully swollen lips.

"Indeed there is, sir," replied the boy, carefully handing the glass to the man who snatched it from the Vendor, and greedily swallowed the contents in one ravenous gulp.

Muriel bent down to pick up the scattered money from the desert floor. When she stood up the beggar was gone. Muriel looked around, but only the Vendor remained. Muriel threw the bundle of notes into the boy's handcart.

"Value is a hat!" exclaimed the lad, putting on a ladies' wide-brimmed hat which had a bunch of ornamental bananas on the crown.

Muriel laughed and shook her head.

The lad swapped this hat for a gentleman's Victorian black silk topper.

Muriel laughed again and continued to shake her head.

"As you go through life's interactions, with other people," advised the boy, swapping the topper for a cloth cap.

Muriel nodded her approval.

"Always offer a hat that both suits and fits."

Muriel smiled, she was beginning to warm to the Vendor.

"Excuse me," said a man approaching the pair. "Would either of you have a light?"

The man had an unlit cigarette stuck to his lower lip.

"Sorry, I don't smoke," replied Muriel.

"I think I may be able to accommodate you, sir," replied the Vendor, producing two lighters from his pocket. "This one is two pounds, and this one is twenty pounds."

The man examined the two lighters carefully. "They look exactly the same," he remarked.

"Indeed they do, sir," agreed the Vendor.

"What's the difference then, apart from the price?" asked the man.

"The difference is in the *quality*, sir," replied the boy. "This one will always work, will last for ages and comes with a guarantee. This one, well, it will work most of the time, will last for as long as it lasts, and there is no guarantee. You pay your money and take your chance with that one."

The man examined the two lighters carefully, trying to make up his mind. "I'll take the cheap one, it's only a lighter," he said. The man paid the Vendor, lit his cigarette after several attempts to get the lighter to work, and then wandered off.

"Another satisfied customer?" asked Muriel when the man had gone.

"For now," agreed the Vendor.

Muriel reached up as she felt a hat appear on her head. She took it off to look at it. It was a white beret, which she liked, she placed it on the side of her head, and examined herself in a mirror which had appeared behind her. She liked what she saw.

Muriel had to admit the beret suited her, and it was the perfect fit. When Muriel turned back around the Vendor was gone.

In the Garden of Idols, Patrick was munching a mouthful of weeds when he stopped and noticed the small statue of a woman's purse begin to change. Patrick stopped chewing as he watched the purse expand and swell as though it was stuffed with money. Two elegant lady's hands, adorned with beautiful bejewelled rings held the purse open. "She's met the Vendor," said Patrick, smiling.

Muriel adjusted her beret, she liked her new hat, and hoped she might see the Vendor again, so she could thank him properly for it. She was turning the knotty concepts of value and quality over in her mind as she came upon the great Arch of Pons, when suddenly a small spider ran down her face. Muriel shrieked, snatched the beret from her head and wiped her face furiously with it.

"Ah, I hate spiders!" she screamed.

The archway itself was a colossal structure, high and wide, spanning one long and multi-laned highway, where armies of Fornix Runners, all looking exactly the same, jogged in long snaking processions in both directions through the yawning mouth of the great arch.

"Where are all these people going?" asked Muriel to herself, as she watched the crowds pass through the giant arch and disappear down the Great Southern Highway and out of sight.

"They go everywhere from here," replied a familiar voice from behind her.

"Get your maps of the Great Industrial South, only five pounds."

Muriel spun around to see the Vendor again.

"Oh, it's you," she exclaimed. "Thanks for my new beret, I love it!"

"It suits you," he replied, "and it fits."

"What are you selling now?" asked Muriel.

"A map of the Industrial South," replied the Vendor. "Everything down from here is automated and industrialised. Unless you like machinery you wouldn't like it much down there."

"May I see the map?" asked Muriel.

"Sure," replied the Vendor, handing her a copy.

"Mmm…" mused Muriel, "it does look very industrial."

"It's all automatic," replied the vendor. "The Fornix Runners keep the place going with their constant messages, but that's it really. It's far more interesting up here."

"Your map looks so fresh and new," observed Muriel, "the one Bron gave me is old and faded."

"Yours was created when the world was new," replied the Vendor. "Mine were printed yesterday, we sell so many we have to keep making more, do you see?"

Muriel nodded, she could see that.

"Is my map okay for you?" ventured the lad.

"What do the tool rooms do?" asked Muriel, regarding her new map.

"Generally they make things," he replied. "They're very clever down there, I must say."

"What sort of things?" asked Muriel.

"Anything we ask them to make," replied the boy. "It all depends on the circumstances the universe finds itself in at the time."

"And the farm supplies all the food?" asked Muriel.

"The farm supplies, and processes the food," said the Vendor, "to keep us all going."

"And the coach station?" Muriel didn't realise there was so much to learn about this place, or how organised it all seemed to be.

"The coach station will take you anyplace you want to go to."

"What are the turbines for?" asked Muriel. "They look like windmills."

"They are windmills," replied the boy. "They harness the natural forces of nature, the power of the wind, and turn it into energy."

"To power the factory, I suppose?" asked Muriel.

"I'm not really sure where the power for the factory comes from," confessed the boy. "Anyway the factory is closed at the moment."

Muriel nodded. "And why is the factory closed?"

"The Client isn't ready yet for the production process to start," replied the Vendor. "We'll all be notified when the time comes."

"Oh, I see," replied Muriel, who, unlike the Great Egg, didn't really see at all.

High in its isolated cave, hidden deep in the folds of the Twisted Mountains, the developing thing now had a pair of hands. Its fingers ended in long claws that scratched continually at the floor of the cave, tearing lumps from the soft rock. It had become fully wake in the last few days, and although it could not move from its prostrate position, it could see, hear and move its hands.

With a great effort it pushed one hand down into the floor of the cave which turned its torso onto its side. Then moving its other hand to the floor it was able to push with both hands until the thing was supported only by the growing power of its arms. In this position it was able to begin crawling along the floor of the cave. It seemed enthusiastic about this new discovery, as it scurried as fast as it could along the floor, until it came to the mouth of the cave. The monster peered out from the cave entrance where it was able to gaze with wondering eyes upon the Crucible of Creation stretching away below it, as far as the thing could see.

Chapter Six

Bron's Other Map

Muriel entered the Camp of the Hippos to find Bron sitting in a deckchair outside his tent, getting himself a nice sun tan. He was talking to what appeared to be a ghostly apparition standing next to him.

"No work today, Bron?" asked Muriel, trying not to look at the ghost.

"It's quiet right now," he replied lazily. "But I have a feeling it's going to be busy later on."

Muriel nodded to Bron, trying her best to appear completely indifferent to the fact that a hooded ghost was standing right there.

"This is the Ghost of Old Memories, or Gom for short," said Bron indicating the spectre with a lazy sweep of his foreleg. "And this of course is our Client, Miss Muriel Mason."

Gom the ghost bowed politely to Muriel.

"Hello," faltered Muriel.

"Gom remembers everything from the distant past," explained Bron. "All the little incidents that happened years ago that we think we have forgotten about. Gom can play back all of them for you, can't you Gom?"

Gom the ghost again bowed in deep respect before The Client.

"Don't you have all that stuff in your library anyway?" asked Muriel.

"Sure we do. But in order to find something that is ancient, we would first have to search the great index, then we would have to go to the archives and search there.

"All that is very time consuming, it's easier just to ask Gom," replied Bron, smiling appreciatively at his ghostly friend.

When Muriel looked at the hooded figure it raised its head, and for the first time Muriel could see the face of the ghost; she jumped back in alarm.

"It's got my face!" shouted Muriel. "It looks like me!"

Bron raised his eyes for heavenly support, and sighed deeply. "It's *your* memories," he explained patiently, "whose face would it have but yours?"

Muriel rubbed her face and hair again gingerly with her fingers, making sure the spider was gone.

"What's wrong?" asked the hippo, noticing her agitation.

"There was a spider on me a while ago," replied Muriel. "I hate spiders. They scare me."

"Fears and phobias are Gom's speciality," said Bron.

Gom bowed again to Muriel.

"It isn't a phobia to be frightened of spiders," said Muriel.

"That depends on where you live in the world of matter," replied Bron. "Explain it to her, Gom."

"The difference between a fear and a phobia," began the ghost, speaking with Muriel's own voice, "is in the level of danger present in the situation."

"What do you mean?" asked Muriel.

"Whether you can come to any real harm or not," explained Gom. "For instance, it is a fear to be frightened of a tiger, as the tiger could easily kill you, the danger is real. Whereas it is a phobia to be frightened of a butterfly, as the danger is not real, the butterfly can do you no harm."

"Spiders can kill you, so the danger is real," replied Muriel, confidently.

"As I said before, that depends on where you live in the world of matter," replied Bron.

"If you live in Africa or Australia," said Gom, "and you are frightened of spiders, then that is a fear, as some spiders in those countries are genuinely dangerous.

"If you are frightened of spiders and you live in England, that is a phobia, as spiders in that country are harmless."

"I still hate spiders wherever they live," insisted Muriel.

"Actually you don't," replied Gom. "You hate one particular spider from long ago in your past, a spider which has been dead for many years now."

"Show her, Gom," suggested Bron.

The Ghost of Old Memories raised its hands high above its head, and then inscribed a great circle in front of itself with a downward sweep of each arm. Muriel saw a scene forming in the vortex of an ancient and long forgotten memory. Muriel felt her consciousness being separated into two distinct halves. She was suddenly both outside the vortex looking in at the developing scene, and she was inside the scene itself, as a five-year-old playing with a puppy in the garden of a house she lived in ten years ago.

The sense of being in two places at once was a new one for the schoolgirl, she wasn't sure she liked it.

"Oh, my dog Patch!" said Muriel. "He died a few years ago."

"He was only a puppy then," replied Gom.

Patch was rooting under a bush, digging a hole and Muriel reached forwards to pull him away, when a spider suddenly dropped onto her hand. Muriel screamed, and fell backwards.

"There!" said Gom. "The original cause of your current phobia."

Gom closed the portal. Even now, years later Muriel could feel her heartbeat had quickened with the thought of that spider running across her hand.

"Now, let us go back again," said Gom. "You know what is going to happen, but this time do not scream, do not be frightened, and allow the spider to run on your hand."

Muriel shook her head violently.

"Trust me," said Gom.

Muriel nodded, but she didn't really mean it.

Once again Gom inscribed the magic portal with its arms, and Muriel watched in fascination. Patch was digging under the bush as before. Muriel reached forwards to grab the puppy.

"Now allow the spider to land in peace," said Gom.

Muriel's heart was racing, but when the spider landed on her hand she did not flinch. The spider ran across her hand and jumped back into the bush. Muriel laughed nervously when it was gone.

"There," said Gom, "nothing to worry about," as it closed the portal for the last time.

"It didn't hurt me," observed Muriel.

"Nor will it ever cause you to fear it again," said Gom. "The phobia of it has gone from your old memories."

"So, I'm not frightened of spiders anymore?" asked Muriel.

"Not the ones in England," replied Gom.

"Thank you," said Muriel to the ghost, which bowed low in deep respect to its Client before fading away.

"That was interesting," remarked Bron. "Did you want to see me about something?"

"I wanted to talk to you about this map of yours," replied Muriel.

"All compliments about my work are both appreciated, and thoroughly deserved," announced the hippo modestly.

"It has no scale on it," replied Muriel.

Bron looked puzzled. "What do you mean?" he asked.

"It doesn't show relative distance, between one place and another," replied Muriel, "and the buildings are not in relative size to each other. Your tent is far too big, for instance."

Bron looked mightily offended. "My tent is the size it is because of its importance!" explained the hippo, patiently.

"That's not how you draw a map," stated Muriel, flatly.

The Chief of the Hippopotami removed his sunglasses and twisted uneasily in the deckchair. He blinked momentarily in the bright sunlight, and then focused on the form of his troublesome visitor. Normally he would have launched into a torrid argument with anyone who dared to question the utter genius of his map, but he had to be more tactful than that with Muriel, she was The Client, after all.

"I give you the greatest map in the universe for absolutely nothing!" replied Bron, sitting upright in the deckchair. "A document absolutely unique in the annals of cartography, and you have the cheek to tell me how I could have made it better?"

"I was only saying," replied Muriel, wondering if she had gone too far with the hippo.

Bron took a deep breath, he was not used to being challenged like this. "Scale as you call it, doesn't matter very much here, anyway."

"But all maps have a scale on them," insisted Muriel.

"Not that one, it doesn't need a scale!" argued Bron.

"Show her the other map!" called the voice of a hippo, from inside one of the tents.

"What other map?" asked Muriel.

"The one with the scale on it," replied the voice again.

"You get back to your work!" shouted Bron. "I was getting around to that!"

"There is another map?" prodded Muriel.

"As you say there is no scale on the first one," said Bron. "The Fornix Runners needed to know where they were in relation to the rest of the landscape, and an idea of time and distance, so I produced a second map for them."

"That's what I need too," replied Muriel.

"Then I suppose you must have the other one as well," sighed the hippo.

Bron rose from the creaking deckchair, which seemed to let out a loud sigh of relief when the hippo finally stood up. Bron went into his tent to retrieve the second map, returning only seconds later with another parchment, again yellowed by the footsteps of time.

"This map will show you where you are right now in relative proportion and distance to every other place in existence," began the Hippo. "It will give you the exact position of all places in the universe, and will show you how the individual items of creation are spaced, relative to this camp."

"Wow!" exclaimed Muriel. "You really are very clever, Bron," she said. "I am sorry for what I said earlier."

"This other map," continued the hippo, ignoring the apology, and expanding his chest with the importance of what he was saying, "took a great deal of ingenuity, time and creative thought, it was very difficult to get absolutely Right."

"I appreciate that, Bron," replied Muriel, becoming very impressed with her new friend's map drawing skills.

"Once again I urge you to take very special care of it," urged Bron. "Never let this map fall into the wrong hands, or the consequences could be catastrophic for all of us."

"I promise," vowed Muriel, earnestly, now eager to see such an enlightened document for herself.

Bron's chest swelled with pride. He handed his other map to Muriel, with an animated flourish.

Muriel's mouth fell open when she saw Bron's Other Map for the first time. A sense of incredulity, giving way to anger gradually began to steal over her.

"Are you trying to be funny?" she hissed at the hippo.

Bron looked both deflated and surprised. "What do you mean?" he asked.

"What is *this* supposed to be?" asked Muriel, waving the parchment at the startled hippo.

"I told you what it is," replied Bron, defensively.

"The greatest map in the universe?" Muriel looked at the document again. "*A lot more up than down?* Are you kidding me?"

"It explains *everything*," replied Bron in a secretive whisper, trying to get Muriel to lower her voice.

"And you can't spell!" persisted Muriel. "I thought you were a librarian?"

"I am a librarian!" squealed the hippo defensively.

"You don't spell *here*, H-E-A-R," said Muriel. "That's hearing with your ear, not being *here*! That kind of here is H-E-R-E."

"I know!" whispered the tortured Hippo.

"Then you should take more care!" replied Muriel. "This thing is useless to me!"

Muriel threw the second map onto the sand. Bron gasped and immediately snatched it up again. Gingerly, he handed it back to Muriel. "Please keep it safe," he whispered.

Muriel snatched the map from Bron, stuffed it into her bag with the other one, and strode out of the camp, her anger and frustration enveloping her face like the folds of a great black hood. She was angry with the hippo, she didn't like to be made a fool of.

High in the isolated peaks of the Twisted Mountains the developing thing felt more physical change come upon itself. At the lower portion of its head another hole appeared as the tissue of its face began to dissolve. The thing lay still on its back, allowing nature to take its course. It moved its lower jaw several times trying to understand what had happened to it, when the jaw dropped a gaping hole was evident, witnessed only by the silent rocks above. Rows of white teeth glistened in the twilight from the roof and floor of this new hole, as the thing opened and closed its new mouth in a series of rapid biting actions.

As Muriel marched in temper across the sands she could see a man trying to light a cigarette. Time after time he clicked the lighter, but the little flame refused to come out to play. In frustration the man threw the lighter away, then threw his cigarette away and stormed off muttering to himself.

"You should have gone for quality!" shouted Muriel angrily at the man.

Bron shook his head as Muriel marched away. "She is so young, yet," observed the hippo to Muriel's retreating back. "With so much still to learn."

A distant roar could be heard from the Twisted Mountains and Bron spun around to face them.

"What was that?" asked the other hippos, suddenly darting out of their tents, and looking to Bron for an explanation.

"I think the monster has just awoken," said Bron, his voice cracking with emotion.

In the Garden of Idols, Patrick began to walk away from the developing statue.

He noticed for the first time that it now had a mouth with teeth, and looked suddenly very dangerous.

"I feel so afraid for the future when I look at this one," said Patrick.

The gardener nodded his head in agreement. "They are not our statues, Patrick," he said. "We only tend the garden, these all belong to The Client. The fears you see are hers alone."

"They have become mine too," said Patrick. "What The Client does affects all of us. And this thing, will have a great deal of effect on all of us sooner or later, you mark my words."

Muriel stomped away from the Camp of the Hippos in frustration. She wasn't sure if Bron was a genius or a complete fool. Or if he was playing some sort of mind game with her.

When Muriel was clear of the camp, she stopped and took Bron's Other Map from her bag to look at it again. She examined the document carefully, taking her time to take in every aspect of it, to see if she could understand what Bron meant about the relative distances of everything in the universe in relation to his camp.

"I still don't get it," she said to herself at last, shaking her head. "How can *a bit more up* mean anything on a map?"

Muriel sat down on the sand to study the new map in comfort. "If everything is in relation to Bron's camp," she said, "then *a lot more up than down*, must be the location of that camp."

Muriel took out the first map, and then laid both maps together, side by side on the sand before her. She noticed that on the first map *The Right Road* was drawn between the Camp of the Hippos and the Fornix Tavern, a road that led to the foothills of the Twisted Mountains, and on the second map *Right over there*, was featured too. It suddenly dawned on Muriel that "Right" on the maps might refer to an actual place, rather than a simple direction. Maybe there was a place called 'Right,' that wasn't shown on either map? Even if that was the case she mused, and Bron was a lot more clever than she had at first realised, he still couldn't spell.

Muriel put the two maps back in her schoolbag, and began to wander away thoughtfully. As Muriel tramped across the desert sands going in no particular direction, she saw in the distance ahead of her the Silver Knight cantering on Spero.

"Hello!" she shouted, waving her arms above her head.

Spero veered towards her, and the magnificent knight, his plate armour glistening in the mid-day brilliance, moved majestically closer, until Spero came to a halt before the schoolgirl.

"Well met, my lady," said the knight. "I hope the day finds you well?"

"I am well enough, thank you," replied Muriel. "How have you been getting on in your quest?"

"We have challenged the beast!" announced the Silver Knight proudly. "Although as yet the creature will not come down to face me in combat."

"And I can't climb up the mountain," added Spero. "But I am Hopeful."

"What do you two do here all day?" asked Muriel. "When there are no monsters to fight?"

"We patrol the Crucible," replied Spero. "I get plenty of exercise."

"It is not so much what we do," responded the Silver Knight. "It is more what we are."

"How do you mean?" asked Muriel.

"We are a reassuring presence here," replied the knight. "The creatures who reside here know we are available should they ever need us, that is our main function."

"Oh, I see," said Muriel. "That's quite a cushy job really."

"Being the Silver Knight is enormously demanding!" replied the knight, being slightly offended that the young girl should think he had an easy time of it. "My duties and responsibilities are endless!"

Muriel smiled. "If you say so." The Silver Knight suddenly reminded Muriel of the Traffic Warden at the Great Egg. Another employee exaggerating the importance of his job.

"Maybe you can help me with something?" asked Muriel, pulling out Bron's Other Map from her school satchel. "Bron says this map is the most important map in the whole universe. In fact, he says it *is* a map of the whole universe."

"Ah, Bron's Other Map," said Spero, looking at the document. "Bron is probably Right about that."

"But how can *a bit more up*, really mean anything on a map?" asked Muriel.

"Or *a lot more up than down*?"

Spero turned his head back to face his rider, as though he were asking permission for something. The Silver Knight merely nodded his helmet forward once, as if he had acceded to the request.

"This map shows all there is to see in the universe," began Spero, turning back to face Muriel. "Its knowledge is ancient and sacred. Very few are even aware of its existence."

"But what does it mean?" insisted Muriel.

"I'm not sure I understand your question," replied Spero.

"If my school is five miles away from my house, then any map would give that distance on a scale," said Muriel. "It wouldn't say your school is *a bit over there*!"

Muriel looked at Bron's Other Map again, and shook her head sadly. "This is all so vague."

"The specific distance you mention has no relevance here, though," replied the horse. "Have you not noticed that when you wander about here on your travels, you arrive at places sooner than you expected to?"

Muriel nodded. "Yes I have actually," she agreed. "I noticed that on the first day, when I went to the Garden of Idols, I arrived there after only a few paces, and yet it seemed so far when I looked back."

"The Garden of Idols is not anywhere near the Camp of the Hippos," said Spero.

"Then how was I able to get there so quickly on foot?" asked Muriel.

"Because time and distance are not relevant here," replied Spero. "They are measures that only work in the world of matter. So a scale on a map for this place is quite meaningless."

Muriel began to understand.

"So, *a bit more up*, actually is quite accurate, when you think about it," concluded Spero.

Muriel looked at Bron's Other Map again, and a sense of enlightenment began to dawn within her consciousness.

"We are going to take you down for a scan," said the consultant, as Muriel was awake again.

Muriel nodded her head in compliance. She was getting bored sitting in her hospital bed with nothing to do. Only her time spent in the Crucible captured her interest now.

Muriel lay on the table as the overhead console slipped noiselessly down over her torso, recording the internal images of her body the consultant would examine later.

"There," said the technician. "All done. That didn't hurt, did it?"

Muriel shook her head and smiled as she jumped down from the table.

A terrible sound echoed through the Crucible of Creation, vibrating the ground and making everyone shield their ears. In the Twisted Mountains, deep in the confines of its cave, the monster suffered the agonies of Hades. Placing its palms across its ears, the creature fell onto its back, as its eyes rolled upwards in its head.

"Why are they doing this to me?" shouted the monster at the top of its voice.

"Why can they not leave me alone?"

The monster's agony filled the timbre of its voice with a terrible resolve, and all across the Crucible, those who heard it, shivered with apprehension. Such a creature had never been seen in the Crucible before, and none there knew how to deal with the menace.

Muriel for her part, seemed the least troubled by the advent of the monster, as she saw herself as a visitor to the Crucible, and not one of its inhabitants. She was only passing through as it were, a tourist in the scene who would not sojourn long, and the after-effects of the monster would be left behind her when her time there was done.

Muriel continued to wander around the Crucible referring occasionally to the maps she had been given by Bron and the Vendor, and found herself at last back at the Great Arch of Pons.

Muriel's dad came into the kitchen still wearing his full face, silver motorcycle helmet, he even still had the visor down.

"Been out on your bike today, Dad?" said Muriel, stating the obvious.

"I'm starving," he replied. "What are you making?"

Muriel took a plate out of the microwave oven. "I was just warming up a bacon sandwich," she replied, "I'll share it with you if you like."

Her father shook his head. "I hate them warmed up in the microwave," he said, still wearing the helmet. "It over-cooks the bacon again, and makes the bread all soggy. I wish someone could invent a proper bacon sandwich warmer."

Muriel shrugged her youthful shoulders. "Suit yourself," she replied.

Muriel's dad wandered off, passing as he went, Muriel's mother.

"My Silver Knight!" said Muriel's mother as both females watched the helmeted figure disappear back through the front door.

Chapter Seven

The Industrial South

Muriel stood on the hillside looking down upon the Great Arch, where the hordes of Fornix Runners congregated and milled through the orifice as they moved north and south, carrying their individual messages to all the distant corners of creation.

"You haven't paid me yet for the map I gave you," said a familiar figure who had suddenly appeared beside her.

"Oh, hello again," said Muriel to the Vendor, "I didn't see you there."

"I come and go as the need arises," replied the lad. "Are you going to explore the Industrial South?"

"I was thinking about it," replied Muriel.

"Then you will need a guide," said the boy.

"And how much will that cost me?" asked Muriel.

"I offer my services to the lady for nothing!" replied the boy.

"In that case, I accept," said Muriel.

Muriel and the Vendor began to make their way down the hillside towards the Arch of Pons itself. As they approached the Great Southern Highway which ran north and south under the Great Arch, the Vendor went first, and put out his hand towards Muriel.

"Take my hand, Miss," he said as they entered the enormous crowd of Fornix Runners who all looked exactly the same, and were pushing and shoving each other out of the way as they tried to all pass at once through the arch. "I don't want you to get lost."

Muriel took the boy's hand, and together they jostled through the crowd until they were able to pass through the arch and begin their journey to the Industrial South.

As they walked further away from the Arch of Pons, the crowd thinned out, and they eventually found themselves alone on the Great Southern Highway.

"Why do all the Fornix Runners look the same, except for their numbers?" asked Muriel.

"They have no individual value," replied the Vendor, "they only function as a collective."

Muriel thought about this as they went along. "But each one still has his own number."

"Yes," replied the Vendor. "They are individuals up to a point. A single Fornix Runner would have a very limited impact on the Crucible, but together, they have a considerable impact. In fact, they keep everyone informed of what's happening everywhere else. Taken together they are as strong as an army."

"They're a bit like ants really," said Muriel, "only bigger."

The Vendor smiled at The Client's analogy. "The pumping station is up ahead, if you're interested in it, Miss," he announced.

"What does it pump?" asked Muriel.

"The lifeblood of the Universe," replied the boy. "Existence would end if it ever stopped."

"It's an important place, then," remarked Muriel.

"Strangely enough," replied the boy, "every place here is important. If one part fails, then the entire system starts to fail. Every place here is somehow connected to every other place, they all depend on each other."

The pumping station from the outside at least, was a bit of an anti-climax, thought Muriel. It was a large, square, concrete building, with no ornamentation at all, to demonstrate to the casual observer the crucial work that went on inside.

"Don't let the outside fool you," remarked the boy, as though he had read her mind. "It's a lot more interesting on the inside!"

"Can we go inside?" asked Muriel.

"You can go anywhere you want to," said the Vendor. "There is nowhere forbidden to The Client."

"I've been meaning to ask someone about that," said Muriel. "What does it mean, exactly, that I am The Client?"

The Vendor looked at Muriel closely. "You mean you don't know?" he whispered.

Muriel shook her head.

"This is all for you," said the boy, sweeping his arms left and right towards the distant horizons. "Everything here is for you."

Muriel was still shaking her head.

"This pumping station, the whole of the Industrial South, the Fornix Runners, Bron, the Twisted Mountains, the Garden of Idols, everything in the Crucible of Creation belongs to you!"

Muriel was becoming uneasy with the meaning of this revelation. She wasn't used to being treated as though she were this important.

"I don't understand," confessed Muriel.

"In a strange way," mused the Vendor, "even the monster belongs to you."

"But why?" was all Muriel could think of to say.

"Only Wernicke would know the answer to that one," replied the boy.

"But why is it all for me?" persisted Muriel. "Why am I so special here?"

The lad shrugged his shoulders. "You are that's all," he replied simply, "who knows why?"

"Shall we go inside?" asked Muriel eventually. The Vendor nodded and they went through the gates of the pumping station together, still hand in hand.

Muriel's heart thumped in her chest with apprehension. She lay on the plastic tray and tried not to fidget. Over her head the transparent canopy gave off a strange, pale blue light which made her skin look luminous and not entirely human.

"Don't move," said a voice to her right. Muriel turned only her eyes towards the sound, not daring to move her head. She immediately moved her eyes to the front again, as the overhead canopy began to whirr, and to move very slowly downwards towards her naked feet.

Muriel and the Vendor entered the pumping station and looked around. There was not a single technician to be seen anywhere, they seemed to be quite alone.

"How come there's no-one here?" asked Muriel.

"I told you," said the Vendor, "it's all automatic. They don't really need anyone."

Muriel felt her throat and her mouth go dry with fear as the canopy slid further down, finally enclosing her within itself, like a cocoon. She tried her best not to move, not to even breathe heavily as the outside motor whirred, and this strange contraption sent an eerie light across her face, and then slowly down her torso to her feet at the other end of the tray.

Muriel and the Vendor stood together on the viewing platform and watched in silence as the great machine crashed its giant pistons up and down, firing the lifeblood of creation in pressurised jets through its tubes, and pipes.

"It's working much faster than usual," observed the Vendor at last. "Something's happening."

"What's happening?" asked Muriel.

The Vendor simply shook his head.

The plastic canopy stopped whirring, and the colour of the lighting inside the tube which enclosed Muriel, changed to a more familiar soft white. The canopy began to slide upwards again, exposing Muriel's feet to the world once again, then her knees, her torso, and finally her face.

"All done," announced the technician, brightly. "Now that wasn't too unpleasant, was it?"

Muriel shook her head and sat up on the tray.

"The Consultant will discuss the results with you and your parents in a day or two," said the technician. "You may feel a little sleepy soon, we'll take you back to the ward, and you can rest."

"Now it seems to be slowing down again," observed the Vendor, as the great machine eased its revolutions, as the giant pistons began to decelerate. "I wonder what that was all about?"

Muriel felt a slight dizziness steal over her, and she felt unsteady on her feet. "I have to sit down for a moment," she said.

"Are you alright?" asked the boy, with genuine concern showing on his face.

"Yes, I'll be fine, I just need some fresh air. Let's go outside again," replied Muriel.

"There's nothing more to see in here anyway," remarked the boy, as he held Muriel's arm, guiding her gently to the front door.

When the bright sunlight of the early afternoon fell upon their faces, Muriel felt revived, and quite herself again. "I don't know what came over me in there," she said, "I suddenly felt very weak, as though the strength had been drained out of me."

"How are you feeling now?" asked the Vendor. "Do you want to go back?"

Muriel shook her head, "No, I am fine now, honestly, where are we going next?"

"The next thing we will come to are the twin turbines, there's one on either side of the road," replied the lad.

Muriel nodded, "Well, let's take a look at one of them."

The Great Southern Highway ran the full length of Creation, from the very northernmost point, marked on Bron's Other Map as *A bit more up,* all the way through the Arch of Pons, past the camp of the Hippos, marked on the map as *A lot more up than down,* then running straight as an arrow all the way through the heartlands of the Industrial South, right down to *All the way down*, where the Coach Station could be found at the base of the world.

As Muriel and the boy continued south on the highway, in the far distance a large truck could be seen approaching them.

"There are people here, after all," said Muriel.

"There's no-one here but us two," replied the boy.

"But someone must be driving that lorry!" persisted Muriel, but as the tanker lorry passed them going the other way, Muriel could see the cab was empty. On the side of the huge cylindrical tank was painted, *Liquid Energy*.

"There's no-one driving that lorry!" exclaimed Muriel.

"I told you," replied The Vendor. "It's all automatic down here."

"Liquid Energy?" said Muriel. "What's that?"

"They make it at the farm, and take it up to the pumping station," said the lad.

The two young travellers wandered further down the seemingly endless highway, until the twin turbines rose before them, one on either side of the road, as indicated on the Vendor's own map.

"There they are," said the Vendor. "Which one do you want to see? They're both exactly the same, so it doesn't matter which one we go to."

"You pick then," said Muriel.

They chose and moved off the highway itself, and began to follow a small path towards the front of the turbine.

"They look like windmills," said Muriel. "The word *turbine* makes them sound modern, but they're not really, they're just old-fashioned windmills."

"The design is an ancient one," replied the Vendor. "When the Industrial South was first created the universe was young. Changing the design takes millions of years."

"I see," replied Muriel, who really didn't.

As the pair approached the turbine the wind picked up, and a stiff breeze began to swirl about them, blowing Muriel's long hair out behind her, then swirling the auburn tresses across her face like a mask. The closer they got to the turbine itself, the stronger blew the wind, until at the front door neither of them could stand up straight against the gale.

"Let's go back!" shouted Muriel, through the roaring blast. "The wind's too strong!"

The boy nodded, took Muriel's hand again, and they began to retreat back the way they had come to the Highway.

"I didn't expect that!" said Muriel. "I had no idea it would be so windy over there."

"They process all the air in Creation," replied the boy. "That's what they're for."

"I think we'll just carry on," said Muriel and the Vendor nodded.

"We will come to the Farm next," he said, "it will not be stormy there."

"I like animals," announced Muriel. "I wonder what type of farm it is?"

"That all depends on The Client," replied The Vendor. "It could process meat, or fish, fowl, vegetables, anything organic really."

"But *I am* The Client!" said Muriel. "Or so everyone keeps telling me."

The Vendor nodded. "Exactly!" he replied. "So what type of farm do you have?"

Muriel shrugged her shoulders, she still didn't get it.

The Farm extended in all directions across the front of the Great Southern Highway. It appeared to be much larger than Muriel had imagined, and yet like everywhere in the Industrial South, there were no workers to be seen. The place was as silent as the Twisted Mountains, and as calm and peaceful as the Crucible desert.

"Why is there no activity?" asked Muriel, as they stood in the great farmyard. "Nothing's happening."

"It all goes on behind the scenes, you might say," replied the Vendor. "We can take a look in one of the processing sheds."

Muriel stopped walking to sniff the air, then shook her head.

"What's wrong?" asked the boy.

"I must be going mad," replied Muriel. "I thought I could smell bacon, there for a minute."

When they opened the door to the processing shed, Muriel exclaimed: "I did smell bacon!"

In front of them, in the centre of the shed was placed the largest bacon sandwich, Muriel had ever seen. Plastic tubes had been inserted into the giant sandwich which were injecting some kind of chemical into it, and other tubes seemed to be sucking a liquid out.

"What's happening?" asked Muriel.

"The food is being processed," replied The Vendor. "They inject it with acids to break down the organic structure into a liquid, and then that is sucked out and stored in those tanks." The Vendor pointed to the far end of the shed, where giant storage tanks stood patiently in line, each one with the words *Liquid Energy* painted on the front of them.

Muriel nodded. "Then the trucks take it from here to the Pumping Station," she said.

"Exactly," replied the boy. "And from there it is pumped to all the places in Creation that require it."

"So the farm doesn't actually have any animals at all, does it?" asked Muriel.

"It does," replied the boy, "but only in the form The Client delivers them."

"Me again!" said Muriel. "Why is it all about me?"

The Vendor smiled, "Because you are The Client," he replied simply.

"How long have you been around here?" asked Muriel. "You seem quite young, too young to know all this stuff, I think you're younger than me."

"The concept of *value* is an ancient one," replied the boy. "Even a caveman may prefer one type of meat to another."

"So you too have been here since the beginning?"

"Since The Client was able to determine personal preferences," he replied, "I don't remember much about the very early days."

"Yet you don't seem to have grown any older in all this time."

"The true meaning of *value* is new to most people, they don't really think about it, and so I am young. The lessons I teach are fresh and new, and therefore so am I!" replied the Vendor.

Muriel shook her head, there was so much to learn, so much that was confusing about the Crucible. It didn't help that she had entered the industrial complex from the Left, and so had to view these things logically, she wasn't able to merely understand them intuitively, as she would have been able to had she entered from the Right.

"Shall we carry on?" asked the boy at last.

Muriel nodded and they left the farm together, pressing on further down the Great Southern Highway.

"Which tool room would you like to visit?" asked the Vendor at last, after they had walked in silence for a bit.

"Are they both the same, like the turbines?" asked Muriel.

"One does more work than the other," replied the boy. "The Client gives more work to the one on the Right."

Muriel seemed puzzled by this. "I wonder why that would be?" she asked.

"The tool room on the Left really only assists the one on the Right. It hardly ever does anything by itself."

"Stranger and stranger," said Muriel, more to herself than to her companion.

"We're nearly there," remarked the Vendor, after they had gone on another few paces.

Muriel shook her head. "I'm not bothered about the tool rooms," she said.

"I've never been interested in engineering, let's skip them and go on to the factory."

"As you wish," replied the boy. "But the factory is closed at the moment."

"Yes, why is that?"

"The production process may begin in the next few years, everything is prepared. But The Client hasn't ordered it to start up yet."

"Stop calling me The Client!" announced Muriel. "And I don't know anything about this factory!"

"You will when the time comes," replied the Vendor.

Muriel sighed. The more she found out about this place the less she seemed to understand.

"So there's nothing to see in the factory either?" asked Muriel.

"All the machines are switched off now," replied her companion. "For one week every month they start up the process, and then shut it down again. It's a sort of test run, just to make sure everything is working properly, but apart from that there is nothing to see."

"I'm getting tired of all this walking, now," replied Muriel, "I think we could start to go back."

"Then we can bypass the factory and go straight to the Coach Station, you can go anywhere you want to from there," said the boy.

"Okay," agreed Muriel.

The Coach Station seemed closer than Muriel expected; as soon as she mentioned she wanted to go there, she and the lad found themselves standing in front of a pair of identical coaches, one on the Right and one on the Left.

"We can take one each and have a race back!" announced Muriel, diving into the first coach, and telling the coachman to take her home as fast as he could.

The boy laughed. "They don't work like that!" he shouted, getting into the other coach.

Muriel's coach sped ahead and then stopped, waiting for the other coach to catch up, before moving on again.

The Vendor's coach drew level with Muriel's, and they could see each other through their windows.

"We can't race each other!" shouted the boy. "The coaches have to work side by side, as a pair! First one and then the other!"

Muriel didn't understand why that had to be, but she merely nodded, and then sat back in the seat. She had a lot to think about.

"Here she is!" exclaimed Muriel's mother, as her daughter was wheeled back into the ward. "How are you feeling, darling?"

"She may be a little tired for a while, that's perfectly normal," said the technician. "She needs to rest."

"When will we be able to get the results?" asked Muriel's dad.

"In a few days, the consultant will meet with you both then, to discuss them."

The next few days were days of anxious apprehension in the Mason household.

Muriel slumbered the time away in her hospital bed, but at home neither her mother nor her father could sleep for the worry of what the consultant might be telling them shortly. For his part, Muriel's father tried to keep the family spirits up, by being positive and jovial with Muriel's mother, but her feminine intuition coupled with her natural pessimism, would not allow her spirits to rise. Muriel's mother spent most of the next three days watching television, but not seeing anything, whilst hugging a large cushion, and dabbing her eyes with an endless parade of paper tissues.

"I just know it's going to be bad news," she whispered.

"We don't know that!" replied her husband. "Just wait for the test results."

"Why has she been falling asleep all over the place?" replied Muriel's mother. "And what about that fainting incident at school? There is something seriously wrong, I just know it."

Muriel's father placed his arm around his wife, and pulled her gently into him, where she rested her head upon his shoulder. There they sat watching a programme on the television that neither of them would remember anything about.

The thing that was a forming shape and little more, over the past week had become more clearly defined. From a torso that crawled about the floor of its cave, it now stood upright on two legs, as a man may stand.

"Now I am complete!" it said, walking to the mouth of its cave and looking down upon the desert civilization which stretched far and wide below.

"Now can I act, and fulfil my purpose here," it whispered, its gravelly voice lost upon the natural breeze of the Crucible.

The inhabitants of that extraordinary place went about the functions of their office with a determined stride, focused on the job at hand. Not a single one of them sensed the storm that was brewing above them, nor the impact the strange creature who had lately arrived in the Twisted Mountains would have on all of their futures.

Chapter Eight

The Fornix Tavern

Muriel's father put down the telephone receiver and simply said: "We're wanted at the hospital. The test results have come back."

Muriel's mother clutched the edge of the table to stop herself from falling. "Oh my God!" she gasped.

"Now, there's no point in upsetting yourself," said Muriel's dad, "before we have heard what the consultant has to say."

"I just know it's going to be bad news," observed Muriel's mother. "There has to be something seriously wrong with her, otherwise why would she keep falling asleep and fainting like this?"

The consultant, fingered his white beard with his index finger and thumb, as he watched Muriel's parents progress down the ward towards him. It was a subconscious action he habitually performed when he was trying to make his mind up about something.

"Ah, Mr and Mrs Mason, let's go into my office," he said when the couple drew up to him.

The consultant waited for the unhappy couple to settle themselves into their chairs. There was no easy way to render their approaching anguish into a palatable medicine.

"We have now received the results of Muriel's scan," he began, "and it is not good news, I am afraid."

Muriel's mother caught her breath, and her father nodded to the consultant, asking him to go on.

"Muriel's test results show a collection of cancer cells located on the left side of her Cerebral Cortex," said the consultant. "That is on the upper left side of her brain."

Mr and Mrs Mason stared blankly ahead without speaking. They were trying to take in what the man in the white coat was actually saying to them. Eventually, Muriel's father broke the tender silence.

"Are you telling us, our daughter has brain cancer?" he whispered.

The consultant nodded.

Muriel's mother thought she was going to lose consciousness, and to slip from the chair to become a crumpled mass of destroyed humanity, right there on the floor of the consultant's office. Her husband caught her by the arm to steady her.

"Muriel is a strong, young girl, with a robust constitution," went on the consultant, eager to now impart some more hopeful news. "We must start a course of radiotherapy right away, and we have every reason to be optimistic about our chances."

When Muriel was told the news, she sat in silence for a while trying to take in the possible consequences of her condition. It was difficult for her to think clearly with her mother openly weeping and her father trying through cracked and broken sentences to explain that the consultant had said they were all to be optimistic.

"Am I going to die soon?" asked Muriel at last, when she had been given a chance to speak. She asked the question so flatly and unemotionally that she might have asked, "Do you have the time please?" or, "Excuse me, do you know the way to the bus station?"

Her frantic mother shook her head violently from side to side and stated as emphatically as she could that Muriel was not going to die, and she must never, ever even think such a thing. Muriel thought that under the circumstances her mother was being a little naive to say the least of it.

The time Muriel had spent in the Crucible had changed her. She had begun to develop a subconscious maturity well beyond her physical years, and her outlook, her mental disposition and her intelligence were now working at levels far in advance of her parents. Muriel accepted the news, and decided she needed to spend more time in the Crucible to find out more about this new situation, if she could.

Later that week Muriel was admitted into the local hospital for her first treatment of radiotherapy. At home, Muriel had organised her mother, who was a bundle of nerves, and ordered her father about, who was numb with the portent of the moment. When Muriel had got them both ready, they headed to the hospital where Muriel seated them both in the waiting room, got them something to read, and went off for her treatment.

"This doesn't hurt at all, in fact you won't feel anything," said the technician, as Muriel lay down on the treatment table. "All you will hear is the noise of the machine working, try not to move. It takes about ten minutes."

Muriel nodded that she understood, and settled herself down on the table, her hands by her sides, and her body quite still.

As Muriel wandered through the desert, she began to be filled with a sense of wonder. At last, like the answer to a question she had sought, which was slowly becoming clearer in her mind, her understanding of the Crucible and its strange inhabitants began to take shape. She walked uphill filled with these thoughts when she saw before her a little pub, seemingly situated in the middle of nowhere.

The sounds of laughter and cheering could be heard away down the road before she had even reached the front door.

"The Fornix Tavern," she said to herself, standing outside the pub. Muriel read the sign, "Free CSF. I wonder what that is?"

"Come on in and find out," suggested Fornix Runner 629385147, who had been watching her approach.

"I'm not allowed to go into pubs," said Muriel, "I'm not old enough."

"You would never be refused entry to this one," replied the runner.

"Free CSF," said Muriel, "what's that?"

"Charlie's Special Fermentation," replied the runner, "it's what everyone drinks around here, in fact, it's all there is."

"I'm not allowed alcohol," replied Muriel sadly, "too young again."

"It isn't alcohol," replied the runner. "It's organic nectar. It provides a cushion against the blows of life. You will love it."

"Then I'll give it a try," replied Muriel, who was more than willing to taste the local brew. The hot desert had made her thirsty, and the tavern seemed a nice place to stop for a short while on her travels around the Crucible.

Muriel entered the tavern, and could not help but smile to herself when she saw that all the drinkers were Fornix Runners, who all looked exactly the same. They were all tall, thin men, with shaven heads, wearing the same white t-shirts and red jogging bottoms. Even their non-descript facial features were alike. The only thing that identified them as individuals, was their own unique serial number printed across their chests. A respectful hush fell across the tavern's interior when The Client entered and made her way to the bar.

"What'll you have, Miss?" asked Charlie when Muriel approached the bar.

"I was told you only have one drink here," said Muriel.

"I do," replied Charlie, "so what's it to be?"

"I guess I'll have the CSF," said Muriel. "What's in it?"

"Oh various things," replied Charlie. "Glucose, protein, sodium, potassium, calcium, magnesium, chloride."

"Sounds lovely," replied Muriel, smiling.

Charlie smiled broadly at the compliment. Muriel's sarcasm was as lost upon Charlie as it had been upon Bron.

"One pint of CSF, coming right up!" announced Charlie, as though Muriel had made a wise and informed choice.

Muriel took the pint of CSF from Charlie, and wandered away from the bar.

The tavern was not much more than a large rectangular room, with numerous sets of tables and chairs dotted here and there. Around the walls hung portraits of local characters, Bron the Chief Librarian at the Camp of the Hippos struck a very dignified pose in his picture. Other portraits showed Patrick and the gardener in the Garden of Idols, (Patrick took a nice photograph, thought Muriel, his kindly eyes shining in the light of the camera's flash). Wernick the Magician, Professor Brocas, The Traffic Warden at the Great Egg, (who still looked rather pompous and not very polite, thought Muriel), and the young Vendor, who had taught Muriel the concepts of value and quality, a handsome lad, thought Muriel.

When Muriel placed the pint glass of CSF to her lips for the first time, she thought the drink to be a little sweet.

It tasted a bit like honey, thought Muriel, and it was not at all unpleasant. The CSF warmed her inside and gave her a feeling of belonging, suddenly she no longer felt like a visitor to the tavern, but more like an accepted member of the group who came there to rest and relax after the labours of the day. The CSF had the effect of uniting her spirit with the Crucible itself, it was like a kind of glue perhaps, that sealed the whole of the Crucible together into one solid structure.

High in the Twisted Mountains the monster was in deep meditation. It sat cross-legged on the floor, with its consciousness stilled. Its senses were the acute senses of a predator, and it was aware of everything that was happening around itself. It felt the movement of the air currents as they swept into the cave from outside, it felt the gentle pulsing of the earth beneath its posture as the living mountain pulsed with the drumbeat of life.

Suddenly the monster was recalled to consciousness, it opened its eyes and looked about the cave, its senses tingling with anticipation.

"Something is happening," it said to itself.

The monster rose to its feet and strode to the cave entrance, where it peered down upon the Crucible. It glanced along the panorama from left to right to try and spot some reason for its own sudden sense of anxiety. Everything below it, seemed as it had before. The creature could not see any reason for its sudden alarm, and so it closed its eyes to remove the distraction of sight from its consciousness, it tuned its ears to the hum of the Crucible, listening intently at the mouth of the cave.

When Muriel had swallowed half of her drink, the whole tavern began to vibrate slowly. It was as though the entire building was at the heart of a mini earthquake. Portraits on the walls began to rock from side to side as the building moved beneath the feet of the startled revellers. The picture of the gardener and Patrick, taken in the Garden of Idols, fell from its hook and crashed to the floor.

"What is happening?" asked Muriel.

Charlie shook his head. "I don't know."

Glasses tinkled in their racks under the counter as the vibrations began to slowly increase in severity.

The revellers started to file outside, where the whole of the Crucible seemed to be in a state of motion.

In the Camp of the Hippos the earthquake was felt more keenly, for although none of the inhabitants were aware of it at the time, the epicentre of the earthquake was in the Twisted Mountains, and the closer you were to that point, the more violently shook your vicinity.

Bron steadied himself against a tent pole, as swirls of sand rose up from the desert floor. Great sand dunes began to slide down to the lowest level as the vibration was felt everywhere.

Professor Brocas held a large atlas over his head as the plasterwork from the ceiling began to shower down into the schoolroom below.

"Everyone outside! Quick as you can!" he called as the Muriels ran and crushed together at the door.

"What is it Professor?" asked Muriel, all at once.

"It appears to be an earthquake," replied the Professor, "it's the most extraordinary thing!"

At The Great Egg, alarms were sounding, and the poor little Warden, who wanted no more from existence than the chance to do his job, ran frantically here and there not knowing what to do, or whom to call. The Upside Down People began to disappear once they started to shake with the vibration, and the Great Egg itself began to slow its twisting motion, and eventually slowed to a complete stop, something it had never done since the Warden had come to work there.

In the Garden of Idols, Patrick continued to munch the weeds as though the earthquake was an everyday occurrence, one he was quite used to by now. As Patrick chewed a mouthful of weeds he raised his eyes a little towards the horizon, his only acknowledgement of the strange event.

"Take cover you silly ass!" shouted the gardener from under one of the benches. "The world is coming to an end!"

Patrick stopped chewing momentarily to consider this. "If the world is coming to an end, what is the point in taking cover?" he replied, showing the calm disposition of a worldly wise donkey, in the face of impending catastrophe.

All along the range of the Twisted Mountains the shock waves rampaged across the landscape like the violent surges of an angry sea. In one isolated cave, deep in the heart of the tallest peak, the monster rolled onto its back and shook with a terrible violence. Every fibre of its being vibrated so violently that the creature could focus on the external world no longer and simply closed its eyes.

In the Fornix Tavern, a low grumbling sound started to be heard, as though some monstrous animal had come upon the building and sensed there was food to be had within. The sound rose in pitch, only to fall again a moment later, and then to rise again, over and over. As the pitch rose and fell so did the volume, until everyone in the Crucible of Creation could feel their very bones shiver in response to the lapping pulse.

The poor beleaguered Traffic Warden did not know what to do for the best. He had never expected a situation like this, and his ignorance terrified him. He gawped, open-mouthed at the egg he had sworn to protect, and now he felt as helpless, and as ineffective in the scheme of things as the Upside Down People appeared to be.

Together, the constant vibration and the repetitive sound waves served to pulverise the Crucible, and all its inhabitants into a state of submissive terror. Bron and his fellow hippos knelt in their tents with their hooves embedded in their ears, as the onslaught continued.

In the garden, Patrick, who had been unconcerned about the vibrations could not show such indifference to the sound waves, and stood transfixed to the spot, with his teeth chattering and his eyes rolling, as the gardener screamed at the top of his voice from under the bench, "What have we done to deserve this?"

Professor Brocas tried valiantly to shield his young charges from the merciless attack, but there was little he or anyone else in the Crucible could do.

"We must be brave, Muriel!" he shouted. "We must ride out the storm."

Muriels clung together in a vast clump of terrified humanity. The aspects of Muriel clung together in a pile of shivering flesh and bone, that was so entwined, so meshed together, it was impossible to distinguish any individual within the mass.

High in the Twisted Mountains, the monster lay upon its back in the deepest recess of its cave, unable to move. Hit time and again by the pulsing noise, its hardened flesh began to soften with the repetition of the blows, until at last it began to succumb to the fury. Suddenly it coughed a great gout of blood up out of its mouth, which splattered against the wall of the cave, as the monster lapsed at last into unconsciousness.

The sound waves stopped and the vibrations died away together, and the Crucible of Creation lay still and tender, as though it were a fresh wound in the flesh that had been cleaved only seconds before. Nothing and no-one moved, and now not a sound could be heard throughout the landscape. Only several clouds of dust, which swirled up from the desert floor in the soft breeze of twilight, showed any observer that the scene was real, a living place, an inhabited land, that was in normal times fizzing with the comings and goings of life itself.

In the Camp of the Hippos the records they had kept so meticulously lay scattered across the horizon as far as one could see. Sheets of paper blowing here and there in the winds of the moment, as the hippos themselves lay prostrate on the soft desert floor unable to move. The camp had been all but destroyed, and yet in the greater scheme of things, it was still there, still able to recover its place in the overall design of life, and to resume its situation exactly where it had always been, a bit more up than down.

On the floor of the cave lay the unconscious thing. It had passed out with the severity of the attack, and its breaths came in slow and regular cycles. On the walls of the cave patches of its blood dripped in long strands to the floor.

"That's it," said the technician. "You're all done for today. That didn't hurt did it?"

Muriel sat up on the bed and shook her head.

"You may feel a little queasy later on today," continued the technician. "That's quite normal, it will pass."

Muriel got up from the bed, and went to find her parents.

Chapter Nine

Wernicke's Magic Castle

Muriel entered the Camp of the Hippos to have a rest from her travels. She had been using the camp as a base in the Crucible, and came to see the hippos often.

"A letter came for you this morning," said Bron. "It's on the table."

"A letter for me? Here?" said Muriel. "I don't live here."

"You're here more than I am," muttered Bron.

The letter was from Professor Brocas at the Language School, and was short and to the point, (with no exaggerations).

Dear Miss Mason,

It is with regret that I have to inform you of the temporary suspension of language services at Brocas' Language School, due to severe damage suffered by the school in the recent earthquake.

Rest assured we are working to repair the damage as I write, and hope to have normal service resume in the very near future.

Best Wishes
Professor Brocas.

"They've stopped language services at the school," said Muriel to Bron. "Because of the recent earthquake."

"Oh, dear!" replied the hippo. "That is serious."

"Is it?" said Muriel, not for a moment realising the repercussions of such a turn of events.

Muriel's mother gazed into the face of her only daughter, and felt the same love and devotion she had experienced the day Muriel had first entered the world, fifteen years ago. For Muriel's mother, nothing had changed, the flesh of her flesh, the bones of her bones, the blood of her blood lay before her, damaged with the natural cruelty of fate, and Mrs Mason felt Muriel's pain as though it were her own.

"How are you my darling?" she asked as Muriel opened her eyes and looked about her. Muriel heard the question plainly enough, and replied that she was a little tired but felt alright.

"Me ragged out with monster done daylight so far."

Muriel's mother's smile seemed a little less natural, and she didn't really know how to reply to this. So she ignored it, and pressed on.

"The consultant says the treatment may make you feel a little tired for a while afterwards, darling," said her mother, "just rest and you will be fine."

Muriel nodded, and wanted to reply: *Yes, I think I will have a little sleep now.*

However, what her mother actually heard was: "Ragged by the door in the sky, slap that hippopotamus."

Muriel closed her eyes and fell asleep instantly.

Mrs Mason left Muriel's bedside and sought out the consultant, with the single minded determination of an owl chasing a mouse. She cornered him by the front desk and positioned herself in such a way that he could not get past her.

"Mrs Mason, how are you?" he asked politely.

"Muriel is saying some strange things," said Mrs Mason. "I don't understand what she said to me."

"Ah," replied the consultant, "I thought that might happen. Muriel has developed a condition called Brocas' Fluent Aphasia. It often happens with strokes and brain tumours. We can treat it very successfully with speech therapy."

"What is it? What's happening?" asked Mrs Mason frantically, fearing her only daughter might sound like an idiot for the rest of her life.

"Brocas' Area is a part of the left side of the brain which processes language. It allows us to understand how language is constructed and what individual words mean," replied the consultant.

Muriel's mother was nodding furiously.

"In Muriel's case the tumour has effected Brocas' Area, and her ability to process language has become impaired. She can understand what you say to her perfectly well, it's when she comes to say something herself, it all comes out wrong.

"We can correct it though, don't worry about it."

The creature that had concealed itself in the confines of its cave since the instance of its birth, was becoming restless. It had a tongue but never spoke to anyone. It had eyes but never saw anything except the view from its own habitat. It had ears but listened only to the wind. It had legs but never walked anywhere.

"I must test my power," it said, "I must know what I am capable of."

The monster sat upon the floor and crossed its legs, in the attitude of a holy man at peace. When it had stilled its turbulent mind, the monster began to feel a strength gather in the pit of its torso. A developing power, a strength that could lead it into battle was as yet embryonic in there, but the monster wanted to feel it working, it wanted to understand its own true purpose in the Crucible. Slowly the strength began to expand within the body of the creature, and then to radiate outwards through its hardened flesh into the cave; a faint yellow light surrounding the beast, almost too faint to see in the open, but visible in the darkness of the cave.

In the Garden of Idols Patrick suddenly stopped what he was doing and turned to face the mountains.

"What is it, my friend?" asked the gardener.

"I felt something," replied the donkey.

The man's senses were not as sharp as the animal's.

"I didn't feel anything," said the gardener.

"Something strange," replied the donkey. "Something I have never felt before."

In the cave, the monster felt the strength inside it suddenly drain away without warning. It exhaled deeply, exhausted with its exertions and slipped over sideways, falling unconscious to the floor.

"It's gone now," said Patrick, "how odd!"

"Forget it," suggested the gardener. "It was probably nothing, anyway we have work to do."

Patrick turned back to his work, but something inside him made him feel uneasy. Something told him it wasn't nothing.

Muriel had decided it was time to meet the famous Wernicke the Magician.

She had travelled Right across the map Bron had given to her, and come eventually to Wernicke's Magic Castle, Right where Bron had drawn it. A fairy-tale-like structure, with pointed turrets and stone battlements, the sort of place a wizard would inhabit.

"I have been expecting you, Miss Mason," said Wernicke, as Muriel entered the great hallway.

"I've been wanting to meet you too," replied Muriel.

"Then come in and sit down," replied the Magician. "We have lots to talk about."

"I have so many questions for you," began Muriel.

"I fear I may not have all the answers," replied Wernicke honestly. "But I will try."

"Tell me about the Crucible of Creation," said Muriel. "I want to know all about it."

"This is your first time here, I am guessing?" asked the Magician. "The Crucible must seem a very strange place to you at present."

"I have started to visit here when I fall asleep," replied Muriel. "It has only started to happen recently."

"The Crucible is the home of your inner self," replied Wernicke. "It is where the miracle of life is engineered."

"I see," said Muriel, who clearly did not see at all.

"Something you have in common with the Great Egg, then," replied Wernicke. Who looked like the storybook Magician she had imagined. Except his robe and pointed wizard's hat were both snow white.

"And who am I then?" asked Muriel.

"You are the heavenly creature, named The Client," replied Wernicke. "The Crucible serves no other function than to allow you to operate in the world of matter.

"The Crucible allows you to be conscious of yourself, which in turn allows the universe to become conscious of itself, through you."

"That's what Patrick said," replied Muriel.

"The donkey in the Garden of idols?" asked Wernicke.

Muriel nodded.

"Pay close attention to the lessons taught by that clever ass," replied Wernicke smiling. "He knows a lot of things."

"This is all so confusing," confessed Muriel. "The more I find out, the less I seem to know."

"That is because you are trying to understand a huge concept logically. It would be easier if you were to perceive it intuitively."

"How do I do that?" asked Muriel.

"The best way would be to go to the City of Artists, follow the Right Road," said the Magician. "Everything you could want to know can be answered in that place."

"Even the language you use is confusing," said Muriel.

Wernicke smiled. "Language is a beautiful creation, it is the mark of a heavenly creature."

"But all language can't be beautiful," argued Muriel. "Sometimes language is disgusting, you should see some of the things people write on the bathroom walls at school!"

"All language is beautiful," replied Wernicke. "For it is the visible manifestation of pure thought, and is therefore a magical act of creation." The Magician was nodding his head and blinking rapidly, as though the two actions when performed together emphasised the point.

"Well, I think some of it is disgusting," persisted Muriel.

"You are missing the point," continued Wernicke. "Thought is mind in motion, as wind is air in motion. Written language is the physical manifestation of mind in motion, and therefore an act of pure creation; it is the work of a heavenly creature, no matter what it says."

Muriel shrugged her shoulders, she wasn't convinced. "There are no heavenly creatures at my school, and that's for sure!" she exclaimed.

Wernicke shook his head. "There are nothing *but* heavenly creatures at your school," he replied. "The human condition is a heavenly creation, no matter what it does."

"So even if a person does something really bad, they are still a heavenly creature?" asked the schoolgirl.

"Of course they are," replied the Magician. "What they do does not change what they are."

"But how can someone who is evil, or who does evil things, be a heavenly creature?" persisted Muriel.

"What are good and evil?" asked Wernicke.

"They are the ways people behave, I think," faltered Muriel.

"They are nothing more than points of view," replied the Magician. "Largely created by society to fulfil its needs, and protect its interests at any particular time."

"Evil isn't just a point of view!" said Muriel, surprised that anyone could say such a thing.

"Evil is nothing *but* a point of view," replied the Magician.

Muriel looked shocked.

"In times past the keeping of slaves was considered a good thing," observed the Magician. "Today the keeping of slaves is considered evil. What has changed?"

"The times have changed," said Muriel.

"Time is largely an illusion, and irrelevant," replied the Magician, "what has really changed?"

Muriel shook her head.

"The point of view has changed," stated Wernicke.

"I still don't understand," said Muriel shaking her head.

"In Edwardian England it was commonplace for an eight-year-old girl to be married to an eighty-year-old man. The practice was considered good for both the girl and the man. Today that would be called child abuse and the man would go to prison.

"So what has changed?"

"The times have changed," persisted Muriel.

"But time is illusory," countered Wernicke. "So what has really changed? Has the girl changed? Has the man changed?"

Muriel shook her head.

"Only the point of view has changed," stated the Magician. "What was once viewed to be good, is now viewed to be bad. The practice has not changed at all. Only the point of view we hold towards the practice has changed. Therefore evil is a point of view. As is good."

"But good can't be just a point of view as well," argued Muriel.

"In the seventeenth century the practice of herbal medicine was considered to be witchcraft, and people were burned alive for it. Today herbal medicines are available to anyone who wants them. What has changed? Has the herbal medicine itself changed?"

Muriel smiled. "Our point of view has changed."

The Magician returned her smile. "Exactly."

"I still don't understand all this," admitted Muriel.

"Yes you do, you just don't know you do," replied Wernicke. "Go to the Hall of Inspiration in the City of Artists, and all will become clear to you."

"That's over the Twisted Mountains," replied Muriel. "Bron says I shouldn't go there as the monster is up there somewhere."

"Mmm, that is a consideration," confessed the Magician. "And yet you must always balance the potential gain against the potential loss in every adventure you undertake. What will you gain if you reach the City of Artists, against what you will lose if you reach the monster instead?"

"My life!" exclaimed Muriel. "The monster might kill me!"

Wernicke the Magician nodded in agreement. "Indeed he might. And if you miss the monster, will you then live forever?"

"No-one lives forever," replied Muriel.

"So, you will die anyway," returned the Magician.

"Yes, but I might live to be old before I die if I miss the monster," argued Muriel. "If I meet the monster I will die the age I am now."

"But time is an illusion!" repeated Wernicke. "Even if it was not, what will you do with the extra time you appear to have?"

Muriel shrugged her shoulders, that hardly mattered, she thought.

"Perhaps you should consider the concept of *Quality*," suggested Wernicke.

"I have already met the Vendor," said Muriel.

Wernicke smiled.

"I want to show you something," said Muriel, as she began to root through her schoolbag, which had suddenly appeared on her shoulder. Muriel withdrew Bron's Other Map and handed it carefully to Wernicke.

"Ah," said the Magician. "Bron's Other Map. I haven't seen this in a very long time."

"What is The Great Divide?" asked Muriel.

"The great and deep cavern running the length of the Twisted Mountains, separating the Left and Right mountain ranges. The two worlds of creation."

"Why has Bron misspelt the word *here*?" asked Muriel, pointing to the left side of the document, as Wernicke nodded and smiled.

"Who says he has?" asked Wernicke.

"You don't spell here like that," said Muriel, confident of her facts now. "He has written it like you hear, with your ear."

"Correct," observed Wernicke.

"But that's wrong!" persisted the schoolgirl. "It should say *Look Here.*"

"Perhaps you should consider the geographical position of the Camp of the Hippos," suggested the Magician.

"It's a lot more up than down," replied Muriel.

"On the Left?" suggested Wernicke.

Muriel nodded.

"And X marks the spot?" whispered Wernicke.

Muriel nodded.

"So what is shown by the X on this document?" asked Wernicke, smiling. "It must be something to do with seeing and hearing, must it not?"

Muriel suddenly caught her breath. "Not my eye and ear!" she exclaimed. "The X is my Left eye and ear?"

Wernicke handed the document back to Muriel. "So, he is a rather clever hippopotamus after all, is he not?" observed Wernicke.

Chapter Ten

The Right Road

A soft tapping at her bedroom door was all it took to raise Muriel's spirits instantly, she knew who was on the other side, and when Michelle pushed the door open, Muriel threw her arms wide and offered a huge smile to her best friend. Michelle ran across the room and the two pals fell into an embrace that made them both squeeze the other as though they were holding onto something very precious.

"Tender Mop, door I see the day," said Muriel.

Michelle laughed. "That's hilarious!" she exclaimed. "Say something else."

Muriel laughed with her friend, "Wait the door long you come."

Together the two girls laughed at Muriel's condition without a trace of embarrassment as only really good friends can.

"That's brilliant!" exclaimed Michelle. "I love it. You should come back to school and give a talk like that, the Old Bat wouldn't know what to do!"

The two girls laughed together again.

"You have Brocas' Fluent Aphasia," said Michelle. "Your dad told me, I've been looking it up on the net. All your words get jumbled up, it's *so* chocolate!"

Muriel giggled. It had been a long time since she had been completely at ease with anyone since her diagnosis.

"They say it's only temporary though," said Michelle, "they can cure it with speech therapy."

Muriel nodded.

"I have something to tell you," said Michelle. "I'm pregnant."

Muriel gasped, slapping her hand to her mouth.

"What bad luck eh?" said Michelle. "Not chocolate at all. My first time as well. My dad's gone thermo-nuclear."

"Little Mop how comes tomorrow?" said Muriel touching the stomach of her friend.

"I'm about six weeks," said Michelle.

Muriel reached under her pillow and took out her journal. "Special place later Mop know my hippopotamus," she said.

Michelle grinned at her friend. "Oh, absolutely," she agreed.

"Know Mop my hippopotamus?" asked Muriel.

"Not really," replied Michelle. "But if he's a friend of yours, I'm sure I will like him too."

The two girls laughed together once more.

Michelle came down the stairs and Muriel's mother held the front door open for her. "Thanks for coming, Michelle," she said. "Muriel has been looking forward to seeing you."

"Mop big delight see Mo! Well chocolate!" exclaimed Michelle, then slapped her hand over her mouth. "Oh, my God, it's catching!"

Muriel's mothers face suddenly lost its smile. "That's not funny Michelle!"

Michelle laughed. "Don't worry Mrs Mason, she'll be fine!"

Muriel's mother closed the door behind her daughter's best friend. "Young people!" she said to herself, shaking her head.

Muriel's mother stood with her hand still on the front door when an idea suddenly hit her. She snapped her fingers, and marched upstairs to her daughter's room filled with the energy of her new idea.

"Retail therapy!" announced Muriel's mother as she stood in the bedroom doorway.

"Sorry?" asked Muriel.

"That's what you and I need right now my girl, some retail therapy!" said her mother. "Let's go shopping!"

Muriel had not been shopping with her mother in years. "Why?" asked Muriel.

"To cheer us both up, of course!" replied her mother. "It will get you out of the house and do us both the world of good, come on, put your coat on!"

Muriel smiled and jumped off the bed.

Muriel's mother had felt helpless since her daughter's diagnosis. She had felt in some strange way that the consultant had taken over her role as parent to Muriel, directing the way things were going to go from now on, and Muriel's mother had been left out, her role usurped. She had felt distanced from her daughter during this time, and the shopping expedition if nothing else, might allow them to spend some precious time together, just the two of them.

"This is brilliant!" exclaimed her mother as they jumped into the car. "Can't imagine why I didn't think of it before!"

The two females attacked the shops in town like a pair of plundering Vikings.

"This would look so good on you!" announced her mother, holding up a blue camisole top to Muriel's shoulders. "Blue always looks so nice on you."

Muriel thought about Patrick the donkey, and what she had learned from him in the Garden of Idols. "Short light, thrown in air blue wave atoms only," said Muriel.

Her mother smiled. "Yes dear, that's what I said. Blue suits you."

Muriel stood with her back to the Arch of Pons and gazed steadily up the Right Road, watching it narrow with her perspective towards the Twisted Mountains.

"Where does the Right road go?" asked Muriel.

"To the Right," replied the Fornix Runner.

"But it can't always be the right road," argued Muriel. "If you wanted to go somewhere that was in the other direction, then this would be the wrong road, surely?"

"No, it is always the Right Road," said the runner matter of factly.

"But that doesn't make any sense!" argued Muriel.

"It makes perfect sense!" argued the Runner.

"It's only the right road if either it goes to where you want to go, or it turns to the right," persisted Muriel, she wasn't going to be beaten on this one.

"It's the Right Road even if it turns to the Left, or if it goes to where you don't want to go," replied the Runner, shaking his head at the naïvety of the young girl.

"The Right Road is the Right Road, always has been, and always will be."

Muriel thought about this for a moment or two. "Is there a place called *Right*?" she asked.

The Fornix Runner smiled, perhaps she wasn't so naïve after all. "Of course there is." He nodded sagely. "Everything on the other side of the Great Divide is Right. That's where the City of the Artists is."

"So, that's why it is the *Right Road*. Have you ever been there?" asked Muriel.

"We don't go there. They have their own messengers, that can fly. They're called angels," he replied. "Everything is different there."

"How do you mean?" asked Muriel.

"Logic doesn't apply over there. So it won't make sense to you. Everything is perceived differently there. It's more intuitive, on the Right. If you see what I mean."

"Not really," confessed Muriel, who didn't see at all.

"The Right Road goes to the Right place," explained the runner patiently.

"Everything on the Right is seen intuitively and not logically; over there they value visions, perceptions and the power of imagination. They're a bunch of day-dreamers really, philosophers, artists and the like; they never really get anything done, here is where the action is."

"I suppose they might argue the same cause in the same way," offered Muriel.

The Fornix runner shook his head. "That's not logical, they would agree with me."

Muriel smiled. "Not if it's logical," she said. "They would disagree, surely?"

The Fornix Runner was not as intelligent as Muriel, and felt he could lose this argument, and so he ended the point. "Besides," he said, "there's nothing over there for you, Miss. Stay here with us."

Muriel didn't want to argue with the runner any more, but she had secretly determined to go to the Right, none the less.

"And you would have to cross the Twisted Mountains to get there, and there's a monster up there now," finished the runner, "so you can't go."

Muriel nodded, agreeing that was a problem.

The Right Road spread before Muriel away from the bustle of the Great Arch of Pons, twisting like the body of a fish away into the foothills of the Twisted Mountains, fading away in the distance to a single point.

"It does seem a long way," she mused, "but distance is different here. It might not take me as long as it first appears."

Muriel began to amble along the Right Road at a leisurely pace, she was in no hurry to place herself in danger, and yet she also felt there was something calling to her from the Right, something she could not easily explain. It felt to Muriel as though someone was calling her from very far away, she couldn't see them, nor could she hear the shout, but instinctively she knew she was being called; somehow she just felt the tug of the moment, a deep instinct to go down that particular road, and to follow it no matter where it might take her.

In front of Muriel three Fornix Runners were jogging towards her, as they passed each one shouted to her in turn.

"Turn around!" shouted the first.

"This road doesn't go anywhere!" shouted the second.

"It ends at the mountains!" shouted the third.

"It's okay, I know what I'm doing!" shouted back Muriel, and then as they passed she muttered, "sort of," to herself. Muriel kept following her instinct, one footstep at a time towards the end of the Right Road.

"Get your map of the Right Road here!" shouted a familiar voice, one Muriel instantly recognised as belonging to her friend, the Vendor.

Muriel accepted the map and looked at it. It was just a sheet of paper with a single line drawn upon it, starting at the upper right corner, and ending at the bottom of the page in the middle. Muriel shook her head and handed the map back.

"You won't sell many maps on this road," said Muriel. "There's only me and a few Fornix Runners."

"Ah," said the Vendor, "that's because this road doesn't appear to go anywhere."

Muriel nodded. "Why have a road at all if it doesn't go anywhere?" she asked.

"I said it didn't *appear* to go anywhere," repeated the boy. "It seems to stop at the foothills of the Twisted Mountains."

"So?" exclaimed Muriel.

"But actually it is the Right Road!" said the boy, as though he had imparted some secret that no-one else knew.

"I know it's the Right Road!" said Muriel. "And it does end at the Twisted Mountains, so what?"

The Vendor shook his head. "When you're on the Right Road," he whispered, "it doesn't really matter where it goes, does it?"

Muriel frowned. "Doesn't it?"

The boy shook his head sagely. "When you're on the Right Road, all will become clear, it's just a matter of time, and time is an illusion anyway, do you see now?"

"But it still doesn't go anywhere!" insisted Muriel.

"It doesn't have to!" exclaimed the Vendor. "It's the Right Road anyway!"

Muriel threw her hands up in exasperation. "It is called the Right Road because it bends to the Right, and because it leads towards the place called Right, right?" said Muriel.

"Yes, that's certainly part of it," agreed the Vendor.

"What else is there?" asked Muriel.

"It is also the Right Road," said the boy, winking. Once again giving the impression he had revealed a secret.

"I have never met anyone I wanted to thump more than you," said Muriel.

"Thump me?" squealed the lad. "Why would you want to thump me?"

Muriel smiled. "The Right Road is called the Right Road because it bends to the Right, right?"

"Right."

"And also, because it goes towards a place called Right, right?"

"Right."

"So, it's right as opposed to left, and it's Right as opposed to elsewhere, so what else is there?" asked Muriel, trying to finally nail down this Right Road thing.

"It's also right as opposed to wrong," said the boy.

Muriel thought about this for a minute. "You mean it's also the Right Road, as opposed to the Wrong Road?"

"Right!"

"So, in summary then," began Muriel. "It's Right because it goes to Right, turns to Right, and is not wrong?"

"Right!" said the Vendor.

"But how can it always be not the wrong road?" asked Muriel.

"Because it is always the Right Road," replied the Vendor.

"But if it goes to a place you don't want to go to, then it is the wrong road, surely?" argued Muriel.

The Vendor shook his head patiently. "No matter where you want to go," he said, "as long as you're on the Right Road, you must be successful eventually. Do you see?"

"Mmm," said Muriel, "that's very subtle and sneaky."

"Not at all, Miss," contradicted the Vendor. "If you always follow the Right Road, you will always end up where you are really supposed to be. The Right Road will always lead you to the Right Place, no matter which way it turns or where it goes."

The monster had fully recovered from its first attempt at radiation, and in the time since then it had grown more powerful, more certain of its purpose, and more determined to exercise its power. It had made up its mind to try the procedure once again, even though the first attempt had completely drained away its vitality to the point where it had lapsed into unconsciousness.

The creature sat down in the mouth of the cave as before, and crossed its legs.

"I am much stronger now," it said. "I will do better this time."

As before the creature cleared its mind of the cares of its time, leaving all thoughts of success or failure aside. It began to focus, to concentrate all of its mental powers only on the present moment. Deep inside itself a strength began to stir, began to agitate into motion, building slowly like the charge in a battery, swelling in force until the housing unit could contain the vitality no longer. The creature fought to contain the building pressure within itself. "Not yet!" it said.

The rising tide of power became stronger with each passing moment, and the thing felt it was now struggling to contain the explosion. "Not yet!" it gasped again.

The power rose within the consciousness of the creature until it would be denied access to the world no longer. The monster lifted its head and opened its eyes.

Suddenly a bright light erupted from the form of the monster, a blinding flash that was spent in a moment. The monster felt the vitality surge out of its body in an instant, blasting out into the cave, reducing the creature to a wasted thing, like a deflated balloon, and once more it slumped over sideways, falling to the floor into a state of deep unconsciousness.

Patrick spun around in the Garden. "There it is again!" he exclaimed.

The ground in the garden began to shake violently, a single tremor. The table supporting the three hand bells collapsed and the bells rolled across the path, though only the middle bell could be heard ringing.

"I felt that!" said the gardener.

"It was stronger this time," observed Patrick. "I wonder what it is?"

The gardener shook his head.

In the cave, the monster once more lay comatose on its back, breathing evenly and deeply. A discharged battery, devoid of power, but not of life. Over the coming weeks it would regain its strength, its power, its vitality. It would become stronger each time it radiated, and it would grow in time into what everyone in the Crucible feared it was already, a real monster.

Muriel smiled at the Vendor. "So, you are telling me that I should always follow the Right Road, no matter what, and no matter where it takes me?" she asked.

The Vendor swept the cloth cap from his head and bowed low before The Client in a very theatrical fashion, as though it were the end of a performance, and the culprit had been finally unmasked.

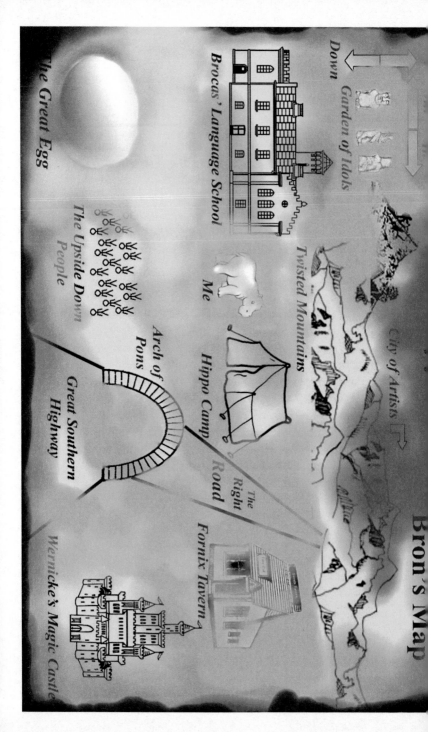

Bron's Map

Down

Garden of Idols

Brocas' Language School

The Great Egg

The Upside Down People

Me

Twisted Mountains

City of Artists

Arch of Pons

Hippo Camp

Great Southern Highway

The Right Road

Fornix Tavern

Wernicke's Magic Castle

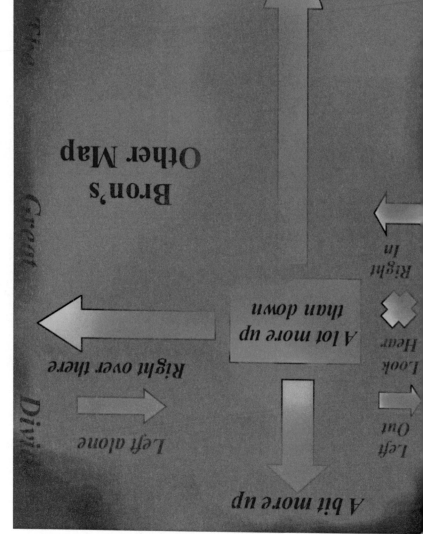

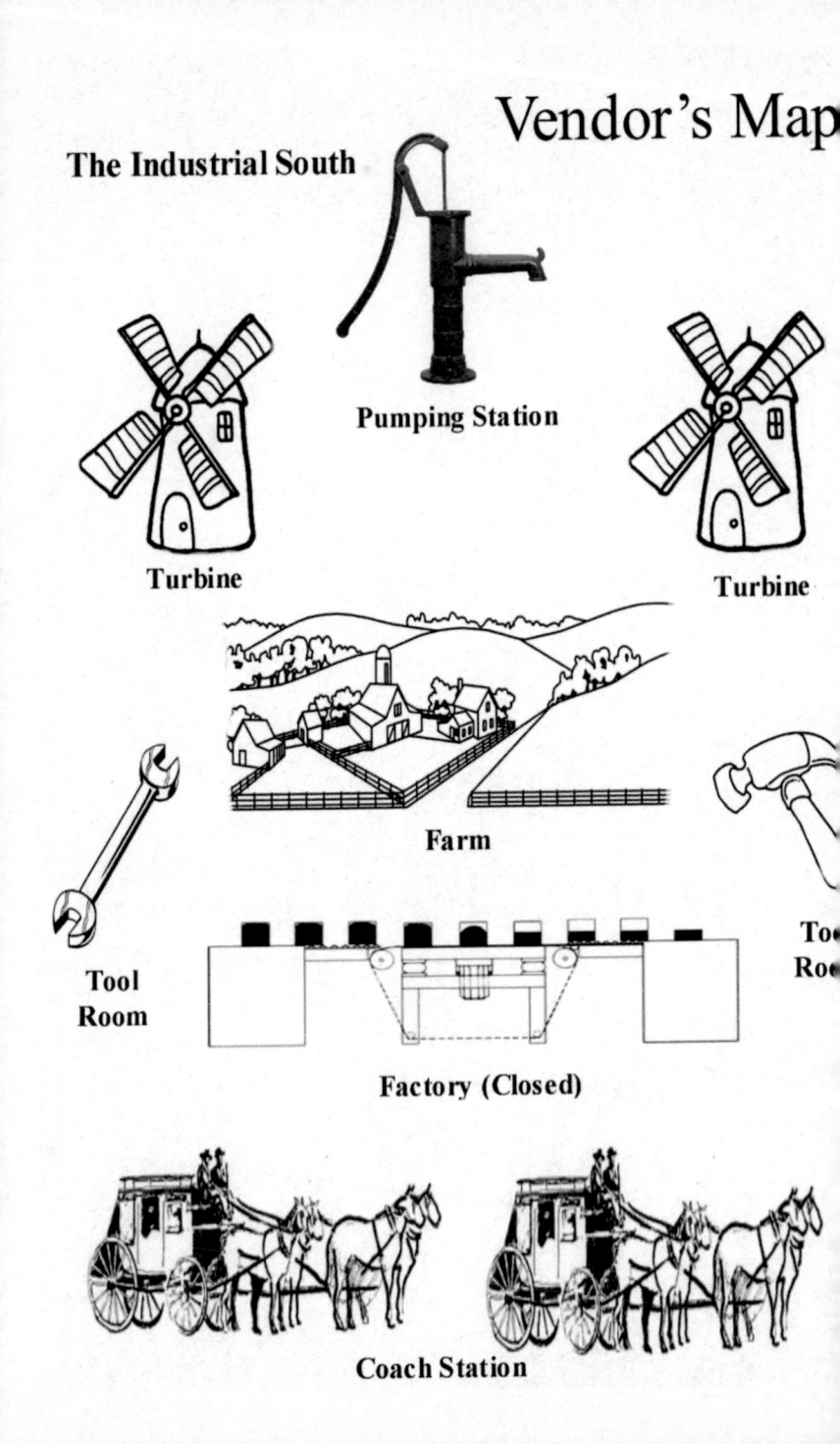

Vendor's Map

The Industrial South

Pumping Station

Turbine

Turbine

Farm

Tool Room

Tool Room

Factory (Closed)

Coach Station

PART TWO

LEARNING TO LOSE

Chapter Eleven

The Twisted Mountains

Muriel entered the speech therapist's office, shook hands with her and sat down on a comfy chair.

"Good morning, Muriel," said the therapist. "My name is Linda, and I am going to be treating your Brocas' Fluent Aphasia over the coming weeks."

Muriel nodded and smiled.

"We are going to try something called MIT which stands for Melodic Intonation Therapy, which means we are going to look at some phrases in a book, and then we are going to sing them together."

Muriel raised her eyebrows.

"The damage to your speech centre is on the left side of your brain," explained Linda. "In a region called Brocas' Area. Singing engages the right side, which, with practice will learn to support the way you vocalise your sentences. In other words we get the right hemisphere of your brain to help recover your speech. Once you can sing a sentence correctly, it will be much easier for you to re-learn how to say it."

A silence fell between them as Muriel processed this. Then Muriel placed her hand on her chest in an operatic fashion and sang out: "OOOH...KAAAY LLINNNNDAAAA!"

They both laughed. There had been no impairment to Muriel's sense of humour.

Climbing in the Twisted Mountains was giving Muriel a sense of freedom she had never before experienced. The view across the Crucible of Creation was breath-taking as she began to ascend the twisted slopes. Muriel could now see the fireflies up close. Bron had called them fireflies, but Bron had obviously never climbed in the mountains, thought Muriel. But then how agile could a hippopotamus be? Up close the little lights were not fireflies at all, but the traces showing through the rock of something electrical that was happening inside the mountain itself.

"How curious," said Muriel. "I must ask someone about this."

In the back of her mind she heard Bron's voice, telling her to avoid this place, as the monster dwelt up here somewhere; but Muriel felt that she would have to face the monster sooner or later anyway, and if she accidentally came face to face with him, she would be able to run away if it came to that. She felt she could not avoid a meeting with the monster forever, and besides, this was her property, she was The Client, everyone said so, and no silly monster was going to stop her from exploring all of a place that really belonged to her.

Climbing in the Twisted Mountains was easier than Muriel thought it would be, and although the terrain arced and undulated, changing direction every few yards or so, she found there were plenty of hand and footholds. The surface of the rocks was soft, unlike any formulation of stone she had ever encountered. She could squeeze the rock itself as she climbed, and her fingers left tiny indentations upon the mountain surface, as she rose, higher and higher, one small step at a time.

As she ascended towards the Roof of the World, as indicated on Bron's original map, Muriel felt a sense of dread steal over her. She kept hearing Bron's warning of the monster returning to her again and again as she climbed, and yet something drove her ever upwards, as though in her heart of hearts she really did want to confront the beast. Secretly, she hoped she would see it, in all its terrifying glory, for she knew that in some strange and unexplained fashion the monster itself was the key to everything.

Muriel climbed higher and higher towards the Roof of the World, and as the time passed and the light faded into a pallid twilight she realised she had become tired.

"I need to rest for a while," she said, and finding a little flat plateau, she sat down to gaze across the vast, sandy expanse of the Crucible of Creation, that spread away below her like a russet coloured rug. As Muriel sat there gazing across the vista she felt something touch her leg, a tiny sensation of touch, nothing more. Muriel looked down to see a spider standing there on the exposed flesh of her leg.

"Hello," she said to the spider, without any trace of fear. Muriel had to smile at the remarkable change in her attitude towards the insect. A vision of Gom floated through her consciousness momentarily, and then disappeared.

"This place is fascinating!" she announced.

"Indeed it is!" replied a growling voice directly behind her, and Muriel spun around screaming.

"I have been wanting to meet you," said the monster, looking over the edge of its cave, and peering down directly into the face of the juvenile climber. "Do not be afraid, I bear you no ill-will."

Muriel gasped, and took in the form and features of the monster. She wanted to escape, to scramble back down the sides of the Twisted Mountain to the flat of the desert as fast as she could, but something told her to stay where she was, to wait just a moment longer, to be brave for ten seconds more. Her heart pounded in her chest so loudly she thought the monster must be able to hear it.

"Come up," said the monster at last, "join me."

The head of the monster disappeared back into the cave, and Muriel was left on all fours neither up nor down against the wall of the mountain. She had to make a decision, and she had to make it right now.

Something deep and secret inside each of us loves to be frightened. A sudden surprise makes us gasp as a river of adrenaline jets through our being and the pounding of our hearts is the drum beat of primordial arousal; add to this blind terror, and the mixture becomes a heady cocktail to make our senses swim with the exhilaration of life itself. Muriel clung to the surface of the spongy rock like a ship's barnacle, as her legs shook violently with fear. Her breaths came rapid and short, as she panted there on the slope, her hair suddenly glued to her face with sweat.

"I said come up!" shouted the monster, peering over the precipice once again, and looking down into the face of the young girl. "You are not in danger from me."

The monster leaned over the edge of its cave and extended a huge arm downwards until its crusty palm and open fingers appeared beside her.

"Take my hand!" commanded the monster.

Muriel could not move, she shook with fear and excitement, her legs shaking that much she thought she must fall away from the cliff face at any second. Slowly she released her grip on the surface of the rock she clung to and reached forwards. The clawed hand of the monster encircled her own little palm and she felt herself torn from the surface of the rock face, as she rose out into open air, and shot upwards. When Muriel felt herself suspended in mid-air, far away from the relative safety of the rock face, and high above the desert floor, which twisted and revolved so far below her, she wanted to scream but the eruption died in her throat, suffocated by the frenzied gasps of her breath.

"I have been waiting to meet you for some time," said the monster as it deposited her gently onto the floor of the cave. "It is fitting that we two should talk together."

The monster released her hand and motioned to a rock beside her. "Please sit down," it said, as though it were a frock-coated gentleman in an Edwardian drawing room, after just receiving a lady visitor.

Muriel sat without a word, as the monster towered over her, its bulk filling the confines of the cave.

"I expect you have many questions for me," said the monster at last. "I will answer them as best I can."

As the threat of imminent harm began to recede in her mind, and the terror began to slowly drain away, Muriel's breathing softened, her heart rate slowed to its natural pace, and she began to focus again.

The monster was obviously waiting for her to recover her composure, demonstrating a level of self-control and patience not normally associated with monsters.

"Why are you doing this?" whispered Muriel at last.

The monster looked genuinely puzzled by the question. "Why am I doing what?" it replied.

"Why are you terrorizing this place?" retorted Muriel, now regaining her faculties, and her courage. "Why are you making everyone fearful of you? Why are you here?"

The monster thought about this for a moment, to gather its thoughts. "It is not my intention to scare anyone," it replied softly, "but I must follow the drive of my nature, as must everyone."

"What does that mean?" asked Muriel, wiping the sweat-plastered tresses away from her face.

"There is an instruction in nature," began the monster, "which every living thing must obey. This instruction applies to everything that lives, everything that exists, from the smallest bacteria all the way up through the plants, insects, fish, birds, and animals, arriving at last at nature's masterpiece, the human condition. Even the planets, and the universe itself must comply. All of creation must obey this instruction, none of them have any choice in the matter, and neither do I."

"And what is the instruction?" asked the schoolgirl.

"Develop or die!" stated the monster.

Muriel shook her head, "I don't understand," she replied.

"When a living thing first exists, it must begin to grow, to develop, to expand its size, to mature. If it cannot do this then it will begin to perish," said the monster.

Muriel nodded, "Okay," she agreed, she could see the logic of that.

"When it has grown to maturity, when its physical size is at the maximum for its condition, it must develop in other ways to survive, but it must continue to grow. It must mature mentally, if it fails at this stage then again it will begin to stagnate mentally, and then to perish."

Muriel thought about this, she was still unsure of what the creature was telling her, but she was willing to go along with it for now. "Okay," she repeated, still not really seeing the point of the story.

"When it has matured to its fullest extent both physically and mentally, it cannot complete the instruction, therefore it will begin to rot, and then it will begin the process of decline into death."

"And what is the point of all this?" asked the schoolgirl bluntly.

"All of nature must comply with this process, including you and I," whispered the creature. "I have no ill-will towards the beings in this place, I mean them no harm, but I too am subject to the instruction. I am merely growing to my fullest extent allowable by my condition."

"But you are causing trouble everywhere!" exclaimed Muriel.

"That is not my fault, and nor is it my concern," replied the monster. "I am following the instruction of all nature. I am growing, developing, becoming stronger. I have little choice in the matter. How that affects others is not my affair."

"That's just an excuse!" replied Muriel. "You can't say it isn't your concern when you are causing devastation everywhere around you."

"I am not consciously causing any devastation," argued the monster. "I am merely following instructions to develop. As I said before, I have no choice but to comply."

"So, you are growing simply because you have to," said Muriel.

"Exactly," replied the beast.

"And everyone is the same?" asked Muriel. "We all have to develop or die?"

"Yes," said the monster. "Not only everything that lives, but also everything created by everything that lives."

Muriel frowned. "Now, you have lost me again."

"When a spider spins its web, the spider who must develop or die, has created a thing that must also develop or die, its web. The spider must tend to it constantly, it must develop its web, or the web itself will begin to perish."

Muriel looked blankly into the face of the beast.

"When a beaver builds a dam, it must develop the dam, or the water will wash it away, the beaver must constantly secure its dam. Not only is the creature subject to the law of all nature, but what it creates is also subject to the same law," explained the monster.

Muriel tried to understand what it was saying, but comprehension was not written on her features.

"If a living thing creates a relationship with another living thing," explained the monster, "that relationship too must also develop or die. If it cannot, then the relationship will become stagnant and start to wither, eventually the relationship will fail and they will part."

Muriel nodded. "So the instruction applies not only to us, but also to what we do?" asked Muriel.

"Indeed," agreed the monster. "If a man starts a business, that business too must develop or die. It must expand and grow in the marketplace. If it does not, it will stagnate and eventually the man will go bankrupt."

Muriel was nodding.

"Develop or Die!" stated the monster. "Is the driving call of all nature. That which cannot develop, must die."

"Why are you telling me all this?" asked Muriel at last.

"So you will understand," replied the monster simply. "When the time comes."

A silence fell between Muriel and the monster that was almost alive, it crackled with its own intensity as neither spoke, each waiting for the other to break the spell.

"When the time comes," whispered Muriel, and the monster nodded.

"I should be going now," said Muriel, wondering if the monster would allow her to leave.

"As you wish," replied the thing. "Come and go as you please."

Muriel turned and stepped quickly to the entrance of the cave, looking back one last time at the creature whose very existence had been the cause of so much stress to so many.

"It has been a privilege to meet you," said the monster. "I don't get any visitors. Come back to me when the time is right."

"I am going to the City of Artists, to find a way to stop you," confessed Muriel. "If I can."

"You must follow your course," replied the creature philosophically. "As must we all."

Muriel looked upon the monster then as a thing which was largely misunderstood. Speaking with it had changed her opinion of the entity. It was still a dangerous creature to be sure, a monster still that must be dealt with if the opportunity arose, but it was not a wild, savage beast. It could communicate, could reason and could explain itself to those who would listen to it.

Muriel exited the monster's cave to resume her journey. She began to climb the steep cliff face of the Twisted Mountains once more, until she reached the summit.

Standing at the Roof of The World she looked back to the Left and could see all the places marked on Bron's original map, exactly as he had drawn it.

Before her lay The Great Divide as depicted on Bron's Other Map, a gargantuan crevice running the length of the Twisted Mountains, as though some angry giant had cleaved the mountain range in two with the blow of a mighty axe.

"Now what do I do?" asked Muriel to herself.

The Great Divide seemed impossible to cross, there were no bridges between the two mountain ranges, and between them a crevice that fell away for ever. Muriel scrambled lightly down into the space between the two halves. She could see the other mountain across The Great Divide, but could not see a way to get there. Muriel stood looking across the divide wondering if this was the end of her adventure in the Twisted Mountains. Was she destined to fail after all? Would she ever reach the City of Artists?

Muriel's consciousness had been expanded during her time in the Crucible. She had come to know that even in the world of matter all was not what it seemed, that everything was made of nothing, and that the will to do a thing, is also the will to learn to be *able* to do a thing. Muriel gazed across the Great Divide before her, the gap was too wide for a leap, too wide even for a running jump. But she was not in the world of matter, she was in the Crucible of Creation itself, where time and distance were reckoned very differently. This was a leap of faith. The knowledge of that entered her consciousness as a whisper heard softly in a dream. A sudden knowing, that once perceived, replaces all that was known before. Belief without proof is the province of the religious, as knowing without education is the province of the mystic. The logical and sceptical scientists have no business here; no place is ever laid at such a table for the men of matter. Without ever knowing why, and without ever needing to understand why, Muriel simply closed her eyes, and stepped forwards off the cliff face into the open air of The Great Divide.

Chapter Twelve

The City of Artists

Muriel landed on the other side of The Great Divide in that single step. In a way she had expected to make it, even though logic told her the leap was impossible. Here in the Crucible, logic was a poor relation to intuition.

Muriel stepped down onto level ground from the last rise of the Twisted Mountain foothills on the Right, and wondered what all the fuss had been about. The Crucible of Creation was a desert here too; it looked exactly the same as where she had Left, and yet Muriel herself felt differently. She felt as though she understood without explanation, perceived without vision, and absorbed without experience. The landscape had not changed, *she* had changed, for knowing without education, is the province of the sage, and Muriel felt as though she had aged in experience but not in years. As she stepped forwards she walked as one with the landscape, not as a traveller might, an individual entity alien to the environment, but as an indigenous weave of the local fabric, a living part of the surroundings, which had always belonged there from the very beginning. She moved across the vista, light as a firefly, feeling in her bones that here she was capable of wonders, as the very air itself filled her with a creative excitement which lapped through her being as she ventured further and further into the mystical realms of the Right.

"I could be a great artist, if I stayed here," she announced to the empty landscape, "or a poet, perhaps."

"You could be anything you wanted to be!" replied the Vendor.

Muriel swung around, startled for a second. "You again!" she exclaimed.

"They are all here, Miss," continued the lad. "Shakespeare, Keats, Dickens, Tolstoy, Da Vinci, all the great ones came here to get their ideas. Every great piece of writing, every great painting, every great idea, was born here, or rather over there," the Vendor indicated a distant city, which Muriel had not been aware of, "in the City of the Artists."

"What are you doing here?" asked Muriel. "I thought your purpose was to demonstrate value on the Left side."

The Vendor shook his head. "Value is a universal concept," he replied. "We instinctively judge everything and everyone by comparative values, how they effect, and what they mean to, us as individuals."

"So?" Muriel was becoming a little irritated by the Vendor who seemed to be able to barge into her experiences as and when he felt like it.

"That locket you always wear around your neck for instance," said the Vendor.

Muriel instinctively reached up to hold the heart-shaped pendant.

"In terms of pure monetary value, it is worth very little," continued the boy, "but to you, it is almost priceless, and why is that?"

"It was given to me by my grandmother before she died," replied Muriel.

"Exactly!" exclaimed the Vendor. "So, we set the value of everything in our lives, don't we? We set a value against every person we know, every duty we have to perform, everything we own, and every idea we have."

"I suppose so," agreed Muriel.

"And against those values, we then compare everything new that comes into our lives; if the newcomer is perceived as having greater value than that which we already possess it is welcomed, and the old item is downgraded. That's why people move house, look for other jobs, change their cars and have love affairs. On the other hand, if the newcomer has less value then it is rejected, and we stay with what we have."

"So, what has all that to do with the City of Artists?" asked Muriel impatiently.

"When Shakespeare first thought of *Hamlet*, he had five other ideas for plays as well. He had to compare the ideas to establish best value. *Hamlet* was written, the others never were."

"William Shakespeare came here," asked Muriel, "to write his plays?"

"He came here for the inspiration, for the first idea, for the spark of genius to fire the imagination," replied the Vendor. "They all did."

"All who?" asked Muriel.

"All the great creative geniuses," responded the boy. "Einstein's Theory of Relativity was born in the City of Artists, in fact it could not have been born anywhere else."

The Vendor raised his arm towards the distant city in a motioning gesture to Muriel. "Shall we go?" he asked.

Within a few paces Muriel and the boy found themselves at the main gate of the City.

"Who approaches this secret place?" whispered a soft voice, as they waited.

"The Client seeks to know this city," replied the Vendor, before Muriel had time to say anything.

"The Client is always welcome here," replied the voice and the gate swung softly ajar.

"You don't need me in there," said the Vendor, smiling at Muriel. "You'll be fine on your own. I'll see you later."

Muriel walked through the gate into the Avenue of the Seeker, the main thoroughfare of the City. She felt an immediate crowding of images in her mind; pictures came to her of future creations she might be responsible for, deeds and tasks she might one day perform to the astonishment of everyone she knew. Here lay the seeds of greatness, the very womb of genius, but there was a discipline required to sort the wheat from the chaff. She needed to focus on what she really wanted to do, in order for the City to work its magic.

"It's all very confusing," said Muriel to herself.

The unrelated images of things that might be, swirled through her consciousness as she walked along, until Muriel saw a sign above a particular shop.

Tourist Information, it said.

"That seems like a good place to start," thought Muriel, as she pushed the door open. A little brass bell tinkled over her head.

"This is indeed an honour," announced an old man in the shop. "I had hoped that one day you might make your way here."

"I'm not really sure why I am here, though," confessed Muriel. "I don't understand very much about all this."

"You are seeking inspiration, perhaps?" suggested the old man.

"Yes, I think so," replied Muriel.

"Then you have come to the Right place!" exclaimed the shopkeeper excitedly. "What exactly are you trying to accomplish?"

"I don't know," faltered Muriel.

"You wish to compose a piece of music?" suggested the shopkeeper.

Muriel shook her head. "I don't read music."

"Do you want to?" asked the old man.

Muriel shook her head again. "No, not really," she replied.

"You want to speak a foreign language?" suggested the old man. "You want to be able to converse with the Poyanawa Tribe of the Amazonian basin, without an accent?"

Muriel laughed and shook her head violently, "No, no, no," she said.

"Mmmm," muttered the old shopkeeper, scratching his chin. "You wish to write a book perhaps?"

"I don't think so." Muriel shook her head again.

"You want to invent something?" pressed the shopkeeper.

Muriel thought about this, "Yes...perhaps," she agreed.

"Now we're getting somewhere!" said the old man. "What is it you want to invent?"

A broad grin came upon Muriel's face as she recalled a conversation with her father. "I want to invent a device for warming up a cold bacon sandwich which doesn't cook the bacon any more, and doesn't leave the bread soggy," she replied, smiling.

"Eureka!" shouted the shopkeeper. "What a wonderful invention!"

Muriel laughed, "Can you help me do that?"

The shopkeeper was nodding furiously. "This is the City of Artists. The Seed of Genius is here. If it is possible, a way to make it manifest can be found in this place."

"What do I need to do?" asked Muriel.

"You must go to the Hall of Inspiration," replied the shopkeeper, "and there you must meditate and let the idea come to you."

"I don't know how to meditate," said Muriel honestly.

The shopkeeper was shaking his head, and smiling at his young customer. "Of course you do," he whispered. "Let me show you."

The elderly man came around from his side of the counter, and stood before the schoolgirl. "You have five senses do you not?" he asked.

"Yes."

"Then use them now. Close your eyes."

Muriel closed her eyes.

"Hold out your hand."

Muriel held out her hand.

"Now imagine I have just placed a warm bacon sandwich in your hand," said the shopkeeper.

Muriel smiled.

"This is your sense of touch. Feel the warmth of the bread in your palm," said the shopkeeper. "Move your thumb over the top slice."

Muriel's thumb moved slowly across the surface of the fresh, warm bread. The shopkeeper nodded his approval.

"Now raise the sandwich up to your eye level, but keep your eyes closed," instructed the shopkeeper.

Muriel's arm rose before her, and her hand came to a stop before her tightly closed eyes.

"This is your sense of sight. In your mind's eye, see the sandwich before you.

"Recognise the white of the bread, the dark red of the bacon, feel it in your hand and see it before you."

Muriel was lost in the moment, absorbed in the spell, she could see the sandwich and she could feel its surface in her hand.

"Now bring the sandwich to your ear," whispered the old man, "we will invoke your sense of hearing. Listen carefully and you can hear the sizzling bacon, it has only just left the pan, it continues to cook; if you concentrate you can hear it sizzle."

Muriel moved her hand to her ear, and the crackle of the bacon, the sight of the bread, and the touch of its texture, and warmth made her mouth suddenly salivate.

"Now bring the sandwich to your nose," said the shopkeeper. "Smell that wonderful bacon, breathe it in, fill your lungs with the aroma."

Muriel took a deep breath when her hand reached her nose, and the heady odour of the freshly cooked bacon filled her nostrils.

"Now open your mouth," said the shopkeeper, "and put the sandwich in your mouth, feel the warmth of the bacon and the bread on your tongue. And take a bite."

Muriel's mouth chewed the sandwich, it was absolutely delicious.

"Now you know how to meditate," said the shopkeeper, breaking the spell.

Muriel opened her eyes. "That was awesome!" she exclaimed. "I could really taste it."

The shopkeeper was nodding furiously.

"I thought meditation was doing nothing, or thinking of nothing," she said, "it never really appealed to me."

"A popular misconception," observed the old shopkeeper. "It is actually impossible to think of nothing, because *nothing* itself is a concept, therefore when you think of nothing you think of something called nothing, which is completely self-defeating, do you see?"

Muriel was trying to see, she just stared blankly at the old man.

"Meditation is the art of invoking all the senses whilst thinking of one, and only one thing at a time. Bringing all five senses to focus on the concept. The subject could be anything, in your case, a bacon sandwich."

"It's funny," said Muriel, "but I was a bit hungry before I came in here, and now I'm not hungry at all."

"Of course you're not hungry now," remarked the old shopkeeper, "your subconscious thinks you have just eaten a bacon sandwich, how could you still be hungry?"

Muriel thought about that for a moment, and then suddenly she understood intuitively how it all worked.

"That was brilliant!" said Muriel. "But how does it help with my invention?"

"Once you are focused, with all five of your senses in play, a secret, sixth sense is triggered, the intuitive sense, which then brings a deeper understanding of the concept into your consciousness, and the answer is perceived. The solution will come to you, don't worry. Now you should go to the Hall of Inspiration, turn right, and it's at the end of the street."

Muriel thanked the shopkeeper, and re-entered the Avenue of the Seeker, turning Right of course, towards her destination. As she passed down the Avenue, Muriel saw several shops with curious signs outside: *New designs for cars, bikes, buses, trains, planes and boats.* She passed another shop, *Totally original musical scores.* Then another little shop window with the sign: *Inspiration for writers and poets, completely original themes, and plots.* At the end of the row yet another small shopfront with the intriguing sign: *Charismatic Speaking, How to inspire others!*

So this is how they all did it! Thought Muriel as she continued to wander towards the mysterious Hall of Inspiration.

As Muriel wandered down the Avenue of the Seeker, a sense of potential started to seep into her consciousness. She started to understand more than most of humanity the possibilities latent within the human condition. She began, even as a young girl to comprehend there was more to life than we ever saw; more to man than molecules, and with her consciousness focused on what she wanted, there was almost nothing she could not accomplish. She began to become filled with a sense of power.

"I could do great things here," she said to herself, "if only I had more time."

As Muriel walked down the Avenue of the Seeker, she was suddenly thrown into shadow by something large passing overhead. The flapping of great wings above her, startled the girl into a defensive posture, as she knelt down and looked up. An angel swept slowly past her overhead, gliding towards the Hall of Inspiration.

Muriel gasped and ran back to the shop, thrusting the little door open.

"I've just seen an Angel!" she shouted to the shopkeeper.

The old man nodded and shrugged his shoulders, "So?"

"Is this Heaven, then?" asked Muriel.

The shopkeeper chuckled. "Don't be silly."

"Then what is it? There are angels here!" exclaimed Muriel.

"They are the messengers of the Right. On the left they run, here they fly. They are the Fornix Flyers," explained the old man.

"So, is this where religion is?" asked Muriel.

The shopkeeper was nodding. "This is the where *everything* is, that is not logical. If it's logical it's on the Left, if it's not logical, it's here. This is where all the mystery and the magic originates!"

Muriel nodded and closed the door again.

The Hall of Inspiration was a cathedral-like edifice, which spanned far and wide the panorama before the young girl. A white colossus made of light, where Muriel entered and found herself in a huge empty room. The ceiling rose above her, and the walls seemed a leisurely stroll away. Muriel walked slowly towards the centre of the room, passing as she went a pedestal upon which lay a great seed. *The Seed of Genius*, announced the plaque on the pedestal. Muriel instinctively knew to go to the centre of the room, where on the floor was a large golden circle, the only colour in the whole place. Muriel knew to sit within the circle and to meditate as she had been shown. She sat on the floor, cross-legged, and tried to relax. Muriel took a few deep breaths to begin with. Images of latent possibilities began to barge into her mind all at once, a violent crowd of unruly salesmen, all pitching at once for her business. Muriel let them come and let them argue and all talk at once, she did not pay attention to any of them, but let the massed images swarm over her and fade away, allowing her perceptions to calm in time.

Muriel remembered the sequence demonstrated to her by the old man in the shop, and she began to invoke her sense of touch. She felt in her hand the texture of the thing she wanted to create, although as yet it had no definite shape. She knew her Bacon Warmer would be an electrical item, most likely, and so she felt the wire extending from the base of it, to a plug at the other end. The device felt alien to her, a gadget she had never seen before and did not know how to use, but she also knew she was only beginning the invention process, and so allowed her perception of the item to develop in its own good time, not forcing it to take any particular shape.

The torrent of unrelated images began to slow down and the pictures now presented to her began to linger in her perception as though some salesperson was showing her wares, one at a time for her consideration. Yet the images she saw were not related to the invention as far as she could understand. A disconnected leg rose before her, old and arthritic; a young pregnant girl who seemed to be in some sort of distress; a man she didn't know drinking beer; a soldier running through the jungle.

Muriel let the images come no matter how bizarre or unrelated they seemed to be.

They floated through her consciousness, one at a time now, as she concentrated on her sense of touch, feeling the weight of the device in her hand, noting the texture and the coldness of its metal parts.

As she had been shown in the shop, Muriel now raised the device to a point directly in front of her face, and began to gaze at her invention through the eyes of her imagination. The device had no constant shape, but twisted and shifted its form as Muriel stared at it, letting it change as it would, without trying to force it to have any particular form. Sometimes it looked like a small television, at other times a miniature engine, then it would suddenly lose all of its metal parts and become a thing of fibre, like the sleeve of a shirt, hanging limply over her outstretched hand.

Muriel lifted her hand to the side of her face, and tuned in to the sounds of her creation. Muriel knew in that instant everything in the universe made a noise; even a pebble on the beach moves its molecules, its atoms vibrate and its electrons whirr in their orbits, the moving symphony of being. Because we think of an item as inanimate, does not mean it has no motion nor sound at the quantum level. There is noise everywhere, above and below that which man may acknowledge. Muriel listened to the continuous hum of her developing concept, as the force of her intuitive sense nursed the formless notion towards a manifest reality.

Moving the creation to the front of her face, Muriel allowed her sense of smell to tune into her idea. At first she could not connect with it in this way, and then as it lingered under her nostrils, a trace of something flirted with her heightened senses. A deep smoky aroma from the dawn of time itself, burning carbon. The electric nature of her invention warmed the material of the universe in her hand and she could smell the effect of heat. Her sense of smell connected with her memory at the deepest of levels, sending her back to the dawn of history, when the molecules of her invention, and the molecules of Muriel herself, were formed together in the atomic furnace of the stars.

Muriel cradled her embryonic creation in the palm of her hand, and moved it towards her mouth, where she allowed her sense of taste to become familiar with the growing embryo of her imagination. She allowed her tongue to touch it, and the purr of its inner electrical nature sent a shiver through her entire body. Muriel could feel the hum of it working; as though it were a thing already, and the electric current which ran through its frame, creating light and heat, transferred to her wet tongue, and connected with Muriel's consciousness. She was beginning to know her invention at the deepest level of her understanding and perception. She did not merely acknowledge its existence, but she knew it intimately, knew its very essence as a mother may know its child.

Moving the new creation an arm's length in front of her, Muriel opened her eyes and gazed for the first time at the offspring of her consciousness. It was a metallic fibre wrap, two sheets of canvas lining where the material was interwoven with metallic threads to help conduct the electrical activity around the surface area of the product. Between the two sheets of canvas ran a series of looping wires which would carry the current to all surface areas. At either end was fastened a Velcro strip for ease of closing, and from one end hung a cable with a plug.

The design was flawless. A deceptively simple device, designed with a cavernously deep understanding, that would work time after time, quickly and efficiently. Because its inventor had been subconsciously connected with the device from its very concept, because all of Muriel's six senses had been focused on the creative process, the child of her imagining had come out perfect at the other end, and could not be improved upon with the technology of its own time. It would require no tweaking and altering, no testing and design re-draws, it was already a finished product as good as the universe could make it.

Universal Mind had made no distinction or allowance for the fact that its user was only a fifteen-year-old, it had merely responded to her subconscious connection as it would to any who linked with it like this. It had read the desire of her mind, had understood what she wanted, and had merely complied, and produced the item requested. As Wernicke the Magician might have said, "It is the work of a heavenly creature."

Muriel smiled.

Chapter Thirteen

Footprints of the Monster

The abandoned debris left behind after an event is often all that is left to show those who fall upon the scene later, that such an event took place at all. The monster had not been seen physically by anyone except Muriel in the Crucible of Creation, and yet the evidence of its presence was visible everywhere.

In the Garden of Idols a new statue had started to form which was solidifying rapidly, yet it was difficult to make out what it was. The new statue had bulk, it had a bulbous head, and what appeared to be eyes, a shapeless body with strong arms and powerful fingers, a demon of sorts, that had only appeared in the garden very recently, and Patrick had come to stare at it every day, observing keenly how each new day had brought more form and structure to the carving.

"This one worries me," said Patrick to the old gardener, one day. "I don't like the look of it at all."

"It's not for us to judge," replied the gardener sagely. "It is the belief of The Client, that takes shape before us, Patrick. We can only observe."

Patrick nodded in acknowledgement of this truth, which was as always beside the point. "I would smash this one if I could," he said.

"Not your decision to make," replied the gardener. "Only The Client can destroy what The Client believes in."

The evolving statue of the monster looked out behind its soulless eyes at the gentle donkey. The eyes of the statue were blind, but portrayed a depth that had known suffering and determination. The hard scales of its skin showed no capacity for a tender embrace, no understanding of gentility or mercy. Its mouth, as yet unformed would never whisper words of comfort to any living thing, or place a gentle kiss upon the cheek of any mortal being. It was a mouth made for biting, and Patrick shook his head and turned away from the new carving, with a very real sense of unease.

Professor Brocas stood alone in his classroom with tears in his eyes. He looked upwards to where the classroom ceiling had once been, only to stare out into the Roof of the World high above him. Part of the classroom ceiling had collapsed inwards, showering the schoolroom desks and chairs with timber, and great shards of plasterwork. The pupils stood around the room in silence, a line of Muriels waiting for guidance and instruction.

"We must repair the damage as best we can, children," observed Professor Brocas. "We cannot let every setback set us back."

"Isn't that what setbacks are for?" asked Muriel.

"A setback is a fork in the road, Muriel," replied the professor. "A chance for us to alter our course, to turn away from our original destination and to seek new horizons, to abandon our goal, for a new adventure. It is a temptation that many would accept."

"Are we going to accept, Professor?" asked Muriel.

"We are not!" stated the old man firmly, with a defiant shake of his head. "Our purpose is a sacred trust, given to us at the dawn of creation. To understand our own language, there can be no other destination for this school.

We shall clear away the rubble and then resume our studies."

Some of the Muriels were disappointed with this, for when a setback occurs, a new direction, leading perhaps to new adventures, often seems more exciting than having to deal with the problem before us, and continue on as before. It takes a resolute heart to turn down the new adventure in favour of an old familiar path, now strewn with debris and disappointment.

"We must be steadfast in our duty, children," said the professor. "We shall not be turned aside from our true path every time there is an obstacle in our way. Let us get to work!"

The Muriels of Brocas' Language School began to pick up the fallen plasterwork and sweep the dust from the floor.

Bron stood in the middle of his violated camp; with his hooves on his hips he surveyed the scene of devastation. All the tents had been blown down as though a hurricane had lately passed though the settlement, and with quite unnecessary violence, had picked up every single record from the ancient archives, and cast them far and wide across the desert sands.

"It will take an age to get all this lot back together," observed the old hippo. "This we did not need, right now."

Thousands of sheets of paper were scattered as far as anyone could see in all directions from the Camp of the Hippos, Upwards to the foothills of the Twisted Mountains, Down to the Arch of Pons, Left to Broca's Language School and Right to the Fornix Tavern. In every direction Bron turned he could see the carefully indexed pages of his life's work strewn to the four corners of creation.

"We must begin at once," said Bron. "Our work here is so important, it cannot be allowed to fail."

"It must fail in the end, though," said one of the hippos nervously. "We cannot stop the monster."

Bron spun around to face his junior. "It is not our job to stop the monster!" he bawled. "It is our job to keep the records safe and secure for when they are required.

"Others have the task of stopping the monster, let them take care of their business, and we shall take care of ours!"

Bron waved his ancient, brown leathery arm across the horizon. "Let's get to work!" he ordered, and all the other hippos started to pick up the scattered records.

At the Great Egg, the Traffic Warden was having a very bad day. The Upside Down People were all bunching up again and causing mayhem on the path.

"Keep moving!" shouted the Warden in frustration. "There is plenty of room for everyone, give each other some space!"

But the Upside Down People took no notice of the Warden, they never did.

As the Warden began to remonstrate with the Upside Down People, yet again the sky suddenly darkened across the Roof of the World, and all the Upside Down People began to overlap each other, causing even more chaos inside the egg.

"What's happening?" shouted the Warden, who had never seen anything like this before.

The Upside Down people began to fade away and disappear.

"Stop! Stop! Come back!" shouted the Warden. "This is not supposed to happen!"

The Great Egg twisted on its base as though the giant structure itself was in pain. The Warden saw the change in the surface of the egg immediately and stopped, open-mouthed at the scene. The egg began to turn from milky white to a pallid grey.

When the egg stopped revolving, trickles of blood began to run in little rivulets from the top to the bottom of the structure, as the petrified warden fell to his knees.

"My God!" he gasped. "What's happening?"

As Muriel lay awake in her hospital bed, her very bones sick with the effects of the radiotherapy, she was still not like any of the other patients. Some of them believed in a life after death, and some did not. Some of them were optimists who believed the doctors would cure them if they could, and others believed death was inevitable, and they might survive if they were lucky. Some had no idea whether they would survive or not, and allowed the tide of fate to wash in their future to their doorstep, accepting whatever that tide may choose to bring with it. The wreckage of chance washed in to the brink of tomorrow, to be accepted by the unprepared. They were all human, and they were all sick, but none of them had ever been to The City of Artists, except the young girl in bed number seven.

Muriel's visit to the Hall of Inspiration had changed her mental state radically.

She now knew as surely as she knew the sun rises in the East, that man is a heavenly creature, as Wernicke had said; and the accomplishments of that angelic condition were limited only by its connection to the source of its power. Muriel took a sheet of paper from her school bag, and a pencil, and began to draw the outline of the Universal Warmer. She knew the design intimately, and the sketch was completed in minutes.

Across the ward from Muriel in the bed opposite an older girl closed her laptop, and lay back on her pillow. Muriel got out of bed and went across to her neighbour.

"Excuse me," said Muriel, "I'm sorry to bother you, but I was wondering if I could borrow your computer for a couple of minutes, I just want to look something up."

The other girl smiled and nodded. "I'm Sarah," she said. "Take it."

Muriel thought the girl looked very depleted of energy, lacking in the vitality of life, as though it had been drained out of her.

"What's wrong with you?" asked Muriel bluntly.

"I have a kidney infection," replied Sarah sadly. "Your left eye is all bloodshot. What's wrong with you?"

Muriel picked up the laptop from Sarah's bed. "Oh, I have a brain tumour," replied Muriel brightly. "Thanks for this, I won't be long, I'll bring it straight back."

Sarah opened her eyes wide and looked at her visitor.

Within minutes Muriel had located a legal firm in London who specialised in patents, and she composed and sent an email to them. She had also contacted a small engineering firm in Liverpool who were able to produce a cloth infused with metal fibres, and a firm in Birmingham who engineered and fitted electrical components into household items. She emailed a marketing firm, whom she asked for advice on a sales campaign, and she had all the web addresses listed on a separate piece of paper when she gave Sarah her laptop back in less than ten minutes.

"Thanks Sarah, I have everything I need now," said Muriel, placing the computer back on Sarah's bed, but her neighbour was now fast asleep.

Muriel thought that the creation of the Universal Warmer was such a wonderfully simple idea, she was astounded that no-one had ever thought of it before.

What she failed to realise was that the creation was born in The City of Artists, where all the best ideas come from, and as so few people visit that sacred place, indeed so few people even knew of its very existence, then it stood to reason that the device and many more like it could not be invented successfully until such an expedition was made by their inventors.

Muriel marched across the desert sands and strode purposefully into the Great Hall of Wernicke's Magic Castle.

Muriel sat down on the chair with a frustrated plop. "Look at all the damage that stupid monster has caused!" she exclaimed. "Why don't you just put a magic spell on it Wernicke?"

"That is beyond my power," observed the old Magician. "I cannot interfere with the Command of Nature, no-one can."

Muriel seemed puzzled by this. "And what is the Command of Nature?" she asked.

"The Command of Nature is *Develop or Die!*" said Wernicke. All living things are subject to that command. All living things must strive to become greater than they are, or they will perish, there are no exceptions. It is the force that drives the engine of evolution."

"But you can't go on growing forever!" said Muriel. "Otherwise people would end up a hundred feet tall! That's just silly."

"There are many forms of growth, Muriel," replied Wernicke. "There is spiritual, physical, emotional, and intellectual growth. To develop, to grow is also to improve."

"Oh, I see," said Muriel, who wasn't really sure that she did. "So, that means everyone has to either grow or die, including me and you?"

"Exactly so, there are no exceptions," stated Wernicke.

"Even the monster?"

There was a pause when the air became as brittle as glass, Muriel felt a chill run through her bones, that made her shiver.

"Even the monster," whispered Wernicke.

"That's just about what it told me itself," said Muriel. "I didn't understand it at the time, I think I do now."

"You have spoken to the monster?" Wernicke gasped out the question.

"Oh yes," replied Muriel. "I went climbing in the Twisted Mountains, and it was there, we sat in its cave and talked. It was quite polite really, for a monster, I mean."

Wernicke the Magician sat on a stool and let his finger and thumb rummage through the snowy folds of his beard, something he habitually did when he was trying to untangle the knot of a problem. "I had no idea," he whispered at last.

"I want to talk to you again about good and evil being points of view," said Muriel. "I'm still not sure about that one."

Wernicke thought for a moment. "Supposing one man stalks another man through the night, and when he gets the opportunity he brutally murders him."

Muriel nodded.

"Is this evil?" asked Wernicke.

"Of course it is!" replied Muriel, certain of her answer.

"Very well then," replied Wernicke. "Supposing we now discover that the man who died was a child killer, who had previously murdered this man's child? A child he had loved since her birth. He tracked down the killer and then killed him?"

"That's different," said Muriel.

"Is it still evil?" asked the Magician.

"Not now," said Muriel, "the murder was justified, I think."

"So what has changed?" asked Wernicke, "have either of the men changed?"

Muriel shook her head.

"So what has changed?" persisted Wernicke.

"My point of view has changed," admitted Muriel.

A silence fell between the old Magician and the young girl, where both of them thought about the nature of good and evil.

"Is the monster evil?" asked Muriel.

"From whose point of view?" teased the Magician.

"From my point of view, I suppose," replied Muriel.

"You have spoken to it. What do you think?" replied the Magician.

"It says it is only following the command of its nature," replied Muriel.

Wernicke nodded. "Exactly so."

"So, is it evil or not?" persisted Muriel.

Wernicke thought about this for a moment.

"When the lion attacks the zebra, who has done nothing to the lion at all," began the Magician. "And the lion tears the throat out of the innocent zebra, subjecting it to terror and agony and then death, is the lion evil?"

Muriel shook her head. "No, it is just following its nature," she said.

Wernicke nodded.

"But I suppose the zebra thinks it is evil!" exclaimed Muriel.

Wernicke smiled. "But the zebra has a different point of view, does it not?"

Muriel nodded.

"There is another side to that question you may not have considered," said Wernicke. "Do you think the lion considers the zebra to be evil?"

Muriel wondered about that.

"I suppose that depends on the viewpoint of the lion," she answered at last.

Wernicke clapped his hands, applauding her response. "Bravo!" he shouted.

"So our perceptions of good and evil depend solely on our point of view at the time?" said Muriel. "And so does the whole of society?"

Wernicke nodded and smiled at his new pupil.

"If you can't put a spell on the monster," said Muriel, "what can be done to stop it? Who could kill the thing before it destroys the Crucible?"

"I couldn't say for sure," replied Wernicke. "Maybe the Silver Knight could engage it in battle, isn't that what knights are supposed to do?"

"I've already sent him there. He has a quest from me to destroy the monster," said Muriel. "But I think the monster will be too much for him."

"Then the future looks uncertain for all of us," observed the old Magician.

"I was thinking of returning to The City of Artists," said Muriel at last. "To the Hall of Inspiration, I might be able to find an answer there."

"It is one thing to find the solution to a problem," said the Magician, again fingering his beard, "it is quite another thing to then take that solution and make it into a reality. A physical solution that can be applied to the problem in the world of matter.

"That requires work, other people to help you, and time. You may not have much of those, none of us may."

Muriel stood up, fired with the enthusiasm of youth. "Then there's no time to be lost, I must go at once!" she announced.

Chapter Fourteen

The Sword of Heaven

Muriel's dad held his daughter's hand as though it were a precious object which he had sought to possess for as long as he could remember. The pair held hands in silence, not needing to speak, but allowing the sense of fear, and apprehension which they both felt, to flow backwards and forwards between them, like the ebb and flow of an emotional tide. At length Muriel gazed into the face of her father and asked a question which she felt she needed to ask, regardless of the answer. Muriel had formed the question carefully in her mind. *If I die, will you please use some of the money from the invention to help with research for brain tumours?*

Muriel took a deep breath and then put this question to her father. "Fight bacon monster with my dead body, Daddy."

Muriel's father immediately felt as though his world, already as brittle as glass, would now shatter for sure, a beautiful and fragile crystal orb, hurled violently against the rocks of tragedy and misfortune.

"You're not going to die my darling," he stammered. "The consultant says that we have the tumour in time, they can cut it out, and you will recover. We can get through this together."

Muriel smiled, "Silver Mum's Knight," she whispered.

"We're ready to take you down to theatre now, Muriel," said a hospital nurse who had appeared at Muriel's bedside.

Muriel was wheeled down to the operating theatre where a team of surgeons surrounded her. "We are going to make you well again, young lady," said the chief surgeon.

"Monster carve up," replied Muriel.

The surgeon smiled as they slipped the intravenous line into her arm in order to administer the anaesthetic. "Start to count backwards from one hundred for me please," he said.

"One hundred...ninety-nine...ninety-eight..."

Muriel awoke to find herself lying on her back in the desert. She must have fallen asleep again, she thought, sitting up and wiping her eyes.

"Today we have a parietal craniotomy," said the surgeon to his team. "We will go in directly above the target zone, through the cranium to the cerebral cortex where the tumour is located, it should be immediately visible once we arrive there, and then we will use the ultrasonic aspirator to remove the offending mass. The patient is young and strong, her vital signs are good, this should be fairly straightforward. As the subject is a young girl we will try and save as much of her hair as we can, so may we have just the top of her head shaved please?"

Muriel stood up and looked about her. None of the familiar landmarks were to be seen anywhere, she could not estimate where she was in the Crucible. As far as she could see in any direction there was only sand, even the Twisted Mountains had somehow disappeared. Muriel felt very groggy, and tired, and she seemed unsteady on her feet. "I don't know where I am," she said to herself. "I have to find Bron."

When Muriel was asleep her head was placed into a three pin skull fixation device which was attached to the table and was designed to hold her head steady during the procedure.

The chief surgeon spoke to two medical students who were watching him carefully. "Now we are going to insert a lumbar puncture into the patient's lower back so we can extract some CSF or cerebrospinal fluid, which will allow the brain to relax."

The students merely nodded in response.

Muriel's cerebrospinal fluid began to drain out.

When The Client was comatose, the Fornix Runners were not needed as much as when The Client was up and about, and so Charlie often declared these times to be Happy Hours in the Fornix Tavern. The bar was packed with runners now, who had suddenly found themselves with very little to do for a few hours, and were all pushing and shoving at the bar to be served.

"Alright! Alright!" shouted Charlie above the din. "One at a time."

Charlie placed a pint glass under the pump and pulled the handle. The nozzle spat and spurted a few drops out and then exhaled only air into the glass.

"We've run out of CSF!" said Charlie.

"Now we need to prepare the scalp with antiseptic," explained the chief surgeon, as the theatre nurse swabbed down the shaved area of Muriel's skin.

"We will now make the first incision. This will be done behind the hairline to ensure a good cosmetic result later."

The chief surgeon began to cut a long thin line across Muriel's scalp, carefully retracing the cut several times, moving a little deeper with each pass. The blood was mopped away each time by the nurse, and when the cut was deep enough, the surgeon turned once more to his students.

"Now we can lift the skin and muscles off the bone, and carefully fold this flap back out of the way," he said.

Again his students nodded.

Muriel continued to wander aimlessly through the featureless landscape, her feet leaving soft indentations in the sand behind her. "Where is everybody?" she asked of the wilderness, but there was only a soft breeze to answer her.

"Now that the scalp has been peeled away, we can clearly see the cranium. We will drill a small burr hole into the cranium," continued the chief surgeon. This will allow the insertion of a craniotome, a special saw which we will use to create the bone flap. Drill please."

The chief surgeon placed the drill tip at one corner of Muriel's shaved skin.

Muriel began to hear a faint humming noise in the distance, she stopped and looked around, it was difficult to pinpoint exactly where the sound was coming from.

Strangely enough it seemed to be coming from the sky. Muriel looked upwards to the Roof of the World, but could see no changes up there. She frowned. Under Muriel the sand began to vibrate very slowly, she could feel the tremor in the soles of her feet.

"What is going on?" she said to herself.

The chief surgeon withdrew the drill bit from Muriel's skull and stood back.

The theatre nurse inserted a swab into the burr hole to wipe away the surrounding mush from the small crater.

"Craniotome, please," said the chief surgeon.

When the theatre nurse had handed the craniotome to the chief surgeon he once more addressed his students. "This is a special saw which will allow us to cut out the bone flap," he said. "Notice the foot plate at the bottom of the device, this we place against the skull so that we know we will not cut too deeply and damage the dura, the soft protective tissue which surrounds the brain itself."

Again the students nodded.

The surgeon inserted the saw into the small burr hole and began to cut. Steadily he moved the saw blade across the shaved skin of Muriel's cranium, describing a rough circle, until he arrived back where he had started at the small burr hole.

Muriel sat down on the sand as the strange vibration in the ground beneath her continued to cause the sand to move. She felt unsteady on her feet today as it was, and the ground moving beneath her only made her already faltering steps even more uncertain. "I wish Bron was here," she said to herself. "He would know what's going on."

"Now we have made the bone flap," explained the chief surgeon, "all we have to do is remove it."

The theatre nurse inserted a small retractor into the burr hole and with a very gentle pressure lifted the corner of the bone flap. The chief surgeon took the corner between his thumb and forefinger, and pulled the entire bone flap clear of Muriel's skull.

The Roof of the World began to tremble, and as the terrified inhabitants of the Crucible of Creation looked upwards, there appeared above their heads a lightning bolt shaped crack, running across the sky from the very edge of Out, all across the heavens to the very edge of Right.

A blinding light descended into the Crucible, sending Bron and the hippos scurrying into the safety of their tents.

"It is the end of days!" shouted the gardener. "The end has come at last!"

Patrick turned his head sideways to view the source of the blinding light. "I don't think so," he mused, squinting his upper eye at the searing brilliance. "This is something else!"

A sharp crack echoed around the Crucible as this new blinding light expanded from that of a hairline splinter to a gaping chasm which allowed the Outlight to bathe the summit of the Twisted Mountains in a never-seen-before radiance of pure colour.

The Twisted Mountains appeared a grey-pink in colour for the first time, and the creatures of the Crucible of Creation wondered how that realm could ever be the same again.

Across the burning sands of the Crucible charged the Silver Knight, his white mount, Spero kicking up plumes of desert sand with every hoof-fall, and the knight's armour reflecting the Light of Heaven like a patchwork of tiny mirrors. "Today we give battle to the monster!" he shouted, and his words filled the Crucible with a terrible determination, that spread fear, excitement and dread through the hearts of the populace.

Patrick nodded. "So, that's it," he whispered to the gardener, who was hiding in a bush. "The monster is to be attacked at last."

"Not before time," hissed the concealed gardener, terrified that the monster might hear him.

In the Garden of Idols, a new figure was rapidly forming, a carving of a young woman on her knees with her arms stretched upwards to the heavens. The features of the girl's face were not depicting any obvious emotion, and so it was unclear whether the pose was meant to depict an act of surrender or supplication; or perhaps it was a gesture of casting some item from her hands to the skies, a dove of peace perhaps? The meaning of the statue was unclear as yet, only The Client could supply the answer.

"This whitish cover we now see below the bone flap cavity is the dura," explained the chief surgeon. "It is a thin membrane which covers and protects the brain itself. We will carefully cut through this, and then fold it back. Scissors, please."

Once again the two students nodded.

Using the surgical scissors, the chief surgeon carefully cut a large semi-circle through the dura. He peeled the membrane back on itself, and held the flap in place, out of the way with retractors. "And there it is!" he said. "The human brain."

When the humming and vibration had stopped, Muriel had stood up again and began to walk around as before. She had not gone many paces when the brilliant Outlight had descended into the Crucible from the Roof of the World and bathed everything in a vibrant colour. The sand beneath Muriel's feet had attained the colour of sand that Muriel was used to, the light in the Crucible suddenly looked normal to her. Muriel shook her head. "I wish I knew what was going on here today," she mused.

"Now we can clearly see the problem," remarked the chief surgeon. "This is the tumour here." He pointed to a dark red mass of cancer cells that straddled the cerebral cortex. "Scalpel, please."

Deep within the safety of its cave in the Twisted Mountains, the monster cowered against the vengeance of the Sword of Heaven. Instinctively it knew the sword had come to attack, sent from the Silver Knight.

"I will lie here very still and quiet," whispered the monster, "and perhaps it will not be able to find me."

The Sword of Heaven lanced downwards through the Roof of the World, slicing back and forth beside the monster, cutting away the sides of the monster's cave. The monster closed its eyes, and realised the hand of fate guided the blade.

"It has found me," sighed the monster, sensing its own death.

With a terrible slashing motion the Sword of Heaven suddenly cut deep into the monster's flesh, slicing off a chunk of its side. Blood spat from the body of the beast across the walls of the cave as it gasped in the throes and agonies of butchery.

"Why are you doing this to me?" screamed the monster. "I have done no wrong, I do only my duty!"

The Sword of Heaven was deaf to its pleading, and continued to slice away the sides of the cave, leaving the body of the monster exposed in the centre of an open cavern.

"Now we have exposed the cancer cells, and separated them from the healthy tissue around them, we can proceed to remove them," said the chief surgeon, "laser please."

The monster folded its arms across its face as an intense pillar of light blasted down from the Roof of the World. The pillar of light moved across the floor beside the monster, burning the ground as it went. The monster shuffled sideways to avoid the shaft, but he had no room. When the pillar touched his flesh he screamed in agony. The pillar of light passed through the monster at waist level effectively cutting him in two.

Great gouts of blood spat from his stomach and mouth across the floor of what had once been its cave. The monster began to crawl away, dragging its severed torso with only the strength left in its fingers.

The pillar of light continued to arc back and forth behind the scurrying beast, carving great chunks out of its severed legs.

"Ultrasonic aspirator, please," said the chief surgeon.

The monster frantically started to dig with its hands into the floor of the cavern.

The severe pain it felt would have caused any other creature to pass out, but the monster was no ordinary creature; agony and terror allowed it to remain conscious, and it dug into the floor beneath itself in a frenzy of movements, driven by the strongest desire in the universe, the desire to survive.

The pillar of light disappeared as suddenly as it had come. In its place came down a long tube from the Roof of the World which hesitated over the decimated lower body of the monster.

The monster had dug a hole in the floor of the cave large enough for what was left of its body to fall into. The creature tipped into the hole head first, and scrambling around inside, frantically righted itself, only its head now showing above the floor.

From the end of the long tube suddenly gushed forth a powerful jet of water, crashing into the cavern above the monster, and washing his severed body pieces clear of the floor. The surging water flooded into the monster's hole.

The jet of water stopped suddenly, and body pieces of the monster floated past its head. Frantically the monster pulled the soft matter it had excavated from the floor back into the hole on top of itself. It scooped the slush into its hole, allowing itself to sink further and further down until only its arm remained outside, sweeping back and forth, pulling the last of the slush into the hole. Then it gently slipped its arm back into the hole, leaving no trace of what remained of its decimated body above ground.

The long tube now began to whirr and the body parts of the monster which had been severed from it and were now scattered across the surface of the cavern, began to move towards the nozzle. One by one they lifted into the air, disappearing inside the mouth of the giant tube. When the last remaining body part of the monster had been removed, the water came again, and washed the whole area clean.

"Now we can see the tumour has been completely removed," said the chief surgeon.

The students nodded.

"All that remains now is for us to close the dura with sutures, replace the bone flap, which will be secured in place with a titanium plate and screws, which will remain permanently in place to support the area, and the muscles and skin sutured back into place. A very successful procedure I think you will all agree."

The students nodded for the final time.

In the weeks that followed, Muriel lay at home, allowing time for her body to recover from its recent ordeal. The consultant had said the operation had been a success, as far as he could tell, and now it was time to let nature begin the long and slow process of healing. Brocas' Fluent Aphasia loosened its grip on her ability to pronounce her words correctly, as the cause of it, the tumour had been removed. As the days passed, Muriel's normal speech had returned.

One day as Muriel lay in bed gazing the day away at her ceiling, her father called in to see her.

"Some letters have arrived for you," he said, sitting on the edge of her bed, and handing her a little pile of official looking envelopes. "We're intrigued!" said her dad. "One of them is from some legal firm in London, what have you been up to?"

Muriel smiled at her dad, and tore open the envelope. She scanned its contents quickly, threw it to her father and opened the next one. Muriel read the contents of each letter in seconds, understood their meaning immediately, and passed each one to her dad, who was completely confused by each missive, until at the end he was as mystified, if not more so, than he had been at the beginning.

"What does it all mean?" he asked.

Muriel touched one of the letters in her father's hand, gently with the tip of her finger. "This one is from a legal practice in London who specialise in world patents.

"We need to ensure we have legal ownership before we go to market."

Muriel touched the next letter. "This one is from a manufacturing firm, with a cost estimate for producing the Universal Warmer, under licence to me."

Muriel's dad looked at his daughter as though she was a person he didn't quite recognise lying there, although he thought he should have known her.

"This one is from a sales and marketing firm who will advertise the product on national television for me, on a sales percentage basis."

Muriel's father's face crinkled into a mask of confusion.

"This one is from a firm of website engineers who will create the website for me to show the product, and how it works, where it can be ordered."

Her dad was trying his best to be the parent here, but he was swimming against a tide that was already lapping against his ears.

"And this one," said Muriel, finally touching the last letter, "is from a completion house, who will store the product, package it and post it out to those who purchase from the website."

Muriel's father shook his head, he suddenly felt very young.

Muriel sighed. "The product will be advertised and demonstrated on television, and the viewer will be guided to my website, people will buy it from the site, and the completion house will send it out. The legal firm will set up the corporation, and everything will work automatically."

Muriel's dad was still floundering. "What product?" he whispered.

Muriel sighed again. "The Universal Warmer. The devise for warming up your bacon sandwiches without cooking the bacon any more and making the bread soggy! I've invented it, it goes into production next week."

Muriel's dad stared at his daughter as though he was seeing her for the very first time. He thought he should say something intelligent at this point, if he could think of something intelligent to say. "Where did you get all the money from?" he stammered at last.

"I didn't need any money," replied Muriel. "The legal firm are my partners, so they get a share of the proceeds, the engineering firm, the internet firm and the completion house are all paid by the website automatically; the income the website generates pays everyone, so the whole cycle is self-funding. When everyone is paid, whatever is left at the end is mine, simple."

Muriel's dad stared at his daughter with his mouth hanging open. "Does your mother know about all this?" was all he could think of to say.

Chapter Fifteen

After The Battle

What was left of the monster lay still in the deep recesses of its shattered cave high in the Twisted Mountains. It had crawled nervously out of its hole in the ground, when the attack had been broken off, scurrying like a wounded animal for shelter, when the light in the Crucible had returned to its more familiar twilight. The Sword of Heaven had sliced it into shreds, and pieces of its flesh had been hauled away skywards, up through the Roof of the World. The wounded thing lay in a state of shock and deep trauma, where it tried to recover its strength as best it could, from the unholy ordeal that had befallen it at the hands of the Silver Knight. The monster surveyed its surroundings carefully, not daring to breathe or make its presence known until it was absolutely satisfied the Sword of Heaven had gone from the Crucible.

When the monster felt sure it was alone, and the avenging blade of the Silver Knight had left the Crucible, perhaps for good, the beast that lived yet, took a deep breath and then with all its remaining strength bellowed into the wilderness. "I am still alive, after all." shouted the monster. "The Silver Knight has failed to kill me. I will lie here and gather my strength, then I will resume my journey. I will grow again in time, I will become twice the creature I once was, and then I will wreak such a vengeance upon all here that it will be the end of days!" The monster took another breath, even shouting had tired it. "The end of days!" it gasped, and then closed its eyes, and quickly fell into a deep, convalescent slumber.

Across the expanse of the Crucible the monster's bellow echoed menacingly from place to place. The librarians at the Camp of the Hippos spun to face the Twisted Mountains, their little ears pricked to the muffled, distant echo. In the Garden of Idols, Patrick momentarily stopped chewing the weeds to listen. In Brocas' Language School, Muriels turned their heads as one towards that high and distant place from where the warning rolled. On the highest parapet of The Magic Castle, the Magician Wernicke gazed towards the Twisted Mountains, and slowly nodded acknowledgement of his fears. At the Fornix Tavern those Runners who were not on duty filed outside to gaze towards the summit of the Twisted Mountains. On the plains far below Wernicke's lofty turrets, Spero rose in alarm, high up on his hind legs, as the Silver Knight pointed his lance at the sound, as though to warn the menace that he yet had a quest unfulfilled from The Client herself, and the final day of destiny was coming for the entire world.

The process of healing is a dance between Therapy and Time. Therapy takes the lead, executing the sequence of steps, one after another as Time sets the tempo; together to the music of creation they waltz a repair to our damaged flesh.

Muriel was drifting like a lily pad upon the gentle current that washes between the states of awake and asleep, when a tapping at her bedroom door recalled her senses to the present.

"Come in," she said, wiping her eyes.

Her dad came into her bedroom with a large rectangular box under one arm. It had been wrapped as a present, with an enormous pink bow cresting the top.

"I have something for you," he said, gently laying the present on her bed.

Muriel unwrapped the box, casting the decorative wrapping aside, and felt a rush of gratitude and excitement when she saw the picture on the box.

"Oh, thanks, Dad!" she exclaimed.

"I thought you might need one, now you're going to be a high-powered executive with your own company," he said, smiling. "Besides, it will save you the trouble of getting out of bed to use my system downstairs."

"My own laptop!" said Muriel. "The very thing I need, thank you so much."

Muriel threw her arms around the neck of her father, who felt a lump come into his throat with the tenderness of the embrace, though he knew not why.

"Don't forget to thank your mother as well," he croaked.

In less time than it takes to make a bacon sandwich, Muriel had the laptop up and running. She responded to her emails from her new business partners, and clicked a link which took her to a trial version of her new website.

The Universal Warmer was now a real item in the world of matter. A photograph of the completed product shone out from the screen of the laptop before her, and Muriel felt a deep knowing in her mind that it would work efficiently at all levels. It was a thing invented, not in the mundane world of matter, where the caprices of conscious thought would produce an item that might or might not work. It was here where faulty products arose, where customer complaints were born, and manufacturers had to deal with product recalls and re-designs, fixing and tweaking the product until it reached a standard that was merely acceptable to both the maker and the user. Instead, this was a thing which had been born in the City of Artists, in the subconscious powerhouse of man's angelic condition, the battery of the soul, connected eternally to Universal Mind, the very engine of evolution, the home of genius itself. The Universal Warmer was an angelic creation, flawless in design and construction, which could not be improved upon with the technology of its own time.

Muriel saw an email come in from a market research company the legal firm had commissioned to test consumer reaction to the new device. Muriel clicked on the entry and opened the report. The research company had found that a device capable of raising the temperature of almost anything was a gift from the gods to the marketplace. Certainly it would warm a bacon sandwich without cooking the bacon any further and making the bread soggy, but it also had a myriad of other uses Muriel had never imagined. Wrapped around the legs it would stop the onset of deep vein thrombosis on long haul flights. It would calm an unborn child when wrapped around the stomach of its pregnant mother. It would raise fermenting beer to the perfect temperature of 24 degrees, and would be a godsend to the home brewers of the world.

Wrapped around the head it would relieve headaches, around the jaw it would relieve toothache. It would combat the onset of frostbite in frozen limbs, fingers and toes. A version with a battery instead of an electric plug had been suggested, which would make the device transportable for use out of doors, where air and sea rescue services, military medics, veterinary surgeons, hikers and campers could take the device into the field and use it where there was no power supply. The Universal Warmer's versatility was limited only by the needs of its user.

Suddenly Muriel remembered the images which had at first been presented to her when she had sat cross-legged in the Hall of Inspiration. The elderly leg, the man drinking beer, the pregnant and distressed woman, the soldier running through the jungle, images which had seemed to be disconnected from her invention at the time, but were now deeply connected: the end users of a product born in the creative centre of human consciousness.

Muriel sent emails approving the battery version of her device, accepting the website layout, and confirming the product design with the manufacturer. Her time in the Crucible had bestowed upon her certain advantages others did not possess. Simply being with the Vendor had given her an insight into the concepts of value and quality, and she instinctively knew the website design was right for her product. Spending time with Bron had improved her memory, and her visit to the Garden of Idols had given her a broader outlook on the human condition. As she closed the lid of her laptop, the telephone started to ring downstairs.

Patrick looked again at the developing statue, and shook his head. The gardener didn't like to see his friend so troubled.

"You're spending too much time with that one, Patrick," observed the gardener.

The statue was as yet unformed, even its outline was uncertain as it seemed to be growing out of the pedestal it stood upon. Only a pair of hands, covered in large scales, with a great claw at the end of each finger were formed, the rest of it was a shapeless mass in the throes of creation. Even the sight of the two hands, reaching upwards out of their pedestal gave Patrick a sense of unease.

"Something terrible is going to happen, because of what this one represents," replied the donkey. "I feel it in my bones."

The gardener placed a reassuring hand on Patrick's back. "You don't know that my friend," he whispered.

"I do," replied Patrick. "Don't ask me how I know. I just know. This thing will bring the end of days to the Crucible, and none will be spared."

"I wish you wouldn't talk like that," said the gardener. "The Client is not foolish. She is young, but she is not foolish. She will not throw her future away, not after what she has learned here."

"She may not have a choice," replied the donkey.

As Muriel sat up in bed she felt her heartbeat suddenly quicken, instinctively she knew something important was about to happen. Moments later she heard the double footsteps of her parents upon the stairs.

"The consultant has just rung," said Muriel's dad as they entered her bedroom.

"They need you to go in for another test. It's nothing to worry about, it's just routine."

Muriel nodded. "They want to see if the tumour is still there or not," she replied. "Their tests will confirm it is."

Muriel's parents cast a downhearted look between themselves, a brief glance of confusion and panic.

"You mustn't say that, darling," said her mother. "The operation was very successful. The surgeon said so."

"He said he thought it went well as far as he could tell at the time," replied Muriel. "But I know the tumour is still there, their tests will confirm it."

Muriel had grown in mental capacity and maturity since her travels through the Crucible, to the point where now she seemed an entirely different person to those who knew her well.

"You can't know that sweetheart," replied her dad, a man from the world of matter, who would never be able to understand about the Crucible, even if Muriel had a mind to explain it to him.

"I know they only got most of it out," replied Muriel. "The rest is too deeply seated, they cannot remove it with a blade as they risk giving me permanent brain damage. So, they will suggest more radiotherapy and some chemotherapy, this time. Which we will agree to and all my hair will fall out. You need to prepare yourselves for that."

Muriel's parents fell against each other and stared with teary eyes, wounded hearts and confused minds at their daughter, who was unexpectedly much stronger than they were.

Muriel looked across the vast expanse of desert, raising a hand to shield her eyes against the glaring light. She narrowed her eyes to glimpse more clearly a seated rider galloping away from the Twisted Mountains, his armour plating reflecting the sunlight in tiny flashes as his moon white charger carried him ever nearer.

"The Silver Knight!" exclaimed Muriel.

Bron looked to where Muriel gazed and nodded his head. "He has completed your quest," observed the hippo. "Now he returns."

"But the monster isn't dead!" said one of the other hippos from inside his tent.

"It has been stopped in its tracks!" replied Bron. "And that is good enough for now."

"It won't be good enough in the end though," muttered the other hippo.

"You get back to work!" shouted Bron. "What the Silver Knight does or does not do is no business of ours."

Spero cantered across the pink desert of the Crucible, flicking up sprays of sand with his hooves as he approached. The Silver Knight seemed prouder today than ever, sitting bolt upright on his worthy steed, his lance held high in the air, as the morning sunshine danced and played across the polished plates of his armour.

"What a show-off!" muttered Bron, as they watched the hero draw nearer to the camp.

Muriel smiled. "I think he's great," she said. "At least he's *trying* to stop the monster, which is more than can be said about quite a few other people around here."

Bron snorted in disgust and went inside his tent, muttering about the fact that some people around here had work to do.

The Silver Knight entered the Camp of the Hippos and, allowing Spero one final rise up on his hind legs, letting him kick forth with his forelegs, the Silver Knight saluted his Lady fair.

"I am returned after your quest, My Lady," he said, as Spero landed on all fours again, shaking his great head, and snorting the desert sands from his nostrils.

"So I see," replied Muriel. "You have done well, but the monster is not slain, Sir Knight, it lives yet. We have all heard it roaring from the mountains."

"It is defeated in its purpose My Lady, and will trouble us no more," replied the valiant knight.

"Then you have my thanks," said Muriel.

"I ask for no more," replied the knight.

"And thank you too, Spero," said Muriel stroking the ghostly white face of the mighty battle steed.

"It is my honour to carry him," replied Spero.

Muriel smiled. "Without you my knight would be Hope-less."

Spero returned The Client's smile. The Silver Knight didn't understand the pun.

The consultant welcomed them into his office with a practised smile. They sat before his desk, Muriel in the middle and a parent on either side, as though they were trying to protect her from an oblique attack. The consultant fingered his white beard and Muriel smiled, he reminded her of Wernicke the Magician.

"The tests have come back," he began. "And I am very sorry to tell you that they show conclusively that part of the tumour remains in the deepest part of the cerebral cortex. I thought we had removed all of it, but it seems the roots of it were too deeply embedded and are still there."

Muriel's mother began to softly sob.

"However, we must not give up hope," continued the consultant. "We will embark upon a course of radiotherapy straight away, and I have great confidence we will achieve positive results."

"But there are no guarantees?" said Muriel's father.

"I am afraid not," confessed the surgeon.

Muriel laughed. "If you want a guarantee you should buy a toaster, Dad," she said.

Her mother looked horrified. "How can you be so flippant at a time like this?" she hissed.

"Or better still, my Universal Warmer, that is going to come with a ten year guarantee!" said Muriel.

Over the next few weeks, Muriel embarked on the course of radiotherapy suggested by the consultant. Muriel attended the hospital at the appointed time, was put into a surgical gown, and brought into the radiotherapy suite. Here she was laid upon a bed at the head of which a large plate was swung into place above her, and a target light shone onto the top of her head. During her surgery, the surgeon had cut away a part of her skull to make a flap, which he had folded back to give his scalpel access to the brain itself. Afterwards the flap had been closed and secured back into place with metal screws. Now the radiotherapy light beam focused on this flap, under which the monster was growing.

Patrick and the gardener had come to look at the strange and troubling statue every day since its first appearance in the Garden of Idols. After the battle with the Silver Knight, where the Sword of Heaven had cleaved the monster in two, the statue in the Garden had shrunk to half its original size. However as the weeks had passed, the statue had begun to develop once more, slowly at first, an inch at a time, and today it was broader, and thicker set than Patrick had ever seen it.

"This thing is growing again," observed Patrick. "I don't like the look of it at all."

"I told you before," replied the gardener. "It isn't for us to judge. These are the representations of The Client's beliefs, and only The Client's. Whether anyone else understands or believes in them is irrelevant."

"I know that," said Patrick. "That doesn't mean I have to like it."

Above Muriel the machine began to whirr.

Suddenly and without warning a great beam of blindingly brilliant light blasted through the Roof of the World, smothering the Twisted Mountains in an incandescence that swallowed the form and structure of everything in the Crucible. The gardener placed his hands over his eyes and fell to his knees, Patrick closed his eyes and hung down his head.

In Brocas' Language School, Muriels shielded their faces as the light spread through the tiny schoolroom stopping the lesson immediately.

"Don't look at the light Muriel!" shouted Professor Brocas.

In the Camp of the Hippos, Bron and his comrades dived into their tents to avoid the searing brilliance, and thousands of Fornix Runners, scattered throughout the Crucible stopped in their track and fell to their knees, as they could see nothing ahead of them.

Spero shied as he suddenly lost his sight, darting sideways mid-step, lost his footing and toppled over, casting the Silver Knight into the sand with a mighty crash, his armour plate reflecting the brilliance of the Angelic Light in all directions from him like a great prism.

High in the recesses of the Twisted Mountains the focal point of the light beam hit the monster squarely in the chest. The scream erupting from the beast echoed around the Twisted Mountains as the voice of doom. In the agonies of the moment the monster coughed a great gout of blood upon the walls of its cave, which killed the scream in its throat. The touch of the light withered the flesh of the creature as easily as a flame destroys paper. The monster rolled back and forth in its cave trying to avoid the touch of the light, but it was too large and the cave too small, for it to hide. Again it screamed its agonies to the Roof of the World, but there was none to listen to its anguished cries.

"Why are you doing this to me?" it shouted. "I am following my nature and that is all." But the savagery of the light was deaf to its cries, and when as suddenly as it had appeared, it vanished, the withered creature fell upon the floor of its cave and passed out.

The machine stopped whirring and the great plate lifted away from Muriel's head. "You can get up now," said the technician. "You may feel a little sick later on. It will pass, don't worry."

A few days later Muriel received a telephone call from the marketing company she had commissioned to promote the Universal Warmer.

"We have been thinking about a television commercial," said the rep. "We think you should explain the product to the viewer, and show them how it works."

Muriel held the telephone receiver in one hand, and with the other she examined a great sheaf of her hair which had fallen from her head to the pillow.

"I'm not sure that is such a good idea," replied Muriel. "I am undergoing a course of radiotherapy, and all my hair is falling out."

There followed an uncomfortable silence, where Muriel sensed the rep was trying to think of something to say.

"I am sorry," came the eventual reply.

Something had troubled Muriel about the conversation with the rep. Before she had ventured into the Crucible, and especially into the City of Artists, Muriel Mason the ordinary schoolgirl would have realised she could not appear on television with her hair falling out, and promote anything. Now she was a different person. Muriel had gained a strength that had crept up inside her by inches since her exposure to the Crucible, and she realised that hair or no hair she was going to promote her own product and that was that.

Muriel felt a twinge of anger inside her when she called the rep back.

"Get the cameras ready," she said. "I will do it. The Universal Warmer deserves my best support, let's get it organised."

"Yes, Miss Mason," came the reply. Muriel smiled as she rang off, that was better.

Muriel stood up and went into her parent's bathroom. She took a good look at herself in the mirror, and didn't like what she saw.

The consultant smiled at the Masons, he liked to smile at people when he had good news to impart to them.

"I am so pleased to be able to tell you," he began, "that Muriel's cancer cells seem to be in complete remission, that is wonderful news."

Muriel's mum and dad hugged each other, a shared euphoria suddenly evident amidst a shared anguish.

"Oh, that's wonderful news!" sobbed Muriel's mother.

Muriel sighed deeply, and spoke softly to the consultant. "The monster has been injured by your science, but you have failed to kill it. Now it rests to recover its strength. Think of it like an animal in hibernation for the winter."

The consultant lost his smile. "I can assure you Muriel, the cancer is in remission," he said. "This is a great step towards your cure."

Muriel smiled. She wasn't going to argue with them.

Chapter Sixteen

The Faceless Army

It was a Saturday morning a few days later when Muriel's parents were having a lie in.

The troubles of the family had taken their toll on the middle-aged couple, and they both seemed to be tired all of the time these days. A gentle tapping at the bedroom door jolted Muriel's father from the light slumber he was floating in.

"Come in," he said, wiping the sleep from his eyes.

Muriel entered the bedroom with a square-shaped box in her hand. It had been gift wrapped, and a blue ribbon crested the top.

"I have something for you," she said, smiling.

Muriel placed the box on the bed and sat down, grinning at her father.

"What is it?" asked her dad.

"Something you have always wanted," replied his daughter.

Mr Mason carefully unwrapped his present, casting the decorative wrapping paper aside, and then gazing with astonished eyes at the carton within.

"Now you can warm your cold bacon sandwiches without cooking the bacon any more, or making the bread soggy," announced Muriel.

"This is your invention!" whispered her dad, who was surprised at the professional packaging, and the general presentation of the product. He was still having a hard time believing the entire device had been invented by his own fifteen-year-old daughter.

"This is just a prototype," said Muriel. "It's the very first one, I wanted to make sure it worked okay before we started to mass produce them."

"I can't believe you've actually done it!" said her dad.

When he looked at Muriel, Mr Mason felt his voice catch in his throat each time. To him she was still the bright, funny little girl she had always been, now her maturity had suddenly risen to an astonishing level, and her hair had all fallen out from the top of her head, leaving her with a bald pate like that of a monk; her long auburn hair still hung to her shoulders from the sides of her head. Mr Mason felt the tears come, fight against them as he might.

"I am going to try this straight away!" He sniffed.

"To do that you will need this as well," replied his daughter, handing him a second present, which had been gift wrapped like the first.

Muriel's dad laughed, when he unwrapped the second present and found a cold bacon sandwich inside.

"I anticipated you would want to try it straight away," said Muriel. "So I cooked that an hour ago and then let it go cold."

Muriel's father shook his head at the foresight of his only daughter. It was hard to believe she was only fifteen years old, she seemed to have grown up so much in the last couple of months.

Muriel's dad extracted the Universal Warmer from the box, and unfolded it on the bed.

"I'll have to plug it in over there," he whispered, nodding to an electric socket under his bedside table.

"No need," replied his daughter. "Just throw that switch on the front, and use the batteries instead."

206

"It has batteries?" said her dad. "You've thought of everything."

Muriel's father placed his cold bacon sandwich into the Universal Warmer and switched it on. Within a minute the aroma of hot bacon filled the bedroom.

"When you have eaten that, Dad, I want you to shave my head for me," said Muriel. "I would rather be completely bald than look like some crazy monk."

Muriel's mother awoke and sat up. "I can smell bacon!" she yawned.

The three of them laughed together, and the magic of that moment would be rendered like a snapshot into the memory of her father, who would think of it often in the quiet, lonely times that would pepper the unfolding years ahead of him.

Muriel's dad took a bite of the bacon sandwich, he let it roll around his mouth as the two females in his life watched him do it.

"It doesn't make the bread soggy!" he shouted in joy.

A week or so later the Masons stood in their living room with their coats on.

"Why won't you tell us where we're going?" asked Muriel's mother.

"It's a surprise," replied Muriel, gazing out of the front window.

"I will have to get some petrol," said her father, "is it far?"

"No need for that," replied Muriel. "A car is coming for us, it will be here in five minutes."

"What car?" asked Muriel's mother, who never handled surprises very well.

"Just a car for our convenience," replied Muriel.

"We've bought you something," said Muriel's mother, who had been holding a paper bag in her hand all morning, and seemed to be waiting for the right moment to mention it.

"If you've got a wig in that bag, you can keep it in there," said Muriel flatly. "I'm not wearing any wig."

"I told you she wouldn't wear it," said Muriel's father.

"But you're so *bald*, darling," observed Muriel's mother.

"I'm bald because I'm receiving chemotherapy, mother," said Muriel. "Lots of people are bald these days, don't worry about it."

"Only babies, young criminals and old men are bald," wailed Muriel's mother. "Not fifteen-year-old schoolgirls!"

Muriel ignored the wail. Still looking out of the front window, she announced, "The car is here."

The television studio had sent a car for Muriel, and as they all sat in the back, Muriel's mother still holding the paper bag with the rejected wig inside, Muriel explained to them both what was going to happen.

"We're going to make a thirty second commercial for the Universal Warmer," she said, "which will suggest people go to the website to purchase the product. They tell me it will take most of the day, you should find it interesting."

Muriel's parents didn't know what to say.

The newly found inner strength, mental maturity and positive outlook of the schoolgirl with brain cancer, had given her a type of charisma that was endearing to all others. Muriel made friends everywhere she went these days, and the producer knew after speaking to Muriel for only a few seconds, that he needed her in the commercial, in fact he didn't need anyone else.

"No-one could sell this product better than you," said the director.

"Very well then," replied Muriel, "I will be in the commercial, but there are a few conditions that would have to be met, or I won't do it."

"Name them," he said.

"Well, first of all, no reference must be made to my medical condition. I want people to buy this product because it is a great product, not because they feel sorry for me."

The director nodded that he accepted and understood.

"Secondly, I will not explain to them why I am bald. They would probably figure that out for themselves anyway."

The director was still nodding.

"However, at the very end of the commercial you can put a line on the screen that a donation of three pounds will be made to Cancer Research from the Right Road Company for every unit purchased through the website."

The director was smiling. "Anything else?"

"Nothing I can think of at the moment," replied Muriel.

"Then I think we're in business, young lady," said the director.

It was Muriel's turn to smile.

"We're going to have to change everything, now," said the director, "all the preparations we made for this morning's shoot will have to be cancelled so we will need to reschedule the commercial for another time."

"Why?" asked Muriel. "I am here now."

"We don't have a shooting script for the new commercial," said the director.

Muriel thought about this.

"Just play the camera on me, and I'll say something. You can judge whether it's good enough or not at the end.

If it's not we can reschedule, if it is, go with it, and we have saved the day."

"You're going to ad lib it?" asked the director.

"I think I can do it," replied Muriel.

"Okay everybody," shouted the director. "Listen up, there has been a change of plan."

Muriel found herself a quiet corner where she could still her mind and think of what she was going to say when the camera started to roll. She recalled the day she went to the City of Artists, and how using her five senses the Universal Warmer was forged into existence. Muriel knew she couldn't say any of that in the commercial itself, no-one would understand it. She merely wanted to recapture that sense of wonder she had first felt about the product in that special moment.

"We're ready when you are," said the director.

Muriel stood up and followed the director to the set. She was completely calm and collected, which surprised the director. He had never worked with someone quite like Muriel before.

"How do you want to do this?" asked the director. He thought he would let Muriel take the lead.

"I will stand behind this table with the product in front of me," said Muriel.

"You just keep the camera on me, and I'll talk straight to the viewer."

"Okay," agreed the director. "Just remember it is a thirty second commercial, so you can't go on longer than that."

"I understand," replied Muriel.

When Muriel stood behind the table, the camera focused in to her.

"Action," said the director, and Muriel began to speak.

"I am going to ask you a series of questions. If you answer 'Yes', to any of these then keep watching. Have you ever been camping? Have you ever had to scrape ice from the windows of your car? Have you ever warmed up a cold bacon sandwich in a microwave oven? Have you ever been stranded in a car? Have you ever brewed your own beer at home? Are you, or do you live with someone who is pregnant? Do you work in the medical profession? Do you work on a farm? Have you ever taken a long haul flight? Have you ever had earache or toothache? If you answered 'yes' to any of those questions, then go to this website now, for a fuller explanation and a demonstration. Thanks for watching."

There was complete silence on the set even after the director shouted "Cut!"

The director wasn't sure what he had on film, until they played it back. Muriel came across in a way that captured the imagination of the viewer from the very first second.

"They'll be intrigued," said the director. "They will have to go to the website to see what it is, then you can pitch them from there."

"That's the general idea," agreed Muriel.

When at last the commercial hit the TV screens Muriel became an overnight minor celebrity. Her beguiling inner strength, complete lack of self-pity, and no nonsense approach, was such an appealing formula that the hits on her website made it a hot topic on many a chat room. No-one who watched the commercial knew what the product actually was, but almost everyone who answered 'yes' to any of Muriel's questions, went to find out more at the website, where a very high proportion of them actually ended up buying the product. Sales of the Universal Warmer began to climb immediately, and

Muriel Mason and her business partners found themselves with a commercial hit on their hands within days.

It did not take the general public long to discover the reason for Muriel's baldness, and this together with the appeal of the product itself gave Muriel a national sense of respect. She received messages of goodwill from around the world, on her website, and other children with life-threatening illnesses wrote to her, thanking her for being so brave and for giving them a reason to be brave as well. Muriel found herself besieged with requests for interviews from local, national and international news agencies, and she often fell asleep in the armchair at home in the middle of writing replies to her growing army of well-wishers, fans and customers.

A middle-aged woman, a stranger to the Crucible stood alone in the arid desert. The woman wore a blue coat, and flat shoes, and she had a shopping bag hung over the crook of her arm. This solitary figure faced the mountains, and was quite still. Standing patiently in that spot she looked like she might be waiting for a bus. The woman seemed so out of place in the Crucible that the hippos at the camp had come out of their tents one after the other to stare at the woman.

Bron nodded his head when he saw her. "It has started, then," he said more to himself than to Muriel who was standing beside him, also watching the woman.

"Who is she?" asked Muriel.

"She is no-one," replied Bron.

"She must be *someone*," suggested Muriel. "Everyone is someone."

"She is no-one," repeated the hippo. "And soon others of her kind will come, and although they will also be no-one, together they will make a statement that will echo across the mountains."

"What do you mean?" asked Muriel. "What does she want?"

"She wants only to be here," said Bron. "That is all any of them will want."

The woman was joined by a younger man who stood beside her, but the two did not speak, nor acknowledge each other's presence in any way. The two did not appear to know each other.

"Now there are two of them," observed Muriel.

"Soon they will be legion," stated Bron.

Muriel squinted hard at the pair as they stood between the Camp of the Hippos and the Twisted Mountains, neither moving nor speaking, just standing there in silence, apparently watching the Twisted Mountains for some reason known only to themselves.

"Tell me what's going on," said Muriel to Bron. "You seem to know everything that happens around here."

"Ask them to turn around," replied Bron. "Take a look at their faces."

The pair had their backs to the camp, and faced the Twisted Mountains.

"They are too far away," replied Muriel, they won't hear me."

"They will hear you," replied the hippo with some conviction. "They *want* to hear you."

"Could you turn around please?" asked Muriel, in a quiet voice, she was certain the couple in the distance would not have heard her, yet immediately they both turned to face the camp.

"Oh my God!" exclaimed Muriel. "They have no faces!"

"They do not need to be known to you personally," replied the hippo. "They have no individuality."

"That is so spooky!" said Muriel. "I don't like this."

"You do not understand them," said Bron. "But you will come to *love* them."

"How can I love strangers with no faces?" asked the schoolgirl.

"*Because* they are strangers with no faces," replied the hippo. "That is their strength, and their power."

Soon the couple were joined by others, and it was not long before a large crowd had gathered in the middle of the desert. They seemed a cross-section of society, and didn't have anything obviously in common with each other. There were the young, the middle-aged and the elderly. They were Asians, Caucasians, Africans, and Latinos. There were males and females, there were fat and thin, tall and short, there were optimists and pessimists, and there were those who sang and those who did not. It would be difficult to find a common thread connecting such disparate specimens together but a vital thread there was. Apart from the fact that not a one of them had any facial features, there was another thread that bound them all together, they had all been touched by a story, and been moved enough to show support. They had gathered in their thousands, this faceless army, to stand as best they could between a moment and a menace, and to make their presence felt.

"Who *are* all those strange people?" asked Muriel.

"That is the faceless army," replied Bron. "They have gathered to show their support."

"But who *are* they?" insisted Muriel. "And where do they come from?"

"They are other Clients. They are individual worlds of their own. They come from Outside of here, and they come because they are human."

Muriel still did not understand. "What do they all want?" she asked.

"They want to show support for the plight of another, a person they do not know," replied Bron. "Their humanity is the thread that binds them, they have nothing else in common."

The faceless army stood in the desert and lit candles when the evening light descended, and there in the darkness of the Crucible they sang hymns as their candle lights flickered in the dusty desert air.

"There is more to humanity than even they know," continued the hippo, "and yet they feel a sense of responsibility towards the tragedy of another. It is a human characteristic which has always been difficult for me to categorise in the library. References to it may be found in many sections."

Muriel wondered who could deserve such unselfish support, and what were the circumstances which gave rise to the gathering, but something deep inside her told her not to ask that question. A silence fell between Muriel and Bron, as they continued to watch the faceless army from a distance, to listen quietly to the hymns, both caressed by the gentility and tenderness of the moment.

"But why are they just standing there, doing nothing?" asked Muriel at last.

"They have chosen their ground carefully," replied the hippo. "And they are doing a great deal."

"I can't see them doing anything expect singing," mused Muriel.

Bron merely smiled, and did not reply.

High in the Twisted Mountains, the monster rolled onto its front, opened its tired eyes, and looked down upon the desert scene with a different perspective. The monster did not see the faceless army as a foe to be faced and defeated, nor did it see the gathering as anything that might have a direct reference to itself at all. The monster merely watched the flickering candle lights with a sense of emotional detachment.

"This will not alter the course of things," sighed the monster, as it closed its eyes again and went back to sleep.

Muriel was getting frustrated with Bron, who never seemed able to give her a simple, straightforward answer to any question she asked him.

"But what *are* they doing?" persisted Muriel. "I can't see them doing anything."

"They are doing all they can just by being here," replied Bron.

"You said they have chosen their ground carefully," said Muriel.

Bron nodded.

"But how?" asked Muriel. "They're just standing in the desert!"

"Where in the desert?" asked the patient hippo.

Muriel thought about this. "Between us and the mountains," she replied.

"Not between us and the mountains," said Bron. "Between you and the monster."

Muriel began to understand. "They have come for me?" she whispered.

"They have come to face the monster," said Bron. "Your story has touched their hearts, and they stand between you and the peril you face."

Tears filled Muriel's eyes as she understood at last.

"Now," whispered the hippo. "Do you still think these faceless people are spooky?"

Muriel shook her head as the tears came.

Chapter Seventeen

The Blue Flame

As the Universal Warmer became more and more well known, as a great product with a versatility to rival anything else in the marketplace, Muriel as the inventor, also became more and more known to the world in general. She was seen by those who knew her as Muriel Mason the local schoolgirl with brain cancer, and by those who did not know her as the genius inventor with a fascinating background. She was asked to speak on the radio, and she was interviewed several times on television. She came across each time as wise beyond her years, but not precocious, interesting but not eccentric, and sad but somehow not tragic. Muriel Mason had caught the imagination of the public, and even the great bat had invited her to speak one morning at her old school.

Muriel was met at the gates by Michelle, who threw her arms around her friend's neck and kissed her on the cheek.

"I've missed you so much!" said Michelle. "How are you?"

"I'm okay," replied Muriel. "Oh my god, look at you!" Muriel pointed to the significant bulge in her friend's stomach. "You can't hide that from your dad."

Michelle shook her head. "I've had to come clean with everyone," she confessed. "Dad is having to deal with it now!"

"You're going to keep it then?" asked Muriel.

Michelle nodded.

"What about the father, where is he in all this?" asked Muriel.

"Nowhere to be seen," said Michelle. "What a loser he turned out to be."

The two girls linked arms and walked together to the Headmaster's office.

"We're all very excited about hearing your talk this morning," said Michelle as the two friends ambled along.

"Why?" asked Muriel. "They all know me here. I can't think why they would be excited."

"Because of everything you have achieved, and your brilliant invention, everyone's got one!"

Muriel smiled.

The two friends parted as Michelle went to join her classmates in the main hall, and to wait there for their special guest of honour. Muriel stood before the Headmaster's door, raised her fist to knock, and hesitated. She saw again the square blocking of the letters on the glass pane, and she recalled the last time she had stood in that very spot. How much had changed since that day.

Muriel knocked on the door.

"Enter!"

The monster's breathing became suddenly less deep and regular. Its eyelids began to flicker, and its lips twitched, as though it were trying to say something. Its crusted eyelids finally clicked open, and it looked about the confines of its cave, first at the ceiling, then at the walls.

"I am recovered at last," it observed, "my period of rest and recuperation is at an end."

The monster sat up, and slowly allowed its consciousness to take in the reconstructed mass of its own body; it was surprised at how large it had grown in the time it had lain dormant. "My hibernation is over." It announced, and its deep, gravelly voice seemed to echo around the walls of its mountainous confinement.

The thing had grown so large during hibernation that it could not stand up in the cave, and so it made its way to the entrance, back bent, stooped like an ancient, until its face broached the natural light of the Crucible of Creation, high up in the summit of the Twisted Mountains.

It wanted to roar at the wind, as it had before, a bellow bursting forth with the sheer exhilaration of life and existence, but it checked itself.

"I shall not roar, I shall not announce my presence to give them time to prepare for my coming. I shall be more stealthy, in this campaign," it whispered. "I shall sneak upon them, and take them by surprise. I will have them all this time."

A smile of excited intent parted the lips of the beast, as it surveyed the desert kingdom, sprawling as far as it could see below the lofty retreat.

The monster spread out its arms and breathed in the life-giving air of creation.

"I shall soon fulfil my destiny to be the Lord of this Kingdom!" it announced, nodding its massive head, and becoming excited at the great adventure which lay before it.

"I need more room now," observed the thing, as it moved back inside the cave.

It placed its craggy hands upon the soft walls of the cave, and then extending its arm outwards from its shoulders, began to push.

Muriel placed her hands against the side of her head when the pain came, and she buckled at the knees, stooping down to the ground, ending in a squatting position.

"What is it?" asked Michelle, stooping down to match her friend's posture.

"Has the pain come back?"

Muriel nodded as the terrible pressure inside her head grew in intensity until her consciousness could take the assault no longer, and with her eyes rolling up and back into the recess of her head, lost consciousness and passed out on the floor.

Michelle stroked the face of her best friend as she felt tears come into her own eyes, "Oh, Muriel!" she whispered.

Michelle searched her bag for her telephone and called Muriel's parents.

Walking once more down the Avenue of The Seeker, Muriel Mason came upon the little shop, where she had been taught to meditate. The shop looked exactly the same as it had before, and yet her last visit seemed like an entire lifetime ago. She had matured so much since then that the City of Artists seemed familiar to her now, and her understanding of her situation was so complete, so deep and thorough, that it was indeed a different girl now, who pushed open the shop door.

"Ah, you've come back, then," observed the old shopkeeper. "Did you find the Hall of Inspiration?"

"I did," replied Muriel. "I completed my invention, and it is working in the world of matter."

"Excellent!" exclaimed the shopkeeper. "Inspiration is of little use unless one follows it up with action."

Muriel nodded.

"What can I do for you this time?" asked the shopkeeper. "Another invention perhaps?"

Muriel shook her head. "I need to understand what is happening to me," she said.

"Ah," nodded the old man. "Then you need the Hall of Understanding.

"Inspiration and Understanding are two completely different things."

"I need to know why the monster is doing this to me," replied Muriel.

"You ask the ultimate question, then," replied the shopkeeper. "The question, '*Why?*' is the greatest question anyone can ask of Creation. '*Why am I here?*' '*Why is this happening to me, and not to someone else?*' '*Why do we exist at all?*'"

Muriel nodded.

"Go to the Hall of Understanding, and make your mind receptive, do not challenge what you learn or see, but merely become an empty pot that will accept whatever is poured into it, and the answer will come. But be warned!" The old shopkeeper gazed intently into the face of his young customer. "There is no guarantee you will like the answer you get!"

"How do I become an empty pot?" asked Muriel, ignoring the warning.

The old man looked about him, searching the bric-a-brac of his store for an answer to the young girl's question. "We are all little pots of one form or another."

Muriel smiled.

The old shopkeeper went into the back of his shop, returning seconds later with an ornate pot, which he placed on the counter top.

"We are all pots!" he said. "Filled to the brim with the trivia of our lives in the world of matter. The little things we think are important, the people we know, the things we do, the places we go to. All these things fill up the space in the pot, leaving no room for Understanding when we need it. This is why throughout history there have been those who have given up the world and gone out into the wilderness, without possessions of any kind. They have emptied their pots entirely, so that true Understanding has had room to flood in."

Muriel looked at the pot on the counter. She wondered what was inside it. The pot had an ornate lid, shielding its secrets from curious eyes like hers.

"Let's see what is inside this pot," said the old shopkeeper, lifting the lid.

Muriel gazed inside, and frowned.

"What does this pot contain?" asked the old man.

Muriel reached inside, and then began to extract the contents of the pot, one item at a time, and laying them down carefully on the shop's countertop.

"A hairbrush, a toy fire engine, a broken pencil, a shoe, some dice, a light bulb, and some assorted buttons," she said, when the pot was empty.

"The treasure and the trivia of this pot's life," observed the old shopkeeper.

"It's just junk," said Muriel.

"To you, perhaps," replied the old man. "But to the pot...?"

Muriel began to understand. "I think I get it now," she said, looking at the scattered contents of the pot in a new light.

"Explain it to me then, so I know you understand," asked the shopkeeper.

"When I go to the Hall of Understanding," said Muriel. "I have to let go of everything first, all the bits and pieces of my own life, everyone and everything."

"The treasure and the trivia," said the shopkeeper.

"But how exactly do I do that?" asked Muriel.

"How did you empty *this* pot?" asked the old man, indicating the contents of the pot now strewn across the countertop, with a gentle sweep of his arm.

"I took out the items one at a time, and laid them aside," replied Muriel.

"Exactly!" said the old man. "Now you are ready to know everything."

Muriel opened her eyes and began to look around. It was immediately obvious to her she was in hospital again. This time she seemed to be in a private room.

"Oh darling, you passed out again," said Muriel's mother, who was sitting by her bedside reading a magazine which she now dropped on the floor and sat on the bedside. "We've all been so worried about you again."

Muriel smiled at her mom. "The monster has come back," she whispered.

Muriel's mother didn't understand. "What do you mean?" she asked.

My tumour has returned," said Muriel. "They didn't get it all the last time, and now it has come back."

Muriel's mother didn't want to hear this. "You don't know that darling!" she urged, frantically. "You mustn't say such things!"

Muriel looked away from her parent, and gazed nonchalantly up at the ceiling.

Muriel realised then that she was going to have to be the strong one in this relationship. Muriel closed her eyes again.

The great Hall of Understanding rose before the schoolgirl like a cathedral. In fact it did look like a cathedral, with its great spires and stained glass windows. Muriel supposed there was a psychological connection between religion and understanding; both required the faith of the subject in order to manifest in the world of matter. One cannot understand anything, unless one is willing to believe, and one cannot believe anything, unless one is willing to set doubt aside, and one cannot set doubt aside, unless one is willing to understand. Here was a sacred place that would allow the traveller to experience both wonder and understanding, the very heart of the City of Artists.

"Here is where I will finally learn the truth," whispered Muriel to herself, as she entered the great edifice.

Muriel walked casually through the main entrance, and along the marbled hallway, letting the solitude and stillness of the place sweep over her. She thought of nothing in particular until she came to a large wooden door at the far end of the long hallway, which she pushed gently open.

"Muriel! Muriel! The consultant is here," said Muriel's mother.

The consultant smiled at Muriel. "We didn't expect to see you again quite so soon," he said.

"The monster has returned," replied Muriel.

The consultant frowned, he did not understand. "We are going to run a series of tests in the morning, Muriel. We need to know what is happening."

"I have told you what is happening," replied the schoolgirl. "The monster has come back, now I need to rest if you don't mind."

The consultant and Muriel's mother were both going to gently chide the patient for saying such things. They were going to remind her that *they* would let her know what was happening with the sophistication of their expensive technology, with the balance of their weights and measures; but Muriel knew more than they did, for she had already been to the City of Artists and was a matured soul now, she did not need their science to know what was happening to her. Before they had a chance to argue their case Muriel had already withdrawn her consciousness from them.

Muriel crossed the marble floor to the centre of the room, where a circular dais was raised from the floor with three small steps. She stepped lightly to the top and stood in the centre of the Hall of Understanding, which itself stood in the centre of the City of Artists, which was located in the very centre of the Right, which stood at the centre of Creation itself.

Muriel sat in the centre of the circle, crossed her legs and began to relax.

"I am a pot that must now be emptied of all things," she said, closing her eyes.

Muriel began to imagine the shape of her physical being slowly changing into that of a large pot. She knew this mental exercise was something she had to do slowly and precisely, it was a process that should not be rushed. In fact the slower she could do it, the better and more intense the final experience would become. Muriel could not think of a pot at home which she could use as a model to copy, and so she decided to model herself on the pot she had just seen in the shop, as the image of it was still fresh and clear in her mind.

The pot in the shop had been a fat, urn-shaped affair, with a yellow Chinese glaze, emblazoned with red and blue orchid flowers around the outside; and Muriel began to visualise her own body slowly becoming fluid, melting like wax, and changing shape to that of the pot. She imagined her arms and legs receding into her torso, and her head sinking down into her shoulders, until all that remained of her original shape was a limbless torso. Very slowly this torso widened at the top and narrowed at the bottom, until the pot shape began to emerge, complete with lid. When the shape was right, Muriel began to colour her being with a faded yellow Chinese glaze, and she focused her mind until she was able to clearly depict the red and blue lotus flowers cresting the bulbous pot, encircling the new shape of her being all the way around.

When this was done, Muriel concentrated on the darkness and oblique vacancy inside the vessel.

"Now it is time to remove my lid and allow in the light," she whispered to herself.

In Muriel's mind's eye, she imagined the natural light streaming into her, as her lid was removed and set aside. She was now ready to empty the contents of her life out onto the floor of the great Hall of Understanding.

"Muriel! Muriel! Don't go back to sleep, I want to talk to you, this is very important!" urged Muriel's mother.

Muriel opened her eyes and smiled into the concerned face of her parent.

"What do you want to talk about, Mum?" asked Muriel casually.

"This! This! Everything!" exclaimed Muriel's mother, becoming frantic with alarm. "Who is this monster of yours? What do you mean by that?"

Muriel felt a calmness pervade her soul that she had never experienced before. The young girl was more in tune with the mechanics and systems of creation than her own mother could ever be, and she smiled caringly back at her parent.

"The monster is my tumour, Mother," she whispered. "It was not killed by the surgery. It has rested, recovered and has come back, their tests will confirm this tomorrow. Now please let me go back to sleep, there is something very important I have to do. I will speak to you again later, don't worry."

"But, but, I don't understand…" replied the unknowing and confused parent, as her daughter's consciousness once more withdrew voluntarily from the world of matter.

In the great Hall of Understanding, the magnificent, yellow ceramic pot, Muriel, with its red and blue lotus flowers emblazoned across its surface, began to focus on the contents of its own fifteen-year history. The jumbled items of its life began to come slowly into focus as Muriel searched inside herself. Muriel felt a warmth of friendship steal about the interior of the pot when she saw Michelle come into focus.

Raising her friend from the top of the pile, Muriel lifted Michelle gently outside, setting her down upon the dais.

One after another, the objects and characters of a fifteen-year experience in the world of matter, slowly came into focus and were placed outside the pot. Muriel's parents, her school, the headmaster, the white vulture, Bron the hippopotamus, the Silver Knight, Patrick and the gardener, the Vendor, her aunts and uncles, the traffic warden, her parents, her new found business partners, even her own invention, the Universal Warmer had no place within her now, and had to be set outside. People and places she was very familiar with and ones she hardly had any remembered history with at all. No matter what was presented to her, she accepted the image, and ejected it from the interior of her being. People she had not thought of in years came into focus, distant relatives who were now deceased but were still buried in the bottom of the pot out of sight, came suddenly into view as she began to empty its contents. Scenes not viewed in years because they were hidden from sight by more recent histories lying on top of them, suddenly exploded into sharp relief when the fresher memories of the pot were cleared above them. At last the great ceramic pot, Muriel stood completely empty in the centre of the cavernous Hall of Understanding. The pot, Muriel, now stood devoid of contents, empty and alone, without a history of any kind. It was as though Muriel herself was now a thing born of that very moment, having no yesterday and no tomorrow.

Muriel found herself breaking free of the pot itself and shrinking down, regaining her arms and legs, and now sitting, cross-legged inside the giant pot, now she was its only occupant.

"Now, at last I am ready to receive that which I seek to know," said the pot.

Muriel tried not to expect the information she sought to be delivered to her in any particular way. She wanted to merely receive whatever was offered, however it was offered and be accepting of that. She could not hide a sense of surprise though, when at the bottom of the empty pot, she became aware of the existence of a small bird's egg. It had not been there before, it was not a part of the pot's own history, it must therefore be from the Hall of Understanding, she reasoned.

Muriel accepted the fact the egg was there. She did not try and understand *why* it was there, nor analyse what it *meant* for it to be there. Muriel merely accepted the fact that the egg *was* there, and allowed her feelings towards it to be as non-committal and as neutral as she could make them.

In the absolute silence of the Hall of Understanding, the sound of a split appearing in the egg seemed to rend the atmosphere like a sudden crack of lightening.

Muriel felt her heart beat a little quicker as she watched the hairline crack zigzag across the eggshell from front to back. Focusing on the shell of the bird's egg, which was now entirely covered in splits and small cracks, Muriel tried not to gasp when she watched the egg roll slightly on its side as the creature within began to push against the walls of its prison, making a break for freedom.

The fledgling's tiny head broke the surface of the shell, rising to its shoulders above the ceiling of its former cell. As though time itself was increasing, Muriel watched the bird mature in seconds and then take flight. As soon as the bird became airborne it aged on the wing, lost its feathers, became a skeleton and vanished. Its tiny life lived out in full in a matter of seconds. Several more eggs appeared at the bottom of the pot, and Muriel watched as these too hatched, matured, took to flight and withered. Muriel felt a sense of despair regarding the birds, she began to wonder if their life was actually worth the effort. More and more eggs appeared as the birds above them withered and died. Time seemed to accelerate to Muriel, as the span between hatching and dying became shorter and shorter, to the point where the birds had only taken their first wing flap inside the pot before they were destroyed. Faster and faster ran the cycle until now Muriel could not concentrate on any single bird as the span of its entire existence was numbered in parts of a second. Before her was a blur of creation and destruction, life and death charging so fast after each other that all she was aware of in the end was a curtain of blurred movement, wherein lay the secret generations of an entire species.

Muriel felt tears rise in the corners of her eyes at the hopeless futility of it all.

Why be born at all, when there is only death to look forward to? She thought, and a lump came into her throat as she began to understand the pointlessness of life itself. Faster and faster ran the cycle of life and death, until at last nothing could be seen of the individual birds at all, except a blue flame which hovered over the eggs.

The flame of existence and life itself.

It's all so cruel, she thought, *they are born and want to live, and yet they are doomed from the beginning.* The tears began to run in little rivulets down the schoolgirl's cheeks.

Slowly the frantic chase of life upon death upon life began to slow down again, and the birds seemed to enjoy a longer lifespan. They flew about the inside of the pot with sublime grace before succumbing at last to the fate of all living things. Slower and slower ran the scene, until at last Muriel found herself where she had started, watching the first single hatch, as the inhabitant broke for freedom once more, and raising its head above the confines of its cell, began to look about.

The fledgling forced its shoulders through the shell, and shook its feathers dry.

Muriel blinked the tears away as she concentrated on the determination of the new life before her. The newly awakened life-form blinked in the light of a new existence, and standing up, crashed through the shell, and stepped out. It looked at Muriel but did not appear to see her, it shook its feathers once again with a rippling shiver, sending the last pieces of the eggshell flying away.

The young bird now with its feathers dry, began to look skywards, as though some ancient impulse beckoned it to rise. The bird stretched its wings, arched its neck, pointing its beak to heaven, and with a soft fluttering of feathers, took off.

Muriel gasped with joy as the bird soared into the air before her, and circling her head inside the pot began to glide with its wings rigid, and tilted. Around her head it circled, and on the third lap, suddenly there were two of them, flying together, a mated pair.

Muriel felt a warm glow begin to rise inside her, with the thought that her bird had found itself a mate. Even with so short a life in front of it, there had still been time for the business of life itself; still time for the pursuit of pleasure, and the fulfilment only found in selfless partnerships.

Together the birds circled Muriel once more and then landed in a branch which had grown beside Muriel's shoulder. In the foliage the birds gathered splinters and sang to the rising dawn, as they built a nest from twigs and leaves. Muriel watched the little nest being constructed with such care and attention, she began to lose her sense of hopelessness regarding the span of an individual existence.

When the nest was completed the female sat within and closed her eyes as if she were contemplating the task before her. Her mate continued to circle around Muriel's head, bringing back spiders and worms for his nesting mate to consume.

Suddenly the female stood and regarded the egg beneath her, examining it for structural flaws. Once the inspection was passed, the female sat once more upon the little egg and Muriel could not help but smile.

When the male returned once more, the female stood up and together they watched the egg split apart. The new fledgling broke the confines of its cell as its father had, and stood upright in the nest, shaking its downy feathers dry. With the father to one side, and the mother to the other, the three birds arched their necks, raising their beaks to heaven, before fluttering their wings and launching into the air.

The three birds circled Muriel's head and were gone.

Alone in the centre of the pot, Muriel found herself wrapped in a blanket of quiet solitude, as she began to contemplate what she had just witnessed. Her sense of hopelessness at the apparent futility of life, had been replaced with a sense of awe at the majestic wonder of it all. Time was an illusion she had been told, and even though each individual creature had been born, lived a short span and succumbed to death, the blue flame of life had flickered across the succeeding generations, connecting the first bird to be hatched with the last one to die.

Muriel thought about the fallen human generations that had gone before her; was there so much difference between all those people who had been born, lived and died, and the birds she had witnessed following the same circle of life and death? How much did one individual life really matter when the blue flame was ever present throughout the entire process?

We are the way the Universe can know itself, she had been told, our individual consciousness allowed the Cosmos to understand its own being, and the blue flame of life must flicker through the heavens, across the galaxies of space, and across the time span of every living thing in the eternal conglomeration of life itself.

Muriel felt the large pot dissolve around her, fading away into obscurity as her consciousness slowly returned like a manifesting ghost back into the world of matter.

Standing up, the schoolgirl stretched her arms and shook the numbness from her legs, as she opened her eyes.

"The Blue Flame is the point of it all," she whispered.

Chapter Eighteen

Loose Ends

Once more, the Masons sat facing the man in the white coat, who had an air about him of defiant defeat. He fingered his beard and searched for the words no-one wanted to hear.

"The tests have come back, and I am very sorry to tell you that the tumour has begun to grow again," he said softly.

"I told you that yesterday," replied Muriel, who seemed bored with the whole affair.

Mrs Mason began to sob softly, and Muriel's father received each word as though it were a hammer blow, battering his spirit into submission.

"We must continue the treatment straight away," urged the consultant. "We will increase the dosage, and we will apply a mixture of both chemotherapy and radiotherapy, I am sure we can achieve positive results this time."

Muriel's parents, nodded enthusiastically, clutching like drowning sailors at any floating wreckage they could find.

Muriel held up her hand. The three adults in the room turned to face her.

"There will be no more treatment," she said quietly.

All at once the trio had more to say to the child; they began to argue for life as they saw it, debating for time they could not purchase at any price. Muriel held up her hand again, and they fell into a stunned and brittle silence.

"There will no more treatment," she repeated. "It makes me too sick. There are things I need to do now, and I need to be well enough to complete them. Thank you for your efforts doctor, but our association must end here."

The adults looked at each other for support, but they all knew the inner strength in Muriel was now superior to even their combined mentalities.

"You will not survive without treatment," whispered the man in the white coat.

"I will not survive in either case," replied Muriel. "And I do not wish to fill the time I have left with sickness. My decision is final."

When Muriel Mason had returned from the Hall of Understanding, back into the world of matter, the sojourn of concentrated experience we describe as life, had developed a more complete perspective for her. Gone were the questions and doubts of a mind confused by the clamour of succeeding moments; vanished was the sense of uncertainty we feel as we paddle aimlessly onwards towards an island we cannot see.

Muriel's consciousness was now as old as the planet she walked upon, and her view of the larger perspective had enshrouded her consciousness in a calm certainty that only the mage may know.

Muriel resolved in her mind to tie up the loose ends of her existence, to put into place a scheme of things that would continue to develop after she had finished her journey in the world of matter, and it was with a sense of determination she stepped forwards into the time she had left.

Muriel rang the doorbell and waited.

In the Garden of Idols, Patrick and the gardener stood before the latest statue to take substance and solidify into granite. It was a full size, full length carving of The Client herself, in a striding pose; right leg and left arm forwards, head up, like a marching soldier. The facial expression showed a gentle determination, a defined purpose, as though she were headed to somewhere in particular.

"I like this one," said Patrick. "It shows purpose."

The gardener nodded in agreement. "There is a determination to it, for sure."

The two keepers of the Garden continued to observe the new addition to the collection of statues. At the other end of the flower bed was another carving which was now complete as well. A bust rising from the floor of its plinth, the monster, now fully formed stretched out its craggy arms, not to the heavens in supplication, as a casual observer might mistakenly suppose, but to the marching Client. She walked towards it with a robust gait, and it waited with its arms open to welcome her into its embrace. The connection of the two figures was not lost upon Patrick, who looked from one to the other, realising that sooner or later a clash was coming, a meeting of these two which would have crucial consequences for the whole of the Crucible.

"The fate of the world is prophesised here," said Patrick. "There are momentous days ahead."

The front door was swung ajar by Michelle's mother who welcomed Muriel into her home with a beaming smile and a warm hug.

"Michelle will be thrilled to see you again, Muriel," she said. "Go straight up, she's in her bedroom."

Michelle welcomed her best friend with another embrace which Muriel returned with fervour. The two friends kissed and held hands as they went to sit on the bed together.

"I've been thinking about you a lot recently," said Michelle. "How are things going?"

Muriel took a deep breath. "I need you to be strong, and to do something for me."

"Anything," replied her friend.

"You don't know what it is yet," said Muriel.

"It doesn't matter what it is," replied her friend. "If you need my help, I am here."

At the Great Egg, the Traffic Warden noticed the process of self-lubrication begin once more. He had witnessed the phenomenon a lot recently, where the egg had sent a purifying fluid over its membrane for no noticeable reason, which washed the surface clean. The watering had the side effect of blurring the images of the Upside Down People, so their features were less distinct during the process, as though they suddenly became slightly out of focus, but continued their journey down the path as ever before.

"It's happening again," said the Traffic Warden. "I wonder what it all means?"

Muriel wiped her eyes, and merely whispered, "Thank you."

Michelle held Muriel's hand, and waited for her friend to recompose herself.

"What do you want me to do?" asked Michelle.

In the Camp of the Hippos, Bron and his associates were suddenly under siege. Fornix Runners approached the little camp from all directions at once.

"Something important is about to happen!" shouted Bron. "Everyone prepare for action!"

The hippos lined up behind their leader ready to receive the Fornix Runners as they crowded into the small camp. The Runners all descended at once, shouting out their long serial numbers to the hippos, and thrusting papers at them from their chest bags. "Momentous decision coming up!" shouted a Runner. "Cross referencing with a past anxiety, and a future plan."

"Re-affirmation of trust, friendship, and a request for future action, cross matched with past associations of trust and mutually shared experiences!" shouted another.

The hippos moved forward to meet the surge of Runners, and taking their papers began to make their way into their tents to search the great archives, to find the requested connections, and to offer suggested matching sequences in the Client's memory. When the Fornix Runners were all served, quickly and efficiently, they jogged away to all the other corners of creation, to put into effect the next stage of the developing plan.

"I need you to be brave and to listen to me for a moment," said Muriel. "This is very important, and you are the one I trust above all others to do this for me."

"I will do whatever you want," whispered Michelle.

Professor Brocas sat on his desk before his Muriels and spoke quietly. "When imparting crucial evidence, it is vital that we do not exaggerate, as the listener will instinctively devalue what is coming next if we do. The listener will balance the importance of the message against the words we use to convey it. Therefore if we exaggerate the importance of the communication, the listener will value it less. If we understate the value of our message by carefully choosing our words, the listener will understand the consequences much more clearly and raise the value of it in their mind, thereby paying more attention to it, and acting upon it in a more constructive way."

Muriels were listening attentively, and writing down what the Professor was saying into their exercise books.

"Exaggerating the importance of something which is already important, has the opposite effect of the one intended," he said. "When saying something important,

237

state it plainly and simply, without frills or exaggerations, and let the listener raise its value themselves, then they will remember it later, and act upon it sooner."

In the depths of Wernicke's Magic Castle the old Magician watched intently as a great spell was being forged around him. The air was heavy with portent, as a heavenly creature was casting a powerful spell with words that would enchant another, and keep them spellbound and dedicated to their new purpose for years to come.

"She understands," nodded Wernicke.

"I am dying," whispered Muriel.

Michelle gasped and shook her head as tears immediately sprang into her eyes.

She was about to speak, but Muriel placed her hand gently over her best friend's mouth to silence her.

"Don't say anything," whispered Muriel. "Just listen."

Michelle nodded.

"I don't have much time left," continued Muriel. "And I have to put my affairs into order. The Universal Warmer has become a great success, and it is helping people all over the world; the company needs someone in charge who can drive it forwards in the years to come. I want you to run my business for me. It will give you direction, it will provide a secure future for you and your baby, and it will give me peace knowing my invention has been placed in hands I can trust."

Michelle was staring wide-eyed at her friend. Muriel pressed on with her plan.

"I have given my instructions to a firm of solicitors who are my business partners, and they are drawing up the papers for you to sign as we speak. You will effectively take over from next week. You will need to leave school, the lawyers are arranging that as well. My parents will also receive a royalty payment every month from the lawyers for the rest of their lives. I have nominated them as co-inventors and their names are on the patent as well as mine, so they will be secure financially too, but only you will run the business day to day. You will be in complete charge and control, and your decision will always be final."

Michelle opened her mouth to speak but Muriel placed her hand there again.

"I have engaged a firm of business consultants to help you in the early days, and to teach you how to run a company successfully; rely on their advice. The legal firm will handle everything else."

Muriel withdrew her hand from Michelle's mouth. "Now you can say something if you want to."

Michelle couldn't think of anything to say.

Wernicke the Magician watched the newly cast spell take form and then dissipate into the archives of Universal Mind, where it would remain for years to come, directing the actions of another and producing beneficial results for the human condition the world over.

Wernicke nodded his approval.

"One last thing," said Muriel. "I have been keeping a journal, I have been trying to make sense of what has been happening to me, everything is in there. When the time comes, read it yourself then give it to my parents so they too will understand."

Michelle nodded.

When the Fornix Runners left the Camp of the Hippos, Bron nodded his head approvingly. "The Client has been spurred into action," he said. "Things are starting to happen quickly now. We need to make sure everything is cross referenced correctly. Everything needs to be in its place as soon as possible."

One of the hippos lingered behind Bron, and said softly. "But what difference will it make, now that the monster has returned? Won't all our work be for nothing?"

Bron spun to face his subordinate. "So, you are Wernicke's junior assistant now are you? Suddenly you have magical powers and can see the future?"

The other hippo looked at his feet and shook his head. "No, I can't," he confessed.

"Then it is our duty to perform our services as well as we can, especially at a time like this. It is now when The Client needs our skills more than ever."

The other hippo nodded and went back to work.

Bron turned again to face the Twisted Mountains. "More now than ever," he whispered to himself.

Muriel's mother could hold the torrent back no longer. "You don't know what you're doing to us!" she wailed one morning at the breakfast table. "Why won't you reconsider? How can you be so selfish?"

Muriel's father, who found himself as always between the two females of his family, caught his breath.

"My mind is made up," replied Muriel calmly. "I have already given you my reasons."

"Don't you want to live?" cried her mother.

Muriel's dad put down his knife and fork, and held his head in his hands.

"The treatment cannot be successful," explained Muriel calmly. "The monster is too strong for that now. All more chemotherapy will do at this time is make me even sicker in the short time I have left. I cannot allow that."

"But you don't know that!" returned her mother, determined to argue every point raised for the chance of life.

"I do know that," replied her daughter. "When there was a chance the treatment would work, I took that chance. It did not work, there is no point in continuing it. I would get the discomfort with no benefits, there is no value in the treatment, and there would be no quality in my time left."

The face of the Vendor flashed though Muriel's imagination.

"There is always a chance!" sobbed her mother, and left the table, weeping into her napkin as she went.

"There will come a time, in the not too distant future," said Muriel to her father. "When you and Mum and Michelle are seated together somewhere, possibly in the consultant's office. Michelle will give you a book, it is very important you read it carefully, then explain it to Mum. The book will clarify a few things for you, it will answer some questions you may have."

"What is this book?" asked her dad.

"*Muriel's Monster*. It is a journal I have been keeping," replied Muriel.

"Promise me you will read it?"

"Of course I will," replied her father.

"Excellent! Pass the ketchup, please Dad. These sausages are really good," said Muriel.

"Oh no! Not you again!" wailed the Traffic Warden, when he saw Muriel approach.

Muriel laughed. "Don't worry, I won't go on the path again. I understand about this place now, I didn't before. I have come back to apologise to you for all the trouble I caused the last time I was here."

The Traffic Warden didn't expect this, and his mood visibly softened. "I see," he said. "I accept and appreciate your apology, young Miss."

"I know all about the Upside Down People too," said Muriel, "I've been researching it."

"The reflections?" asked the Traffic Warden as the Upside Down People continued to traverse the long path between the Great Egg and who knew where.

"Actually they are retinal inversions," explained Muriel. "Light enters the eye through the cornea, then the lens inverts the image onto the retina, and the brain reconverts it to the right way up again."

The Traffic Warden didn't understand, he didn't need to, he just had to keep them from bunching up.

"Yes, that's it of course," he agreed.

"Well, I just wanted to apologise for the trouble I caused you," said Muriel, shaking hands with the Warden.

When the mind is tuned to a specific idea, or to a concept, the subconscious continues to knead the idea as a baker may knead their dough, working its texture to the required consistency when the originator of the idea has long stopped thinking of it consciously. This is why suddenly the answer comes to us when we are not expecting it, and we are taken by surprise. We do not realise the creative Right of our consciousness never quit on the concept, working on it tirelessly as we slept, as we ate, as we thought of other things; and now it suddenly presents us with the solution, seemingly out of the blue.

Muriel awoke one chilly morning to the sound of her father outside in the street scraping ice from the windshield of his car. A man across the road was doing the same thing. Muriel watched the two men blow on their frozen fingers in between bouts of frenzied scraping. The vision was all the sharpened consciousness the schoolgirl needed. Immediately an idea sprang into her mind with the suppleness of a gymnast, fully formed and ready to go; the completeness of the idea made Muriel smile. She went

242

back to bed and opened her laptop, then she sent an email to the manufacturer of the Universal Warmer.

We need to produce a version of the UW which is long enough to wrap around all the windows of any car. The driver simply switches on the battery and the UW will clear all the windows of ice in no time, with no effort. Please begin work on the new model straight away. Muriel Mason. PS add a power lead to it which can be plugged into the car's cigarette lighter so it can work from the car's battery, then it could be used as an electric blanket for everyone inside the car as well!

On a whim Muriel sent her idea to the Minister for Trade at the Swedish Embassy in London, telling him she could supply all the drivers in his country with the product for a discounted price during their severe winter months. These two emails would earn the Mason family more money than her father could earn for the rest of his life at work.

Muriel gazed down upon the Arch of Pons once more, and marvelled at the jostling, pushing and shoving of the Fornix Runners as they battled through the Arch on their way North and South.

"I love the new hair cut!" said a familiar voice behind her.

Muriel spun around to see the Vendor. It was like greeting an old friend.

"I wondered if I would find you here," she said. "I wanted to thank you."

"Thank me for what, Miss?" asked the boy.

"You taught me the meaning of value, and the concept of quality," said Muriel. "Both have served me very well."

"Then they were lessons well learned," replied the boy.

Muriel nodded. "Understanding the concept of quality has allowed me to produce a really great product," said Muriel. "And understanding value has allowed me to price it perfectly for the market. My family owes you a considerable debt."

"Neither you nor your family owes me anything at all," replied the boy. "It is merely my job, but I thank you for your kind words."

Muriel stepped forwards and placed a tender kiss upon the cheek of the boy.

His skin felt soft and pliable, like the jelly statues in the Garden of Idols. Muriel smiled at the Vendor and walked away without another word.

"Then my work here is done," said the boy, who began to lose substance with every step The Client made away from him, until at last he had disappeared.

Muriel closed the iron gate at the Garden of Idols behind her with a metallic clang.

Patrick and the gardener were delighted to see her again, and stopped what they were doing to come over and greet her.

Muriel reached into her skirt pocket and drew out a five pound note which she offered to the donkey.

Patrick shook his head. "That lesson has been learned already," he said. "No need to teach it twice."

Muriel replaced the note in her pocket, "I felt I needed to come here once more," said Muriel. "To thank you both for all you taught me."

"The honour was ours," said the gardener. "No thanks are necessary."

"Very few clients ever come here to examine their idols," said Patrick. "They allow them to harden and then they forget the statues are the way they are because The Client is the way *they* are."

"And so the statues never change once they are allowed to harden," continued the gardener.

"But you are different," said the donkey. "You understand this place. You can effect change to these statues for years to come. You can shape and reshape them until they are masterpieces, each and every one."

"If only I had the time," sighed Muriel.

Patrick and the gardener looked at each other briefly, a worried glance passed between them that lived for a moment and then was gone.

"I fear most of them will never become solid, not now," said Muriel. "But I am really grateful for what you have taught me here. I feel special in here."

"You are special, very special," replied Patrick. "There is no-one more important here than you."

"What will happen to this place when I die?" asked Muriel.

The question was a shock to both Patrick and the gardener. "You mustn't talk like that!" said the gardener.

"Why not?" asked The Client. "It is a reasonable question after all. I want to know."

"The whole of the Crucible exists to allow you to function as a heavenly creature in the world of matter," said Patrick. "When you die, its function is served. The Crucible, and everything in it, will fade away."

"Including you two?" asked Muriel.

"Everything and everyone in the Crucible," replied the gardener.

"I am sorry for that," said Muriel. "That seems so unfair."

"It is what it is," replied the donkey. "We are only here for your benefit, while you need us. When you stop needing us, we lose the power to develop; when that happens we cease to exist."

"Then you should know that the end is coming for all of us," said Muriel. "I cannot escape the monster, none of us can."

Muriel ambled into the Camp of the Hippos for the last time, and stood before the ancient librarian, Bron.

"I owe you an apology most of all," she confessed.

The hippo looked genuinely puzzled by her remark. "How so?" he enquired.

Muriel reached into her schoolbag, and took out the first map Bron had given to her.

"I once told you that your tent was too big on this map," she said. "I told you it was not drawn to scale, and you replied it was that size because of its importance."

Bron nodded.

"You were right," said Muriel. "The Camp of the Hippos is one of the most important places in the whole of creation."

Bron seemed very pleased by this, and his chest visibly swelled with pride.

"I am delighted you think so," he whispered.

"It is more what I have learned, than what I think," replied Muriel. "And as for your second map…"

Muriel withdrew Bron's Other Map from her school satchel.

"This *is* the most important document ever written," she said simply.

"You understand it now?" asked the hippo.

"I do," replied Muriel with some conviction. "And I apologise sincerely for what I said about it before."

Bron nodded. "Thank you," he whispered.

"*Look Hear,*" said Muriel pointing to the map. "The physical position of my left eye and ear, in relation to this camp."

Bron smiled.

"*Left Out*, the world of matter, *Right In*, further into the Crucible," explained Muriel to the hippo.

Bron's smile visibly widened.

"*A bit more up*, to the roof of the world," said Muriel, "the top of my head, and *all the way down*, to my feet."

The hippo nodded his approval.

"*Left alone*, this side of me that does not interact with the Right hemisphere, and *Right over there*, where the intuitive hemisphere is located."

Tears filled the eyes of the ancient hippo.

"*The Great Divide*, the separation of the two hemispheres of my brain."

The hippo allowed a tear to fall upon the desert floor. "So few of The Clients ever come to such understanding," he sniffed.

"All I now know and understand, began and ended with you and this camp," said Muriel. "I just wanted you to know that."

Bron was too tearful to reply, he simply nodded, and sniffed.

"This," said Muriel, holding up Bron's Other Map, "is nothing less than a pictorial representation of the Angelic Creature, known as The Client! The living, thinking creature made only of meat. Produced by the Universe so it may come to know itself! Bron, you are a genius!"

The overjoyed hippo burst into tears.

Chapter Nineteen

The Last Embrace

The Muriel Mason who sat with her lawyers directing the future of her new company, was so far removed from the Muriel Mason who had fainted at school, that they could have been two completely different people. Her voyage through the Crucible of Creation had not only widened her outlook, it had expanded her consciousness, increased her intelligence and given her a strength of character few adults could claim to possess. The hardened lawyers did not try to advise her on anything, but accepted their instructions from her, as she laid out her plans for the future of the Universal Warmer. Muriel had her successor already in place, and the lawyers were spending their time and expertise on tutoring Michelle in the ways of international business.

"The Universal Warmer must cross all boundaries and borders," said Muriel. "It cannot be a product available only to those who will use it to warm their bacon sandwiches. It must also be available to the poor and cold everywhere. We must contact the International Red Cross and make the product available for areas of natural disaster. The Universal Warmer must become a necessity in every household in the world of matter."

"The world of matter?" asked one of the lawyers who had been furiously writing down everything she had been saying.

"I'm sorry, I mean in the real world," said Muriel. "It must become available to everyone in the world."

"We are about to register the company," said one of the legal team, "you still haven't told us the name of the business."

Muriel thought about this for a moment. "Call it *The Right Road Company*," said Muriel. "The company logo should be a golden arrow pointing to the right with the words *Right Road* written on it."

The lawyers thought about this.

"Interesting, recognisable, memorable, and different," observed the senior partner. "Very good indeed."

"And a company motto or slogan perhaps?" asked one of the other lawyers.

"Sequi Recto Itinere," replied Muriel without a second's hesitation.

The old lawyers thought back to their ancient schooldays, fumbling in their dark room of faded memories, Fornix Runners dashing to the Camp of the Hippos for long-buried archives. Their individual Goms trying to appear in the world of matter, without success.

"Follow The Right Road," explained Muriel.

The lawyers nodded and smiled.

In the subconscious realm of every living creature lies a ticking clock. It summons the creature to action when the time is right; hence spiders know when to spin their webs, bees know when to swarm, fish to spawn, and birds to build their nests, even cells know when to divide. In the high ranges of the Twisted Mountains, the monster, answering the internal summons of its own clock, knew it was time for it to radiate.

"I would like to congratulate you, Miss Mason," said the senior partner, when Muriel had signed all the paperwork. "It is not often we are able to boast such a capable young lady as one of our clients. We look forward to carrying out your instructions with utmost care, we do indeed."

"Thank you," replied Muriel. "I am certain you will help The Right Road Company to become very successful in the years to come, that is all I ask of you."

"You can be certain of our best efforts at all times," assured the senior partner.

In the narrow confines of its cave the monster sat down upon the floor, crossed its legs, and began to breathe deeply.

"I want you to understand that Michelle Davis, my chosen successor is to be in charge of this company absolutely. You are to take your instructions from her as you have from me. She will run the company as she sees fit, once she has completed the training you have provided for her, and she is ready to take over."

"We understand, completely," agreed the senior partner.

The monster began by clearing its mind of the clutter it had accumulated during its time in the Crucible. The pain it had felt as the Sword of Heaven had cleaved its flesh; the agonies of its trials against the wrath of The Silver Knight. The anger it felt towards those who would hinder its progress. The monster set all its feelings and emotions aside, as it cleared its consciousness of the trivia of its time.

"Are your parents to have a say in the running of the new company?" asked one of the legal team. "You have nominated them as co-inventors, and they are also named as fellow directors."

"No," replied Muriel flatly. "They are appointed in name only, so they can be legally entitled to a salary, bonus shares and pension rights, which I have already agreed with Michelle. They are to be taken care of financially for the rest of their lives, but they are not to become involved."

"Very good," said the senior partner, who was secretly wishing every client he had was just as focused and precise as Muriel Mason.

"I have a folder here that I would like you to keep for me," announced Muriel. "It contains the details, contact names, email addresses, websites and telephone numbers of all the manufacturers, wholesalers, distributors, website designers, and anyone else who will play a part in the design, manufacture or distribution of the Universal Warmer. If you ever need to contact anyone in the future, all the details are in here."

Muriel slid the folder across the desk to the senior partner, who could only smile in genuine admiration at the preparedness of his young client. What the senior partner could not have known, was that his young client had sojourned inside the City of Artists itself; she had bathed in the tide of its brilliance and was now a fully matured consciousness, regardless of her physical years. She was in fact a genius, as were all those who had visited that sacred site.

The monster slipped very slowly into a trance-like state when its mind had been emptied of all its clutter. From this state its consciousness began to focus on the latent energy its condition contained. Like a pot of water placed on a stove, nothing happened for the first few minutes, the water in the pot does not show any visible sign of change. Then in time, tiny bubbles begin to rise, and vapour can be seen to ascend from the surface of the water.

"If there is nothing else, gentlemen," said Muriel. "I think we may say our business for today has been concluded."

The lawyers nodded, and the senior partner rose from his seat to come around the boardroom table to his client. He wanted very much to shake her hand.

The bubbles now are larger and the water in the pot is turbulent, there is visible violence and power within the maelstrom.

The senior partner came face to face with the schoolgirl, and as he extended his hand to her, she knew it was the hand of admiration, gratitude and respect, from one professional to another. Smiling broadly, Muriel shook the hand of the senior partner, securing her hopes and ambitions for the ones she loved.

The monster could contain the surging torrent of energy within itself no longer.

It opened its eyes, opened its mouth, and thrust its arms outwards, displaying the pose that Patrick had seen in the Garden of Idols. The energy bust forth from the thing in shafts of radiant brilliance filling the cave and blasting a blinding light across the entire Crucible of Creation.

The eruption of light, heat and energy exploded out from the Twisted Mountains, and the Silver Knight raised his shield against the blast. Spero shied from the onslaught, turning his head away from the furnace.

Muriel threw her head back as her knees buckled beneath her, and she fell away from the old lawyer, still holding his hand. Her eyes rolled upwards into her cranium, as if she were trying to look at the monster from the outside. As the old man caught her, a trickle of blood ran down from her left nostril, over her lips to her chin.

"Oh my God!" shouted the senior partner. "Someone call an ambulance!"

First came the light, then came the blast. At Brocas' Language School the intrusion of the light made them all stop and look out of the window. When seconds later the blast hit the school, the side wall fell in and the ceiling collapsed. Amid the screaming and crying, the lifeless body of Professor Brocas lay prostrate under the rubble.

The senior partner held his young client in his arms as they both sank to the floor. "Someone call an ambulance!" he cried out again.

The savagery of the blast ripped the flimsy tents at the Camp of the Hippos from their moorings casting them high into the air, the hippos with them. Like a tornado of paper, the great library was strewn across all of creation, the carefully accumulated documents of a specific life, scattered to the corners of that hidden world.

The senior partner lay Muriel carefully down on the expensive carpet of the boardroom floor. The elderly lawyer, a man used to the battles and bloodshed of the courtroom felt his composure melt away with the sight of his young client, stretched out before him.

"Miss Mason! Miss Mason!" he pleaded, as he frantically patted her hand, not knowing what else to do.

Patrick closed his eyes when the blast hit the garden. The high gates, with their secret truth interwoven through the wrought iron, lifted from their hinges, and flapped like an ungainly bird attempting flight, before crashing into the flowerbeds. The statues which were yet of jelly disintegrated into globules, and their more solidified counterparts shattered like glass. The statue of the striding Muriel was broken at its knees and carried away on the torrent. Only the carving of the monster remained, in the pose its living model now displayed, high in the distant mountains.

With the latent force of its being now spent, with the last drop of its power jettisoned out of its body into the world, the monster slumped to the floor. Exhausted, it rolled onto its back and lay still. It breathed deeply, and evenly, allowing its strength to slowly return. Gradually it rose from the floor of the cave and stood upright. Its senses tingled with the expenditure of passion, and it suddenly felt a presence, a knowing that it was no longer alone. The monster turned around slowly to see The Client of the Crucible silhouetted against the twilight, framed like a shadow against the mouth of the cave.

"I knew you would come," it whispered. "This is our time."

The ambulance raced through the grey afternoon traffic, red and blue lights flashing as the sirens wailed.

Muriel felt an icy calm wash over her. "I don't feel frightened anymore," she said, as she was able to look peacefully into the face of the monster, at last.

"That is a good thing," replied the monster. "It was never my intention to destroy you. But I must answer the command of my nature. I am instructed to grow at all costs."

"I understand that now," nodded Muriel. "But you must also know that when you destroy me, you also destroy yourself. As I cannot live with you, you cannot live without me."

The monster nodded. "Our destinies were always intertwined," it said.

Muriel's father took the call from the senior partner and held his breath. He held the telephone receiver away from his ear and stared blankly at his wife who stood in their hallway waiting to hear the news. In one moment she would be nervously expectant, and only a moment later, thrown into a hysterical panic. The seconds ticked away.

Muriel took a deep breath, the time had come and she knew it.

"Are you ready?" whispered the monster, sympathetically.

Muriel again nodded her head, slowly, asserting that she was ready.

Michelle took the call at home, let the telephone drop from her hand to the floor, and fighting back the tears that would come no matter what, raced upstairs to get dressed. Her mother called after her, "What is it? What has happened?"

In a corner of the cave, Mop and Little Mop seemed agitated, moving nervously on their fibres and shaking with apprehension on the sandy floor.

"I am sorry I have to leave you, Mop," said Muriel, "but you know what you have to do later, it is all arranged." Then she turned back to face the monster with confidence.

"Yes, I am ready now," she announced.

The crash team were waiting for Muriel at the hospital entrance. They moved Muriel quickly through the doors and raced with the trolley down the long corridor to the emergency suite.

The monster moved closer to Muriel, one small step at a time, and when it stood before the schoolgirl, its mammoth bulk towering over her, it reached out its arms towards Muriel, who made no attempt to resist the coming embrace.

"Clear!" called the doctor in the emergency room as the team stood back. He placed the pads of the defibrillator onto Muriel's chest, her back arched with the impact of the shock, and the blood ran more freely from her nostril.

The ground shook in the Twisted Mountains, rocks fell from the walls and open mouth of the cave, both Muriel and the monster steadied themselves.

"Flatline!" called one of the technicians, as the doctor with the defibrillator moved back in towards the young girl who lay prostrate before him.

"Clear!" he called again.

The mountain shook with a terrible violence, and Muriel bent her knees to absorb the shock wave. More rocks fell from the roof of the cave. Muriel and the monster stared into each other's eyes, neither speaking as the moment ripened between them into a sacred trust.

"Do it now!" whispered Muriel.

The monster took one more step closer, and enveloped Muriel entirely in an embrace that was so overwhelming that it even blotted out the lights in the cave.

Across the Crucible of Creation the natural light of existence began to fade into a dusky twilight, as the inhabitants of that wonderful realm began to realise the time of the reckoning had come at last.

Bron looked from his decimated camp to the Twisted Mountains and slowly nodded. A tear formed in the corner of his large brown eye, which he made no attempt to wipe away, when it ran like a raindrop down the leathery surface of his ancient face.

In the Garden of Idols Patrick and the old gardener watched the statue of Doom take its final shape and solidify into granite.

"It's too early!" shouted the gardener.

"She is too young for this!" shouted Patrick, at the injustice of it all, but their cries were not heeded, there was no-one to listen, no arbiter to redress the unfairness of life, no God of Justice who could rebalance the scales. Patrick hung his head, as the darkness descended for the last time across the dying flower beds of the Garden of Idols. The old gardener let his shovel fall to the soil he had tended faithfully since the dawn of creation, and placed his arm around the neck of Patrick.

In the corner of Patrick's eye, a single tear began to form, which swelled until his eyelid could contain the drop no longer, and it tipped like a ball over the lip to begin a free fall down the donkey's cheek. But it was a tear drop like no other the garden had ever seen, for the globule was not clear water, as any other tear may be, but a tiny blue and white ball, the very earth itself; Muriel's entire world, the sum total of her existence in the garden. The earth rolled down the face of the donkey, to eventually fall into empty space, descending in one last path of grace downwards upon its final journey, free-falling through the vastness of space until it landed, shattering into a thousand tiny droplets, upon the hoof of the donkey.

"Our time is done, my old friend," said the gardener, "the world has to come to an end."

In the emergency room of the hospital the doctor placed gentle fingers on the neck of his young patient, as he closed his eyes, to allow him to concentrate. He waited for the feint pulse of life to throb across his fingertips from beneath the young girl's skin, but there was no answering call. He waited for life to call to life, but answer came there none. He waited still, but his knowledge and experience knew there was no pulse there to answer his call; yet still he waited, for he was a human, and hoped that from nowhere, out of the gloom a light might suddenly burst forth and banish the darkness, but there was no light for him to see, only The Blue Flame flickered above the carcass of the schoolgirl, invisible to all in the room. The machines which registered Muriel's vital signs told him all he needed to know, and yet he wanted to be certain himself.

"I am afraid Muriel has passed away," said the consultant, a few moments later.

Muriel's mother felt her knees abandon their duty, as she slumped helplessly against the torso of her husband.

"I am so very sorry," said the consultant, "so very sorry, indeed."

The monster held the young girl in its last embrace, knowing in its heart the end of days had come, it had fulfilled the call of its nature, and now there was nothing left to do. With no more development possible, the monster's time had also run its course.

Slowly the monster's hard and dry skin began to change to a pallid grey, and to lose its sensation. The monster felt a sense of oneness with the lifeless body of Muriel, as the loss of consciousness began to creep up the creature's form, up its torso, to its shoulders, neck and head, like a slowly rising tide.

The old gardener, still with his arm around Patrick's neck, began to fade away; he and the donkey became transparent, like figures from a dream, receding in substance and form, until they could be seen no longer. The statues in the garden which had survived the blast, returned to their original state of jelly, losing all structure and form, until nothing was left of shape or silhouette, to inform a passing visitor that there had ever been a sense of structure there; that a young girl had belonged here, a girl with hopes and dreams and fears, that were beginning to take shape and to harden into a sense of self that would carry her like a raft through the turbulent seas of her future, into womanhood.

The Great Egg ceased its movement, and came to a grinding halt for the last time. The Warden and the Upside Down People had all gone, never to return. The long path which had been filled with the population of the Upside

Down People, each with their own panorama and history, each with their own story, separate and unique, a self-contained view of the universe had all faded away into nothingness; they were now not even kept in a memory, their entire existence had been wiped away like the chalk characters on the schoolroom blackboard at Brocas' Language School.

Across the great Crucible of Creation there was nought but empty wilderness.

The giant Arch of Pons lay deserted, still straddling the Great Southern Highway, but the army of Fornix Runners, who had jostled for position, who had elbowed and shoved their way through the arch to carry their sacred trusts to all points in the Crucible were all gone. The top stone of the arch turned to sand and collapsed to the Highway, as the two sides of the great Arch left now unjoined, fell forwards with a silent crash upon the deserted road.

In Brocas' Language School all the facets of Muriel were absent, the body of the Professor too was nowhere to be seen, and the rows of small desks stood empty under the rubble, with no-one to sit at them and experience the secret enchantments of language.

The Camp of the Hippos was a deserted encampment, where the meticulously kept records of a young girl's life were fading into yellowed parchment and crumbling away. The carefully crafted comings and goings of an entire lifetime, documented with the care and precision of a watchmaker, now scattered to the winds of the moment, to blow where the breeze may take them.

In the Industrial South the Pumping Station, the heart of the matter, had stopped, its giant pistons now silent forever. The great tanks, labelled *Liquid Energy*, sat still and silent, their contents already starting to coagulate into putrid slime.

The two turbines had stopped revolving their great sails, as the wind that had powered them had died away. They stood beside the Great Southern Highway, like lost travellers waiting for a lift that would now never come.

The factory, which had never gone into production, even though it had been meticulously maintained year after year for the day when it would be needed, was now abandoned, its services that would call life to life, now eternally deserted, left for the rot and decay to lay waste to such promise. What generations are lost to the world when a single life is lost! The descendants that were to come from Muriel are now the missing multitude, the people who never can be; the chain is broken, and all the links which come behind the break are possibilities no longer, and all of what those individuals might have achieved, might have accomplished in the spans of their own lifetimes, the meagre and the mighty, now tally all to nought.

All across the Crucible of Creation the footprints of the monster had laid waste to the panorama. The only sound that could be heard in all of the Universe was the sound of sobbing. The Silver Knight, his armour tarnished and rusty, knelt beside the lifeless body of Spero and wept. The sound of The Silver Knight's weeping was the only sound in Creation, it echoed through the shattered Arch of Pons, ran up and down the deserted Great Southern Highway, filtered like smoke in and out of the Twisted Mountains, swirled around the Language Schoolroom, Wernicke's Castle and the Fornix Tavern, skipped across the devastated Camp of the Hippos and was heard by none save the grieving Knight himself. The Silver Knight's shield, which had sported a Valentine's

Day heart as his coat of arms, now showed that heart split asunder, torn down the middle, never to be repaired. Beside the devastated form of the Silver Knight lay the lifeless form of the great horse Spero, who had carried the Silver Knight to great adventures in times past when Muriel had been heedless of those exploits. For it had been Spero, and Spero alone who had supported the Silver Knight when misadventure, bad luck and the trials of everyday life had beset the Knight with difficulties during Muriel's infancy. Now that Spero was gone, the optimism that had sustained his rider was also lost, and the Silver Knight, defeated at last, could do nothing but weep for his shattered world.

Muriel's mother put her arm around her husband's shoulder and tried to comfort him, she had never seen him weep before.

"I am so very sorry," repeated the consultant. "So very sorry indeed."

Chapter Twenty

A Need to Understand

Muriel's death had been reported on the television, internet news pages, newspapers and magazines. The fifteen-year-old girl who had brain cancer, and who had invented a device called the Universal Warmer had become a news phenomenon, for a short while at least. Reports about the short life and tragic death of Muriel Mason could been seen everywhere. Her old teachers, the great bat and the white vulture, had been interviewed, where they had said what a wonderful pupil Muriel had been, and what a tragic loss to the school her demise had represented to everyone, staff and pupils alike.

Her parents' house had been laid to siege where every twitch of the curtains had been caught on camera, until at last, Muriel's father had given an interview to the press, where his cracked voice and broken spirit had become exposed to the world. Michelle, as the successor to Muriel's business had also been interviewed, and together with the senior partner by her side, she had told the word that no amount of money would even begin to make up for the loss of her best friend.

A week later, on the morning appointed for Muriel's funeral, hundreds of people began to line the route from her home to the local church. As the funeral procession moved slowly through the town, Muriel's mother gazed out of the window and shook her head. "Who are all these people?" she asked. "I don't know any of them."

"The Faceless Army," replied Michelle, who had been invited to share the car with Muriel's parents.

"Who?" asked Muriel's mother.

"The army of well-wishers who were touched by Muriel's story. The people who didn't know her but sent cards and flowers to the hospital. The people who first saw her on the TV commercial," said Michelle.

"But they didn't know her, not really," replied Muriel's mother.

"That is why Muriel called them the Faceless Army," replied Mop. "They didn't really know her, as you say, but in a strange way they thought they did, they all felt a connection with her. They were moved by her story, and they bought the product."

In the second car, the senior partner looked out of the window too. He didn't really see the people, he was lost in a mental speculation, wondering what Muriel Mason might have gone on to achieve if she had only been granted a little more time.

The small church where Muriel had been baptised was so full, many people had to wait outside in that cold November morning, listening as best as they could to the priest within, eulogising about the vibrant life and tragic death of the girl he had never met, but who had also come into his life through the medium of television.

When the service ended and the family, business associates and friends filed outside, they formed a line to read each wreath in turn, which had been placed on the ground in a long line for the purpose. The messages from people who had been touched by Muriel; people in hospital, people in nursing homes, people of her own age who were feeling abandoned and directionless, the lost and the lonely.

Muriel had inspired many with a renewed sense of purpose, and given a feeling of courage to others, and those who felt they knew her, had come to say goodbye.

Around the graveside stood Muriel's parents, Michelle, the senior partner and the priest. The well-wishers of the Faceless Army were kept back for this last, and final farewell to the young girl who had touched them all.

They lowered the wooden casket into the ground on straps, and as it descended to the bottom of the hole they each threw in a flower.

In the deserted realm of the Crucible, nothing stirred, even the wind had died way. The whole of the Crucible of Creation was as quiet and as still as the vast ocean of space. Brocas' Language School was a deserted ruin, a shapeless structure with three leaning walls and a missing roof. Wernicke's Magic Castle was crumbling into dust, becoming one with the desert floor itself. The Camp of the Hippos was an oasis of desolation in the desert, the tents had all fallen down, the papers of the library scattered like autumn leaves to the far corners of creation. The Great Egg had long ago ceased to move or function, the Upside Down People were all gone. The deserted factory lay ruined and abandoned, as were the farm, the tool rooms, the pumping station, the turbines, and the coach station, all deserted. In the Garden of Idols the statues had all returned to formless jelly, and then they had become rancid, returning to liquid, and spilling down their plinths, to form a lake of lost possibilities. The whole of the Crucible was a civilization no more, and never could be again. Throughout the entire panorama of the Crucible only one body remained. High in the far reaches of the Twisted Mountains lay the slowly decomposing corpse of the monster.

A few days later, the consultant opened his office door, and gestured for the small group to join him inside.

"You too Mop," said Muriel's mother, to Michelle. "She would have wanted you in here as well."

Mop, with Little Mop cradled in her arms entered the office with Muriel's parents and they all sat down.

"First of all let me say how sorry I am for your loss," began the man in the white coat. "Muriel was an extraordinary girl. Quite extraordinary."

Muriel's mum wiped her eyes, and nodded. "Thank you," she sniffed.

"What can I tell you?" asked the consultant.

"We have a need to understand," said Muriel's father, simply. "We just want to know exactly what happened to our daughter."

The consultant nodded. "Your daughter, Muriel was diagnosed with an intracranial neoplasm, or primary brain tumour," he began. "Primary means it started in the brain, and did not spread there from somewhere else in Muriel's body."

"How did it get there?" asked Muriel's mum.

"No-one knows how they begin," continued the surgeon. "Early symptoms may include drowsiness, lethargy, vomiting and bouts of unconsciousness."

"She was often sick in the mornings," said Muriel's dad. "And she fainted once or twice, as you know."

"We thought she might be pregnant," said Muriel's mum.

"She wasn't pregnant," said the surgeon. "The tumour was classed as malignant, meaning it was spreading, and was a threat to Muriel's life. That was why we had to act fast once the test results came back confirming our suspicions."

"Where was the tumour?" asked Muriel's dad.

"The tumour was located within the cerebral cortex," said the surgeon, "the top of the brain."

"The Twisted Mountains," muttered Mop, under her breath, but no-one heard her.

"Because of its location, we decided to operate and to physically cut out the growth, this is when Muriel underwent her brain operation," continued the consultant.

"The Sword of Heaven," muttered Mop again, to herself, reading Muriel's notebook.

"Unfortunately," went on the consultant, "we were unable to get all of the tumour, as it lay deeper inside the brain tissue than we first imagined. We then had to begin a course of radiotherapy, to try and kill what was left of the cancer cells."

"After the Battle," sighed Mop, as tears filled her eyes.

"Her friends at school, and all the people who wrote to the paper, and sent flowers to the hospital, were so supportive," sighed Mrs Mason.

"The Faceless Army," whispered Mop, allowing a tear to fall unchecked, onto the page of Muriel's journal. Michelle dabbed it away with a tissue.

"As you know," ended the consultant, "the radiotherapy was ultimately unsuccessful."

Everyone nodded. A silence descended into the small office, which was like the silence in church.

"What areas of her brain were affected?" asked Muriel's dad, breaking the spell.

"What does it matter now?" replied Muriel's mum, with a stifled sob.

"I just want to understand as much as I can," whispered Muriel's father. "I did the best I could, but it just wasn't enough. I was useless in the end."

"You mustn't think like that Mr Mason," replied the consultant. "We all did the very best we could for Muriel."

"You were always her Silver Knight," said Michelle. "And she saw you like that."

Muriel's father looked at Mop with curious eyes.

"It's all in her journal," continued Michelle. "She wrote everything down so she could try and make sense of it all, it's all in here."

Mop handed the journal to the Silver Knight.

"Why was her speech all mixed up, like that?" asked Muriel's mother, who had had the answer to this question explained to her once before by the same consultant.

"The tumour affected many different parts of Muriel's brain," replied the consultant. "One of the areas it affected was Brocas' Area, a part of the brain which deals with the understanding and construction of language."

"Brocas' Language School," said Mop, smiling.

"It also had an adverse effect on the Pons, which is the area that links the Temporal Lobe to the Medulla Oblongata," said the consultant, forgetting who he was talking to for a moment.

Everyone looked blankly at the modern Magician. "The lower part of the brain to the brain stem," he explained.

"The Arch of Pons straddles the Crucible floor and the Great Southern Highway," said Michelle. "Muriel called her spinal column the Great Southern Highway. It's all in her journal."

Muriel's dad opened his daughter's journal as though he had found a treasure he had never before been aware of. "I will read this," he said.

"It explains everything," replied Michelle. "Even how she thought of the Universal Warmer."

"She was a very clever girl indeed," replied the consultant, fingering his white beard thoughtfully.

Muriel's dad let the journal fall open where it may, and gazed at Muriel's reproduction of the Vendor's Map.

"The Industrial South?" he asked, looking quizzically at Mop.

"The rest of Muriel's body below her head," replied Michelle. "The Pumping Station is her heart, the Twin Turbines, her lungs, the Tool Rooms her hands, the Coach Station her feet, and so on. She was trying to understand her body and what was happening to her. She renamed all the areas, so they were more real to her. In her journal the areas of her body became real places, and some of their functions became characters she interacted with."

"The Factory?" asked Muriel's dad.

"Muriel's reproductive system," explained Michelle. "It was closed because she never became pregnant."

The Silver Knight nodded and flicked to another page, where he looked at Bron's Map. "The Camp of the Hippos?" he asked.

"The Hippocampus is an area on the left side of the brain which stores memory," interjected the man in the white coat. "It might help if you think of it as a great library."

"Bron is the chief librarian there," explained Michelle, with a smile, "he's a hippopotamus."

Muriel's dad nodded and smiled. "The Great Egg?" he asked.

"Muriel's left eye," replied Michelle, "and the Upside Down People are the refracted images of the world, inverted by the lens of the inner eye. It's all in her journal. You really should read it, Mr Mason."

"I will," replied Muriel's father, continuing to flick through the journal. "The Fornix Tavern?" he asked. "Free CSF?"

"CSF means Cerebrospinal Fluid," explained the consultant. "A liquid cushion which protects the brain in the case of an external impact."

"Charlie's Special Fermentation," said Michelle, smiling. "She renamed everything so she could understand it better."

"Wernicke's Magic Castle?" asked Muriel's dad, as he gazed at his daughter's drawing of Bron's original map.

"Wernicke's Area is an area of the brain which allows us to understand the nuances of language, more than just its construction," said the consultant. "Which is handled mainly in Brocas' Area."

"The magic of language," said Michelle. "Wernicke's Magic Castle. Muriel also used real people she knew as the models for some of the characters in her journal. She saw you as a Magician, a wizard."

The consultant smiled at this, aware that whatever magic his modern procedures might have held, they were ultimately unsuccessful in this case.

"So I was The Silver Knight," observed Mr Mason. "Why was my horse called Spero?"

Michelle smiled. "Spero is Latin for 'hope', Mr Mason. Spero, or hope, carried you forwards. When Spero died, hope died, and all was lost."

Muriel's father closed the journal, and caressed the outer binding as though it were made of gold leaf. "We should read this together," he said to his wife, who simply nodded.

It was a cold and drizzly morning when the small party left the office of the consultant, and ventured out into the world of matter.

"Buy a copy of The Big Issue, Miss?" asked a young lad as Michelle walked past.

Michelle smiled and paid the lad for the magazine. Something about the boy seemed vaguely familiar to Michelle, but she couldn't place it, the cloth cap he wore shielded his eyes as Michelle briefly looked at him. "Thank you," she said putting the magazine in her shoulder bag.

"You're very welcome, Miss," replied the vendor, with a smile. "That magazine represents both value and quality, for a very small price."

Michelle darted a look straight into the face of the vendor, when she heard those words. Michelle didn't know what to say.

"Is there anything else I can do for you, Miss?" asked the vendor.

Michelle felt tears suddenly flood into her eyes. She shook her head and walked away.

"We're going home now," said Muriel's father to Michelle. "But I want you come and see us, Michelle, whenever you can. You will always be welcome at our house."

"I will, I promise," replied Michelle.

Mop, still cradling Little Mop in her arms, then said a final farewell to The Silver Knight and his lady. They parted as friends, inextricably linked together forever by the tie of Muriel's presence and their shared memories of her. The Silver Knight held on to Muriel's journal tightly. He would read it and he would understand in the days to come what his daughter had experienced in the Crucible of Creation, and perhaps he would come to examine the statues in his own Garden of Idols, and to even reshape some of them if he could, although for him they were long since solidified and difficult to change. He would make the effort for his daughter's sake, and after all, the gardener and Patrick would be there to help him.

THE END